THE HARDY BOYS®

UNDERCOVER BROTHERS™

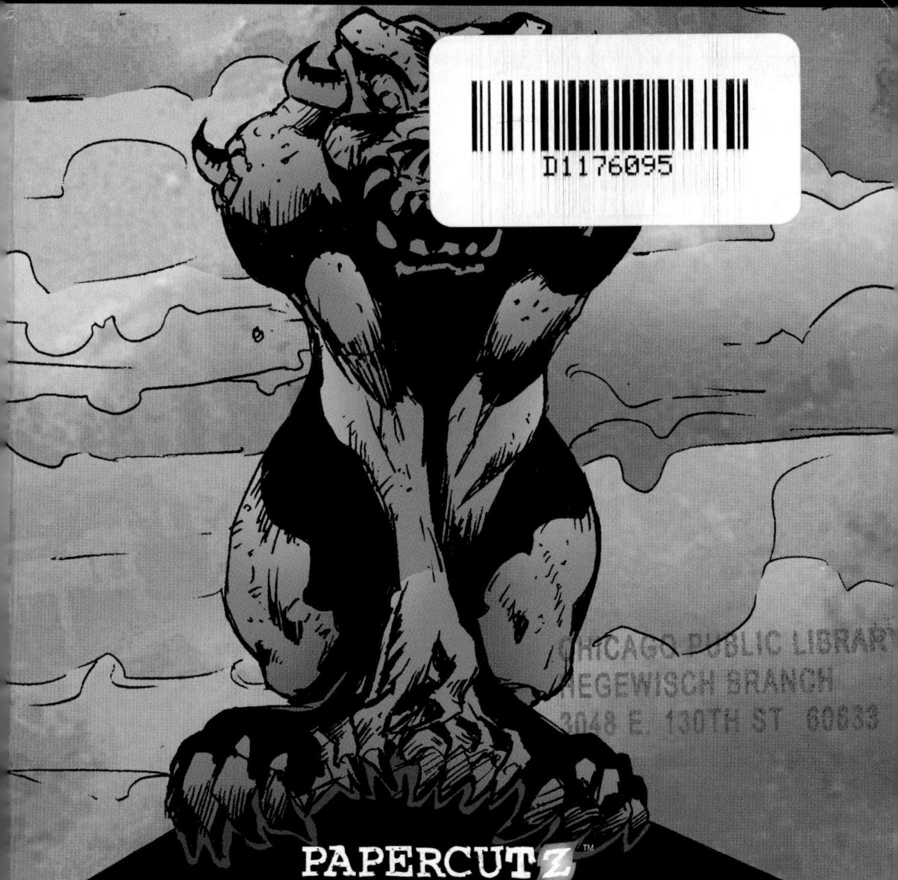

PAPERCUTZ™

THE HARDY BOYS GRAPHIC NOVELS AVAILABLE FROM PAPERCUTZ

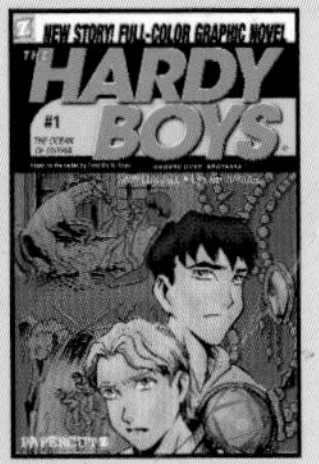
NEW STORY! FULL-COLOR GRAPHIC NOVEL
HARDY BOYS
#1
PAPERCUTZ
#1 "The Ocean of Osyria"

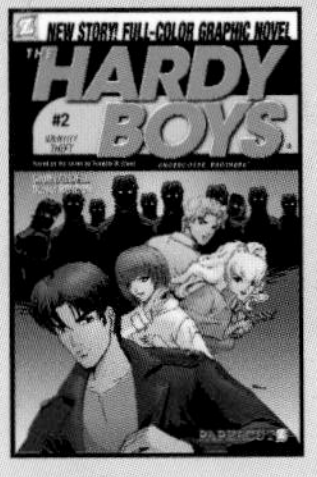
NEW STORY! FULL-COLOR GRAPHIC NOVEL
HARDY BOYS
#2
PAPERCUTZ
#2 "Identity Theft"

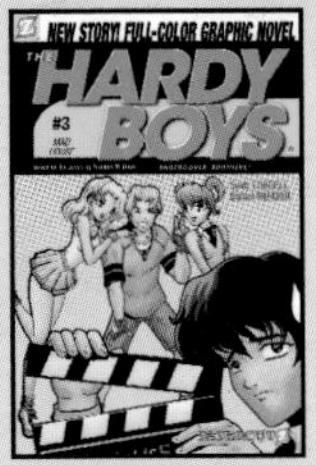
NEW STORY! FULL-COLOR GRAPHIC NOVEL
HARDY BOYS
#3
#3 "Mad House"

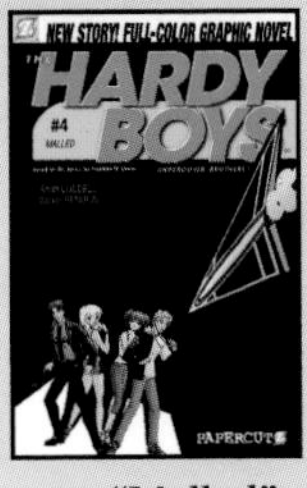
NEW STORY! FULL-COLOR GRAPHIC NOVEL
HARDY BOYS
#4
PAPERCUTZ
#4 "Malled"

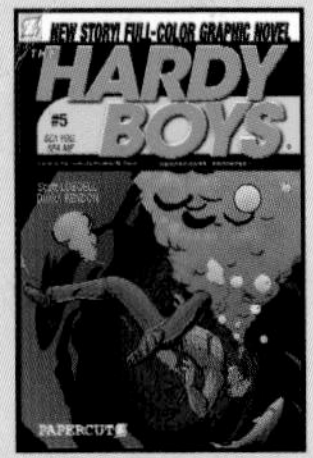
NEW STORY! FULL-COLOR GRAPHIC NOVEL
HARDY BOYS
#5
PAPERCUTZ
#5 "Sea You, Sea Me!"

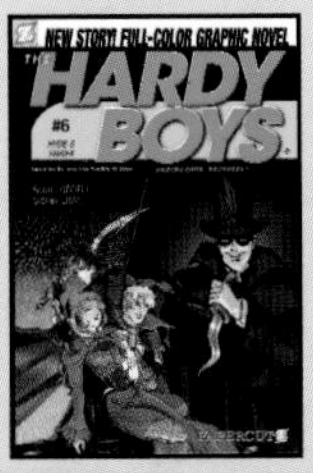
NEW STORY! FULL-COLOR GRAPHIC NOVEL
HARDY BOYS
#6
PAPERCUTZ
#6 "Hyde & Shriek"

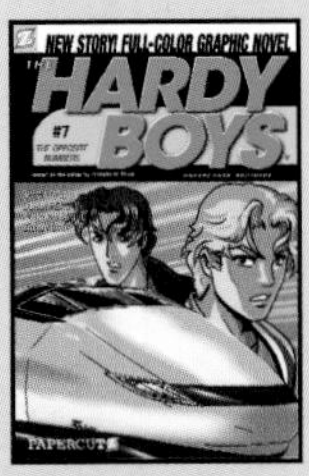
NEW STORY! FULL-COLOR GRAPHIC NOVEL
HARDY BOYS
#7
PAPERCUTZ
#7 "The Opposite Numbers..."

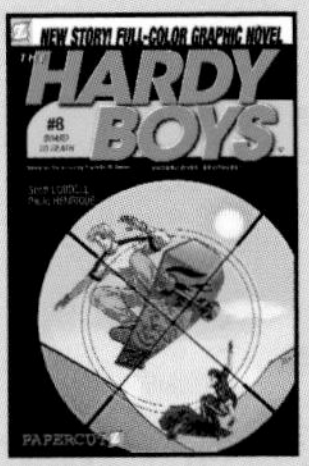
NEW STORY! FULL-COLOR GRAPHIC NOVEL
HARDY BOYS
#8
PAPERCUTZ
#8 "Board To Death"

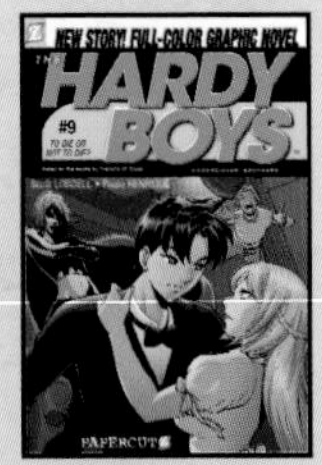
NEW STORY! FULL-COLOR GRAPHIC NOVEL
HARDY BOYS
#9
PAPERCUTZ
#9 "To Die Or Not To Die?

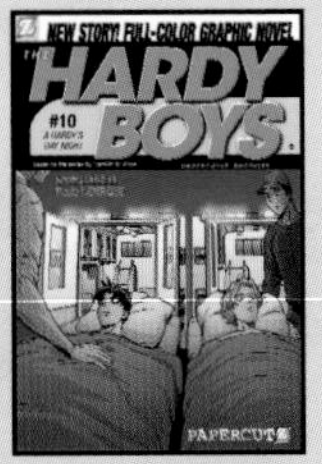
NEW STORY! FULL-COLOR GRAPHIC NOVEL
HARDY BOYS
#10
PAPERCUTZ
#10 "A Hardy Day's Night"

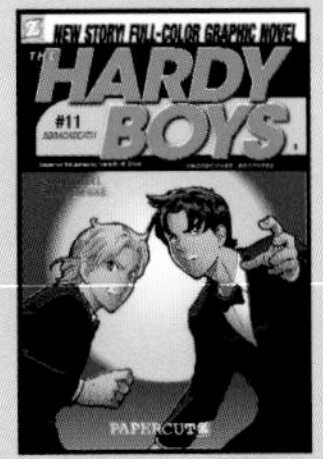
NEW STORY! FULL-COLOR GRAPHIC NOVEL
HARDY BOYS
#11
PAPERCUTZ
#11 "Abracadeath"

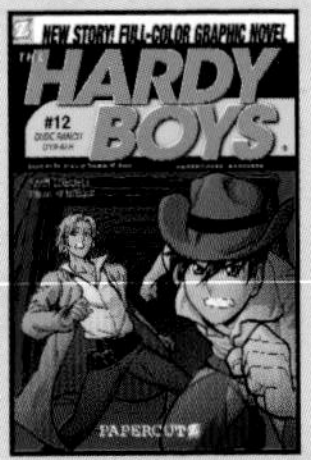
NEW STORY! FULL-COLOR GRAPHIC NOVEL
HARDY BOYS
#12
PAPERCUTZ
#12 "Dude Ranch O' Death"

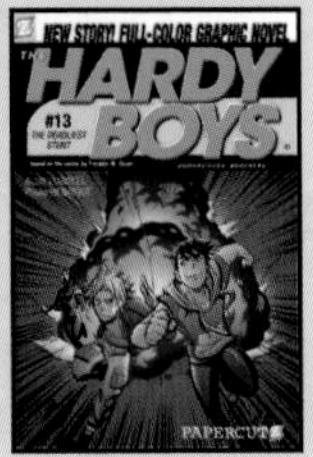
NEW STORY! FULL-COLOR GRAPHIC NOVEL
HARDY BOYS
#13
PAPERCUTZ
Coming Soon!
#13 "The Deadliest Stunt"

$7.95 each in paperback, $12.95 each in hardcover.

Please add $3.00 for postage and handling for the first book, add $1.00 for each additional book. Please make check payable to NBM Publishing. Send to: **Papercutz, 40 Exchange Place, Suite 1308 New York, NY 10005** • www.papercutz.com

THE HARDY BOYS

#6

®

UNDERCOVER BROTHERS™

Hyde & Shriek

SCOTT LOBDELL • Writer
SIDNEY LIMA, PAULO HENRIQUE • Artists
Preview art by DANIEL RENDON
Based on the series by
FRANKLIN W. DIXON

New York

Hyde & Shriek
SCOTT LOBDELL – Writer
SIDNEY LIMA and PAULO HENRIQUE — Artists
MARK LERER – Letterer
LAURIE E. SMITH — Colorist
JIM SALICRUP — Editor-in-Chief

ISBN-10: 1-59707-028-9 paperback edition
ISBN-13: 978-1-59707-028-7 paperback edition
ISBN-10: 1-59707-029-7 hardcover edition
ISBN-13: 978-1-59707-029-4 hardcover edition

Published by arrangement with Aladdin Paperbacks,
an imprint of Simon & Schuster Children's Publishing Division.

Printed in China
Distributed by Macmillan.

10 9 8 7 6 5 4 3

CHAPTER ONE: "WITH LIBERTY AND JUSTICE FOR ALL..."

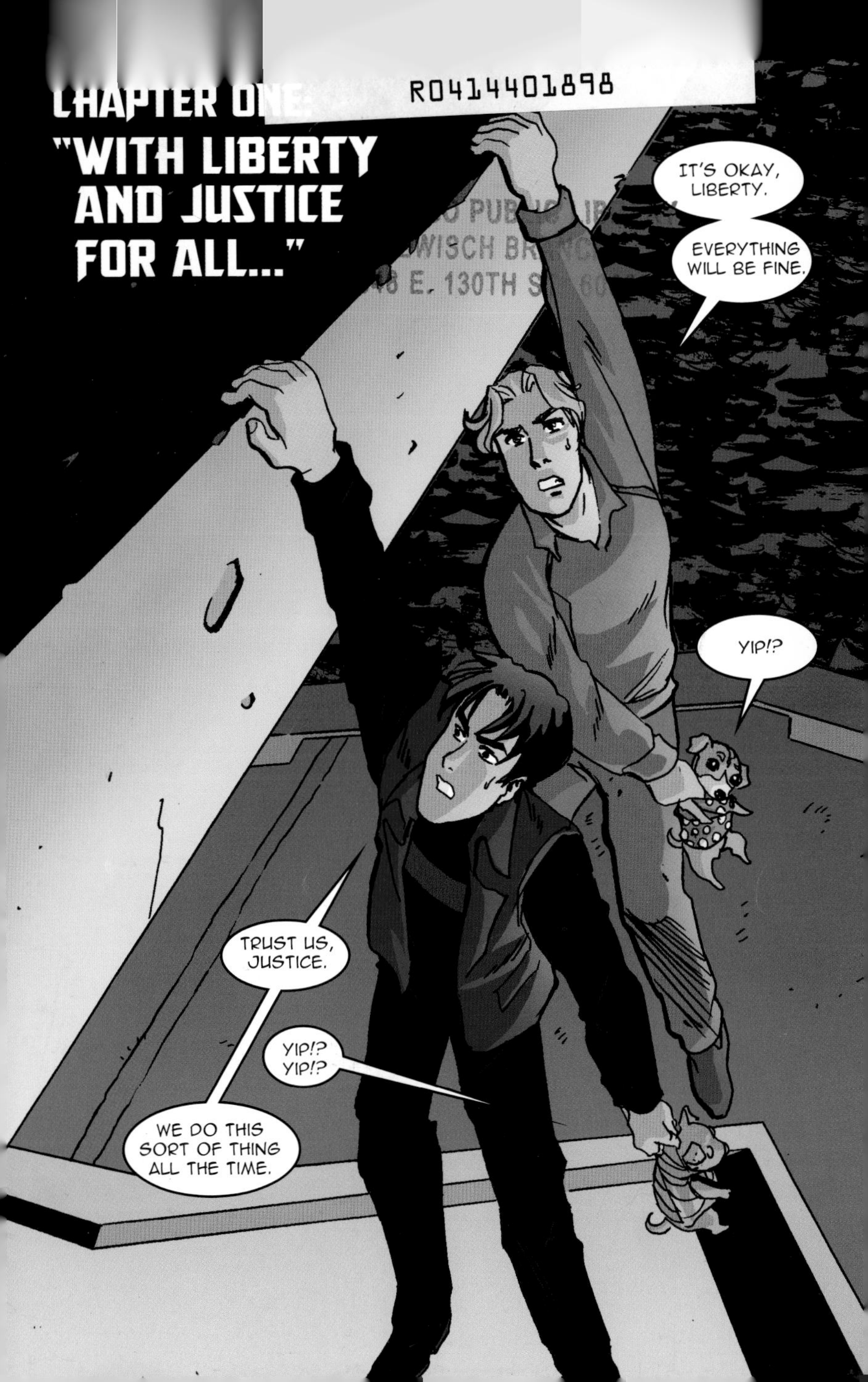
IT'S OKAY, LIBERTY.
EVERYTHING WILL BE FINE.
YIP!?
TRUST US, JUSTICE.
YIP!? YIP!?
WE DO THIS SORT OF THING ALL THE TIME.

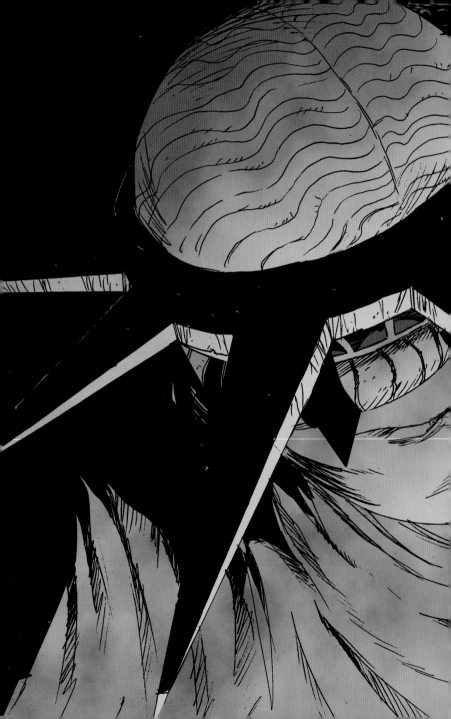

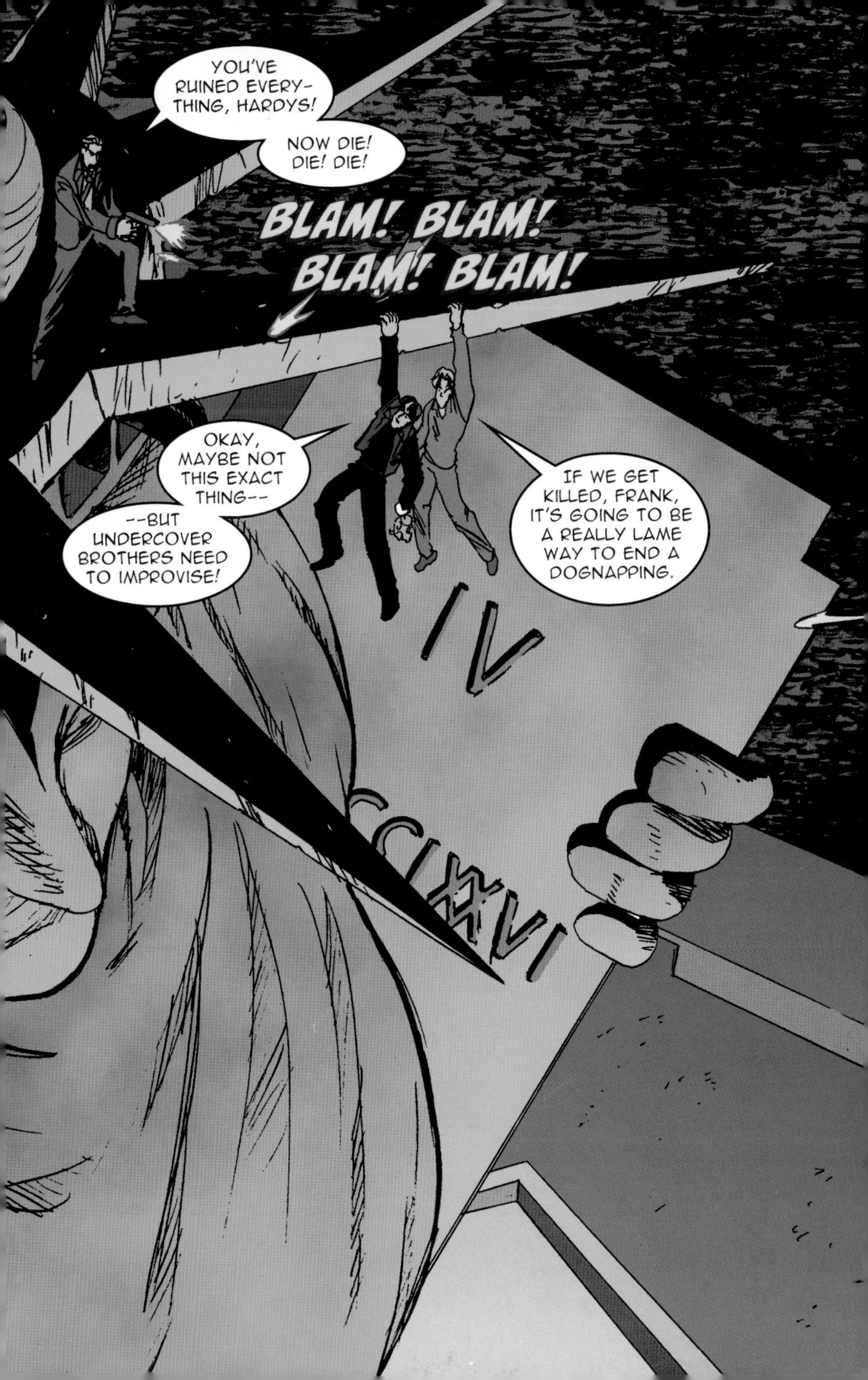
YOU'VE RUINED EVERY-THING, HARDYS!
NOW DIE! DIE! DIE!
BLAM! BLAM! BLAM! BLAM!
IF WE GET KILLED, FRANK, IT'S GOING TO BE A REALLY LAME WAY TO END A DOGNAPPING.
OKAY, MAYBE NOT THIS EXACT THING--
--BUT UNDERCOVER BROTHERS NEED TO IMPROVISE!
IV
CCLXXVI

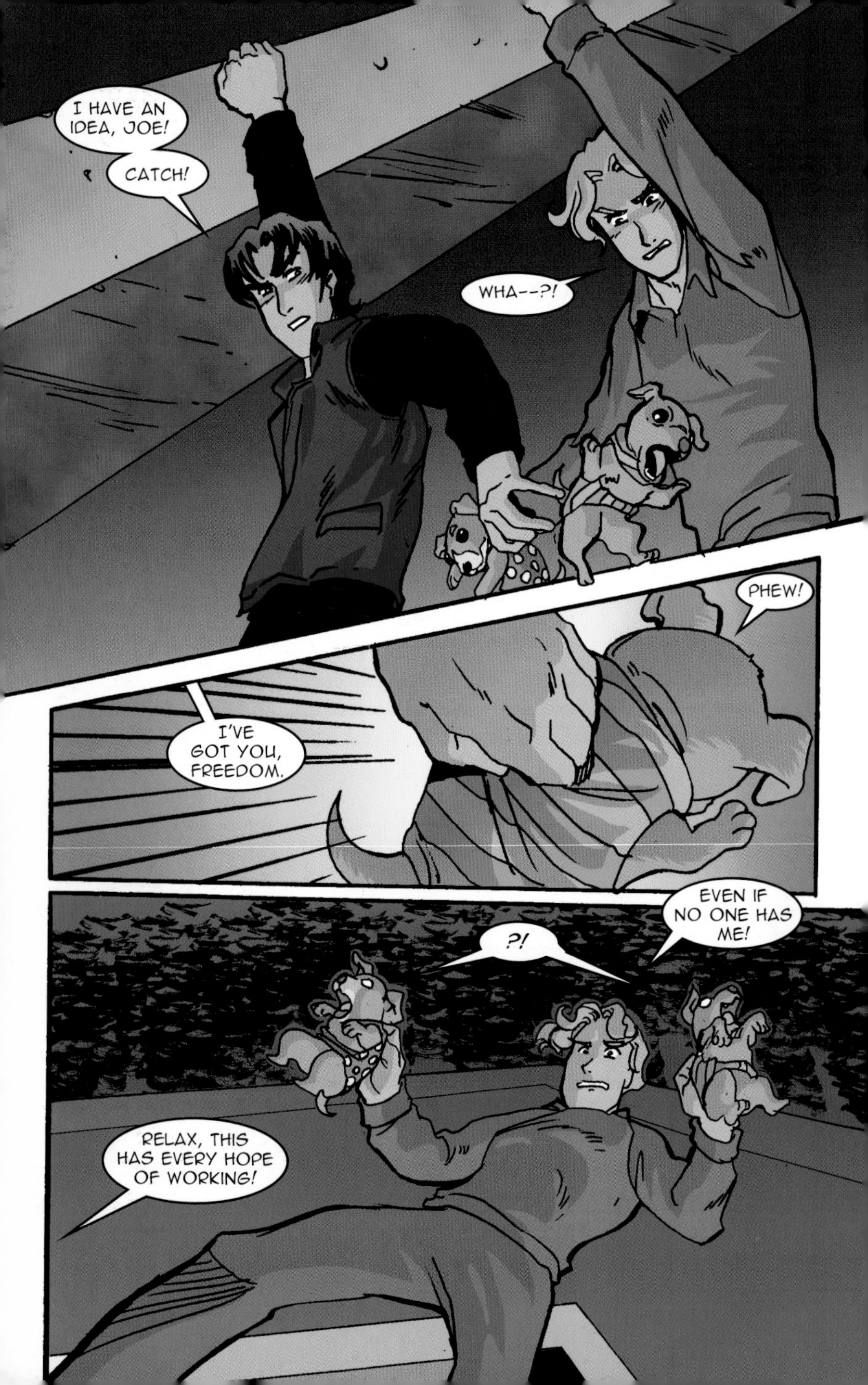
I HAVE AN IDEA, JOE!
CATCH!
WHA--?!
PHEW!
I'VE GOT YOU, FREEDOM.
?!
EVEN IF NO ONE HAS ME!
RELAX, THIS HAS EVERY HOPE OF WORKING!

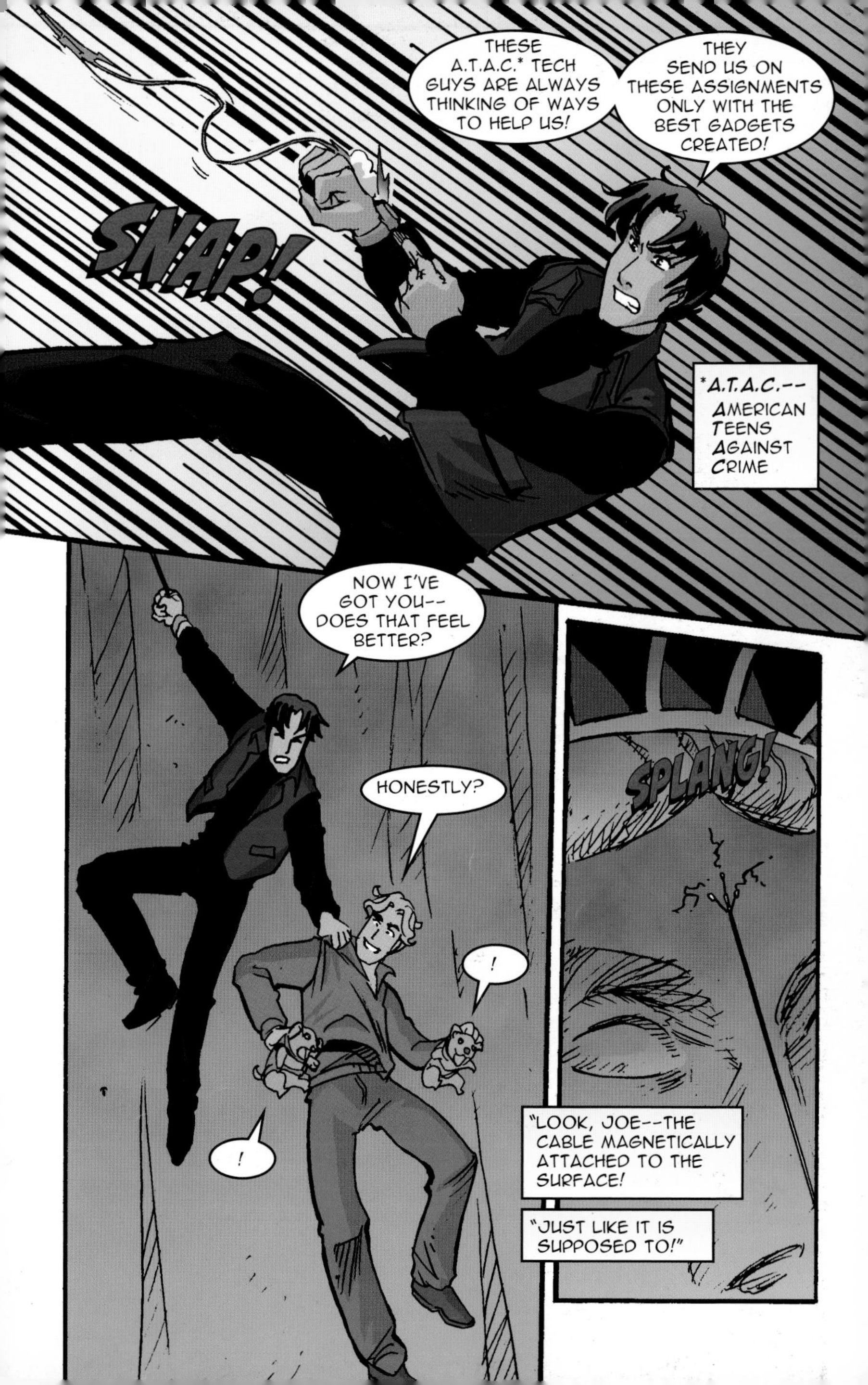
THESE A.T.A.C.* TECH GUYS ARE ALWAYS THINKING OF WAYS TO HELP US!
THEY SEND US ON THESE ASSIGNMENTS ONLY WITH THE BEST GADGETS CREATED!
SNAP!
*A.T.A.C.-- AMERICAN TEENS AGAINST CRIME
NOW I'VE GOT YOU-- DOES THAT FEEL BETTER?
HONESTLY?
!
!
SPLANG!
"LOOK, JOE--THE CABLE MAGNETICALLY ATTACHED TO THE SURFACE!
"JUST LIKE IT IS SUPPOSED TO!"

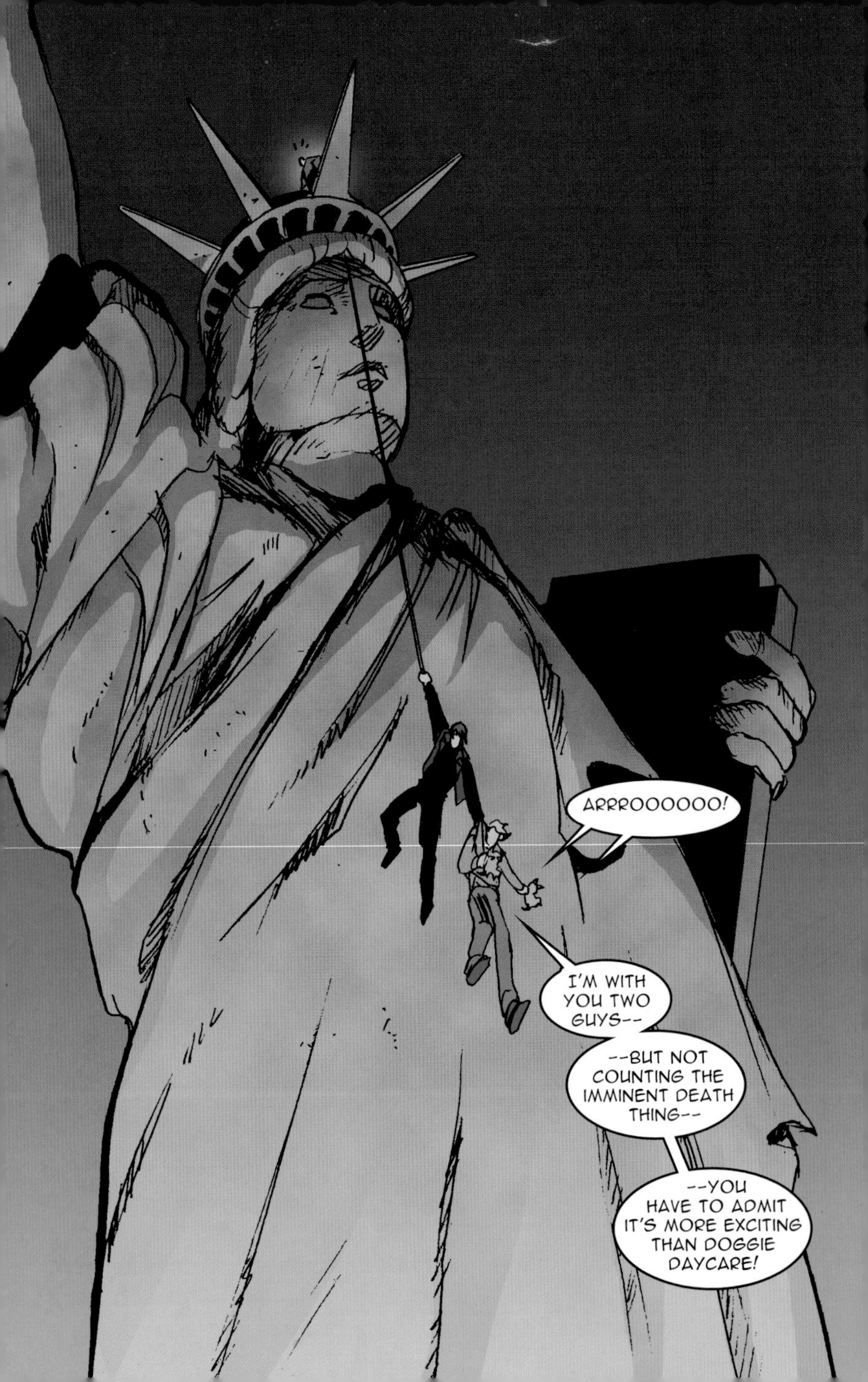
ARRROOOOOOO!
I'M WITH YOU TWO GUYS--
--BUT NOT COUNTING THE IMMINENT DEATH THING--
--YOU HAVE TO ADMIT IT'S MORE EXCITING THAN DOGGIE DAYCARE!

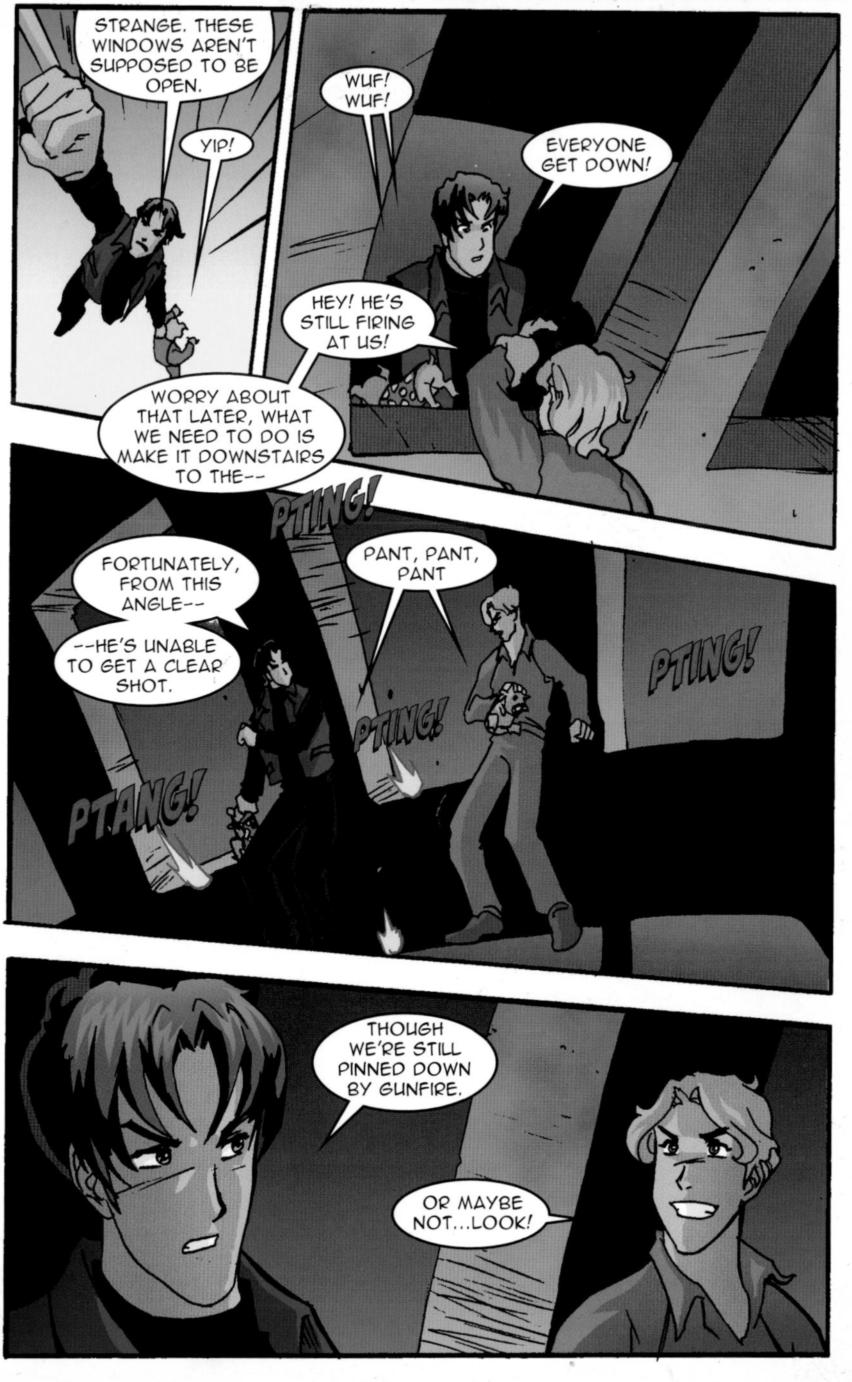
STRANGE. THESE WINDOWS AREN'T SUPPOSED TO BE OPEN.
YIP!
WUF! WUF!
EVERYONE GET DOWN!
HEY! HE'S STILL FIRING AT US!
WORRY ABOUT THAT LATER, WHAT WE NEED TO DO IS MAKE IT DOWNSTAIRS TO THE--
PTING!
FORTUNATELY, FROM THIS ANGLE--
--HE'S UNABLE TO GET A CLEAR SHOT.
PANT, PANT, PANT
PTING!
PTING!
PTANG!
THOUGH WE'RE STILL PINNED DOWN BY GUNFIRE.
OR MAYBE NOT...LOOK!

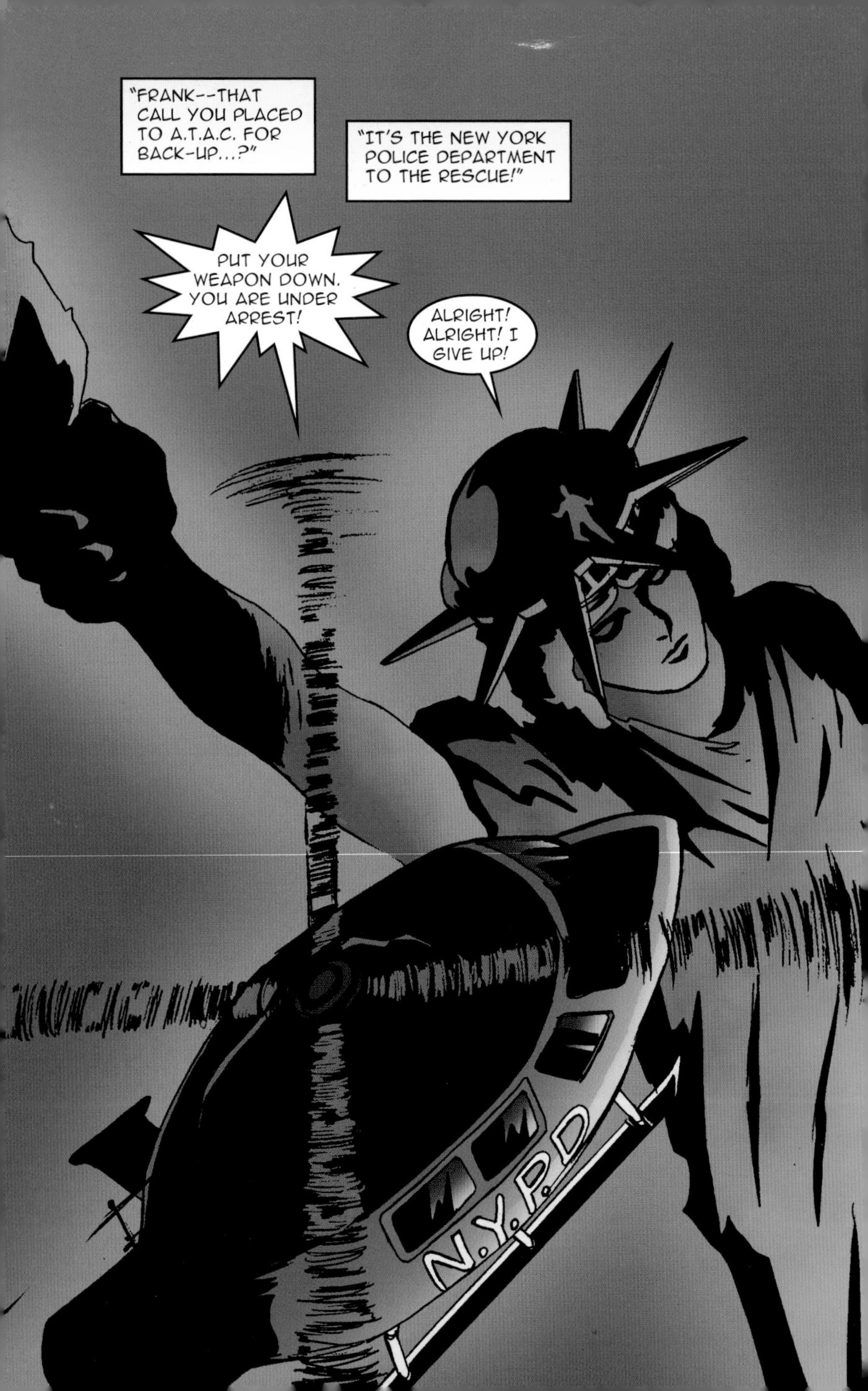
"FRANK--THAT CALL YOU PLACED TO A.T.A.C. FOR BACK-UP...?"
"IT'S THE NEW YORK POLICE DEPARTMENT TO THE RESCUE!"
PUT YOUR WEAPON DOWN. YOU ARE UNDER ARREST!
ALRIGHT! ALRIGHT! I GIVE UP!
N.Y.P.D.

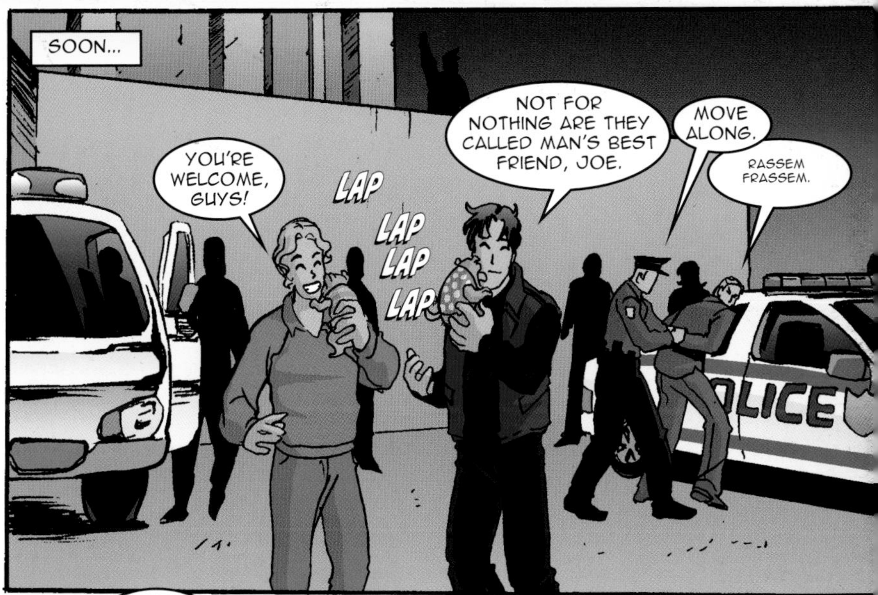
SOON...
YOU'RE WELCOME, GUYS!
LAP
LAP
LAP
LAP
NOT FOR NOTHING ARE THEY CALLED MAN'S BEST FRIEND, JOE.
MOVE ALONG.
RASSEM FRASSEM.
POLICE

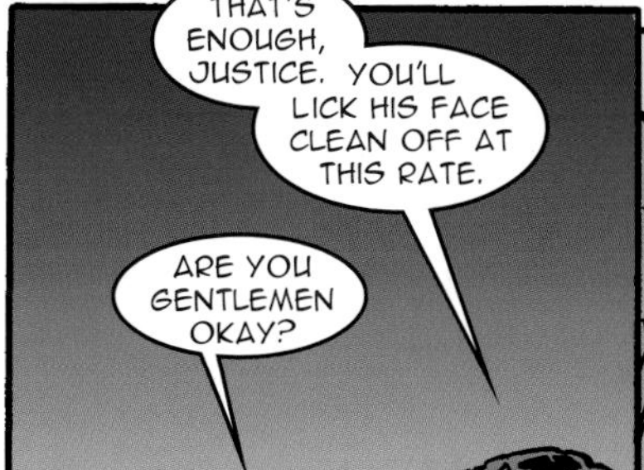
THAT'S ENOUGH, JUSTICE. YOU'LL LICK HIS FACE CLEAN OFF AT THIS RATE.
ARE YOU GENTLEMEN OKAY?

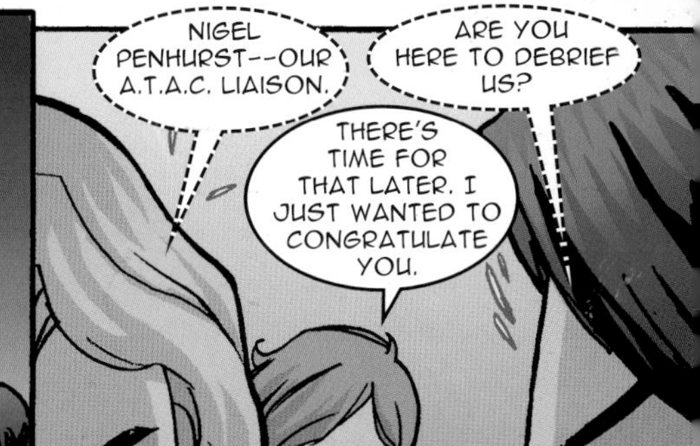
NIGEL PENHURST--OUR A.T.A.C. LIAISON.
ARE YOU HERE TO DEBRIEF US?
THERE'S TIME FOR THAT LATER. I JUST WANTED TO CONGRATULATE YOU.

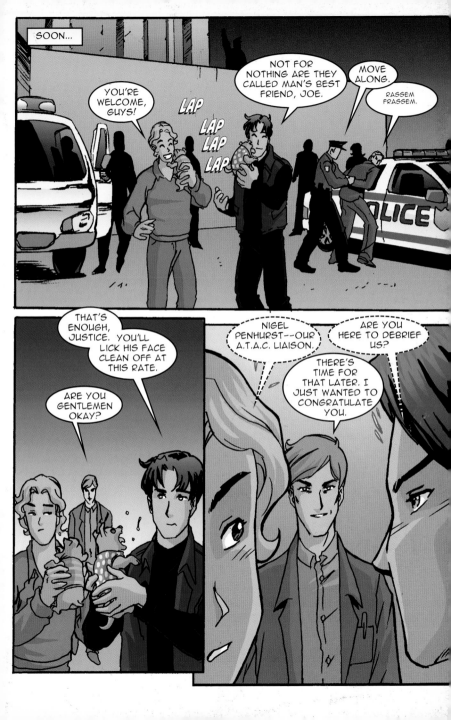

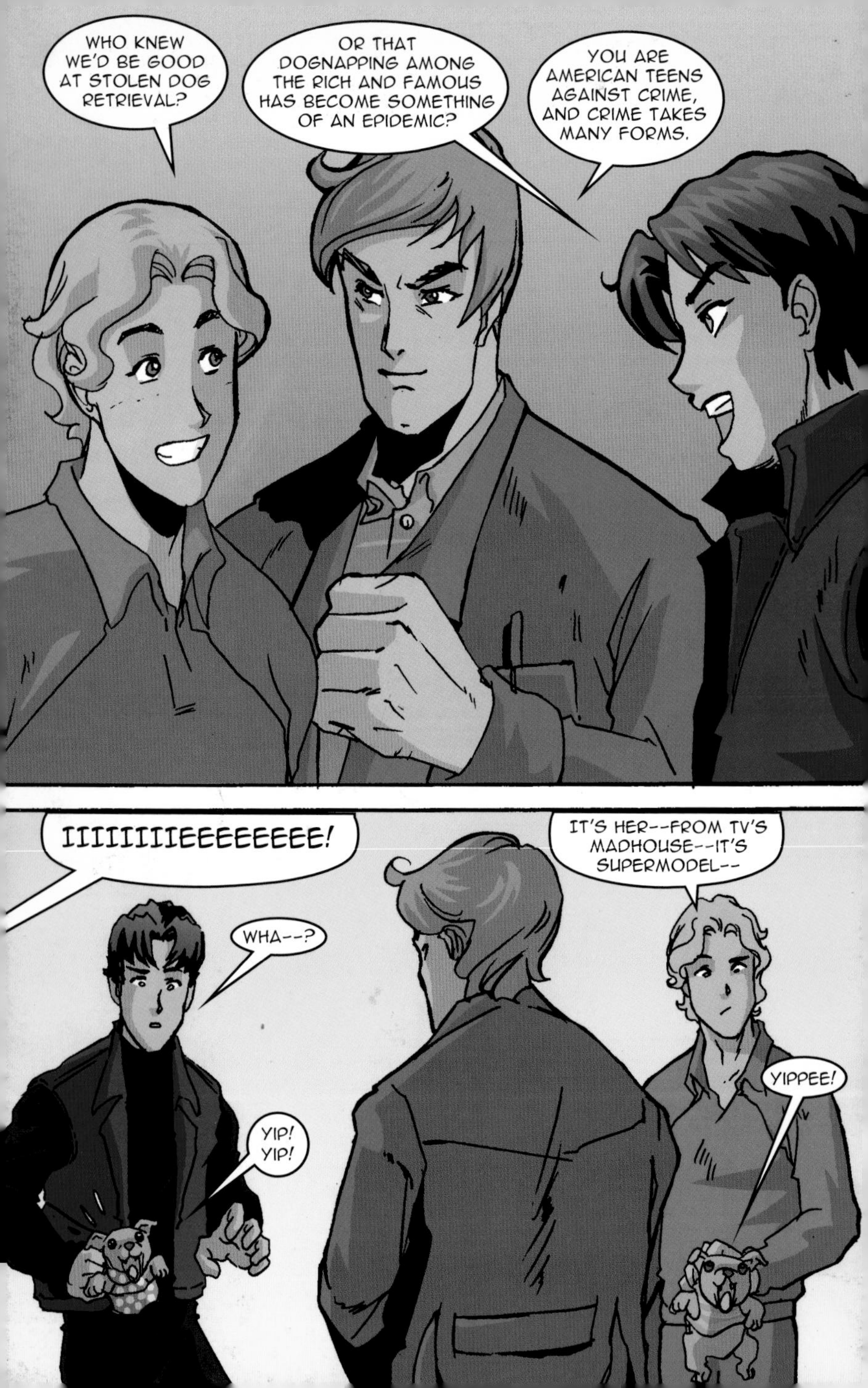
WHO KNEW WE'D BE GOOD AT STOLEN DOG RETRIEVAL?
OR THAT DOGNAPPING AMONG THE RICH AND FAMOUS HAS BECOME SOMETHING OF AN EPIDEMIC?
YOU ARE AMERICAN TEENS AGAINST CRIME, AND CRIME TAKES MANY FORMS.
IIIIIIIEEEEEEEEE!
IT'S HER--FROM TV'S MADHOUSE--IT'S SUPERMODEL--
WHA--?
YIP! YIP!
YIPPEE!

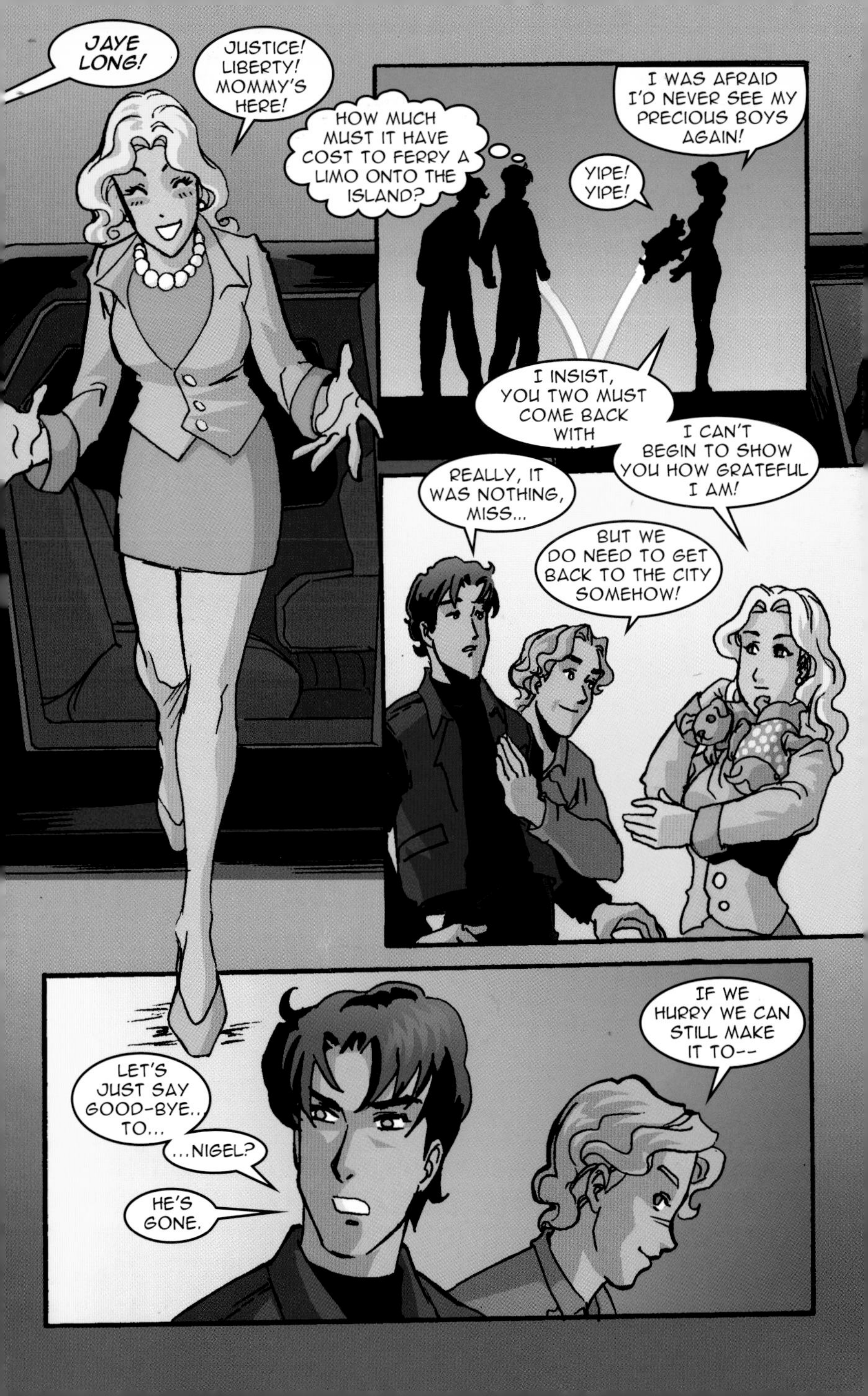
JAYE LONG!
JUSTICE! LIBERTY! MOMMY'S HERE!
HOW MUCH MUST IT HAVE COST TO FERRY A LIMO ONTO THE ISLAND?
I WAS AFRAID I'D NEVER SEE MY PRECIOUS BOYS AGAIN!
YIPE! YIPE!
I INSIST, YOU TWO MUST COME BACK WITH
I CAN'T BEGIN TO SHOW YOU HOW GRATEFUL I AM!
REALLY, IT WAS NOTHING, MISS...
BUT WE DO NEED TO GET BACK TO THE CITY SOMEHOW!
IF WE HURRY WE CAN STILL MAKE IT TO--
LET'S JUST SAY GOOD-BYE... TO...
...NIGEL?
HE'S GONE.

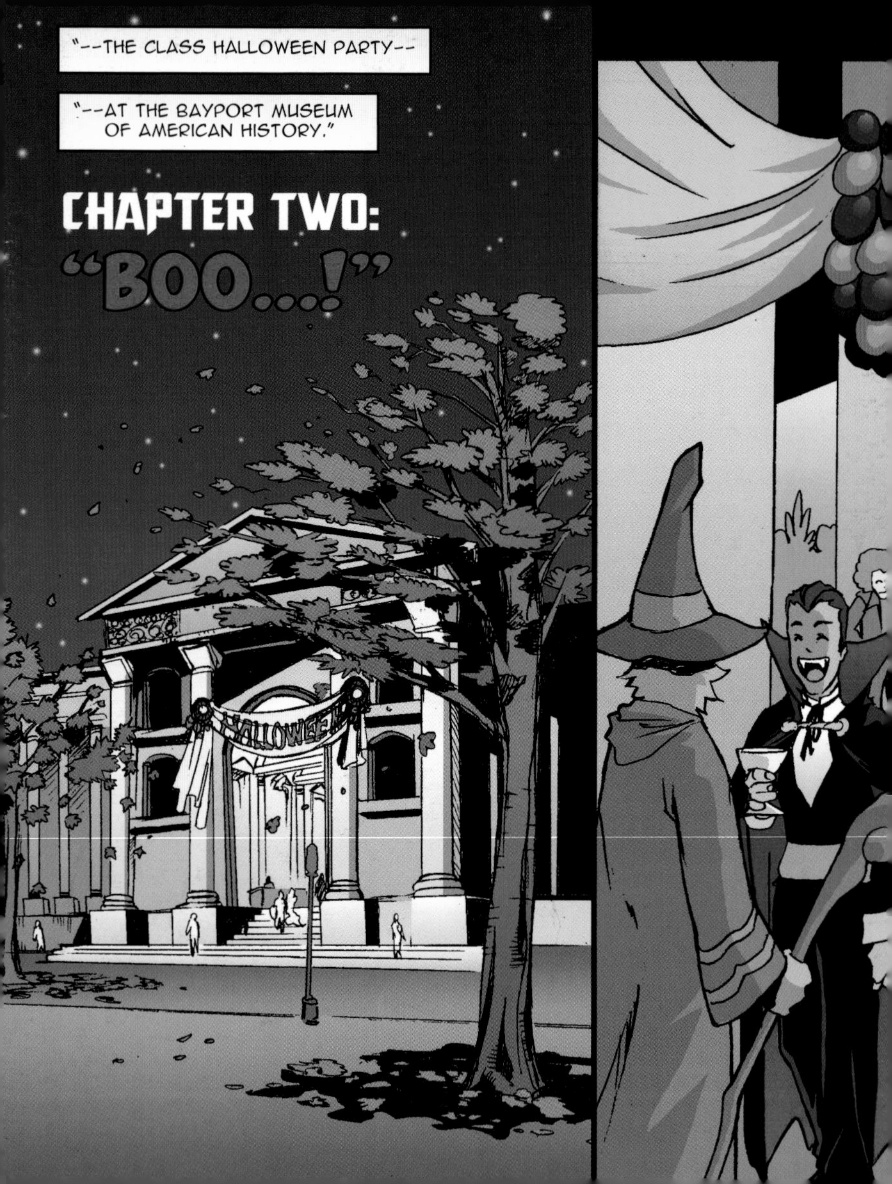
"--THE CLASS HALLOWEEN PARTY--
"--AT THE BAYPORT MUSEUM OF AMERICAN HISTORY."
CHAPTER TWO:
"BOO...!"

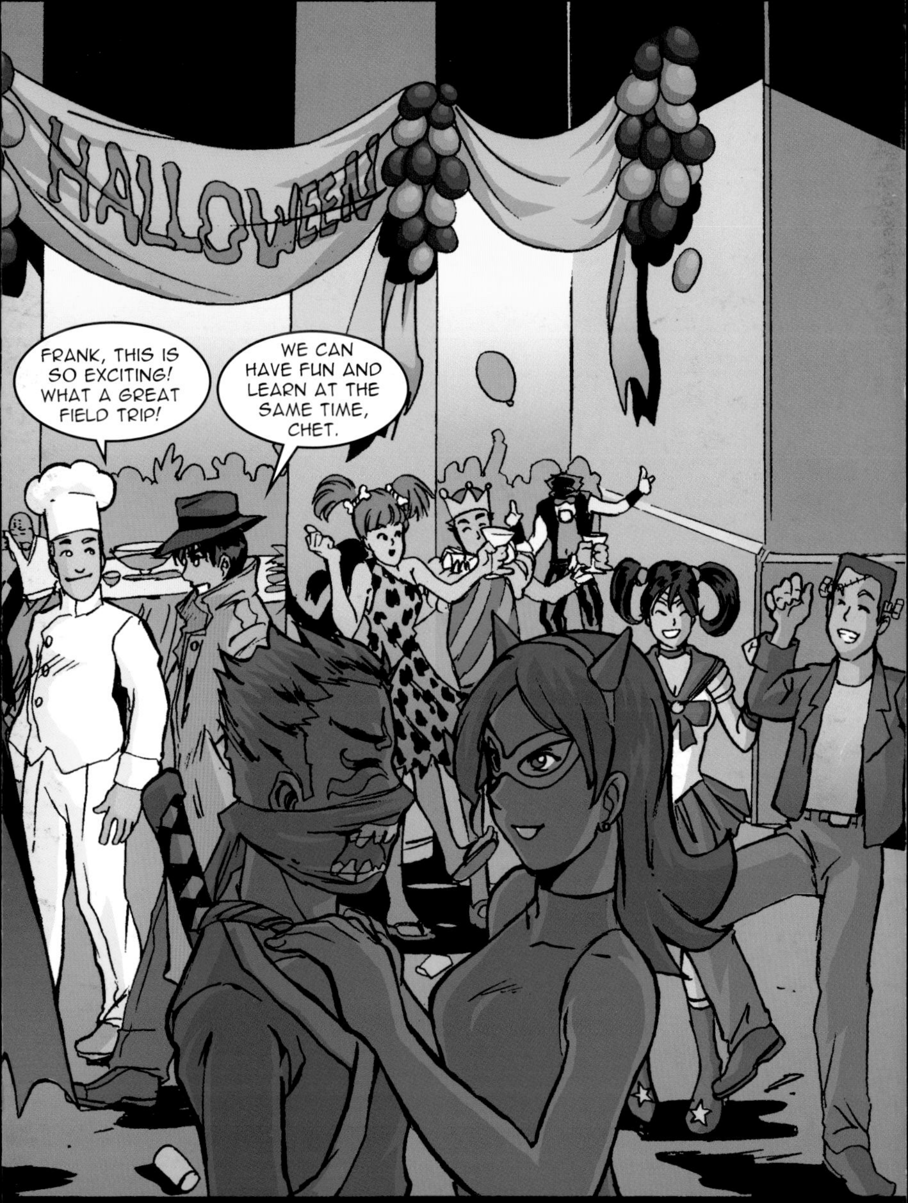
HALLOWEEN
FRANK, THIS IS SO EXCITING! WHAT A GREAT FIELD TRIP!
WE CAN HAVE FUN AND LEARN AT THE SAME TIME, CHET.

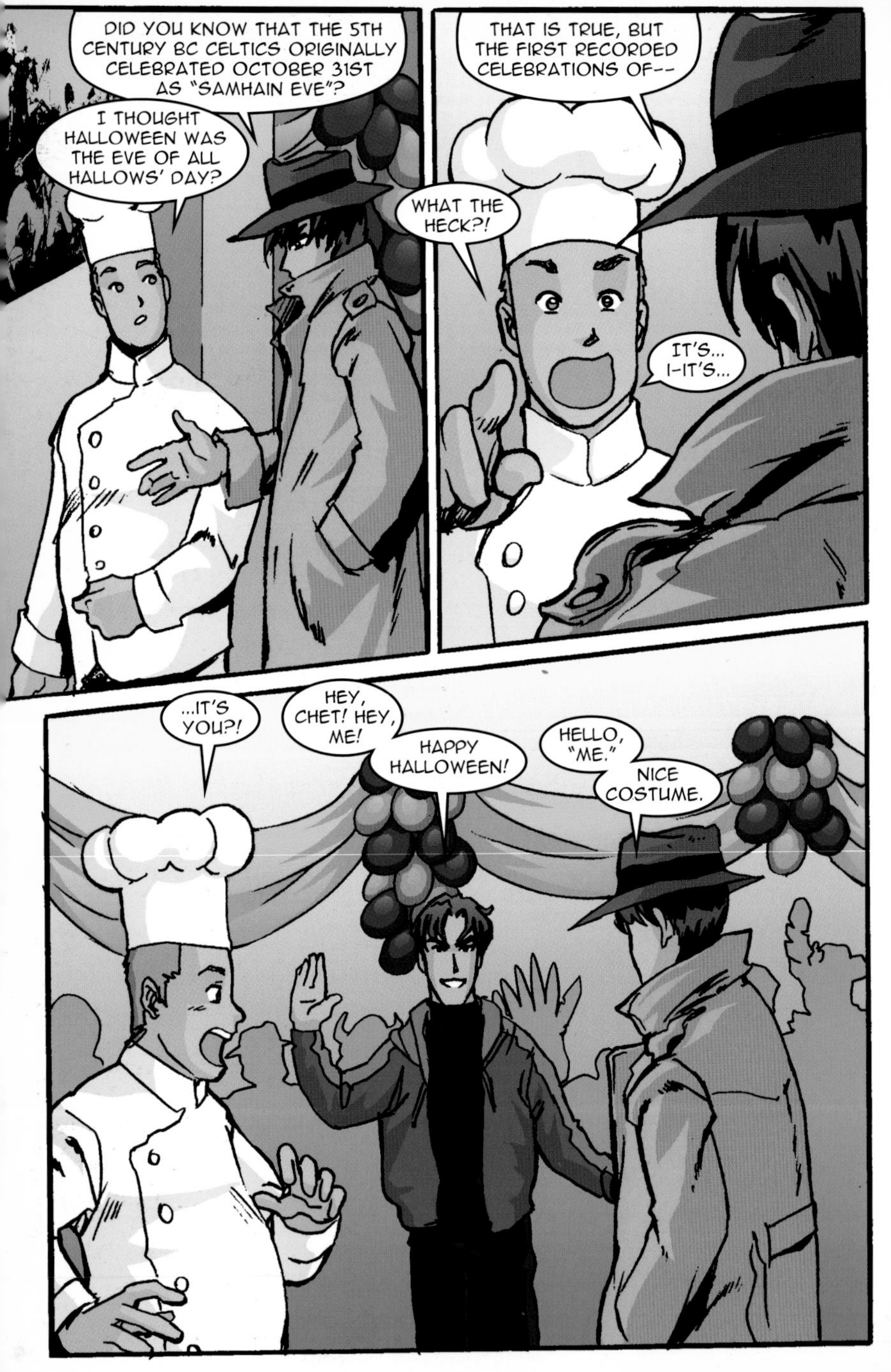
DID YOU KNOW THAT THE 5TH CENTURY BC CELTICS ORIGINALLY CELEBRATED OCTOBER 31ST AS "SAMHAIN EVE"?
I THOUGHT HALLOWEEN WAS THE EVE OF ALL HALLOWS' DAY?
THAT IS TRUE, BUT THE FIRST RECORDED CELEBRATIONS OF--
WHAT THE HECK?!
IT'S... I-IT'S...
...IT'S YOU?!
HEY, CHET! HEY, ME!
HAPPY HALLOWEEN!
HELLO, "ME."
NICE COSTUME.

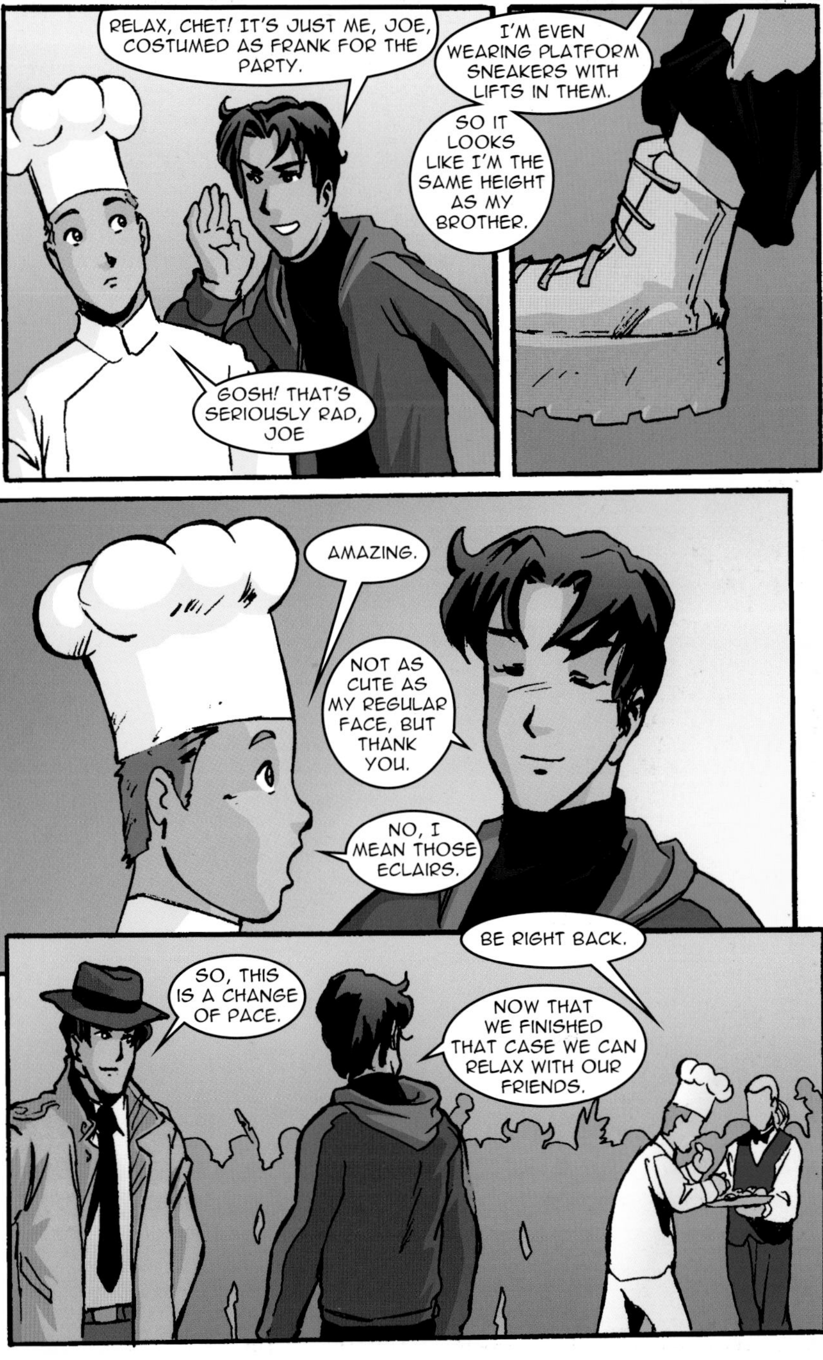
RELAX, CHET! IT'S JUST ME, JOE, COSTUMED AS FRANK FOR THE PARTY.
GOSH! THAT'S SERIOUSLY RAD, JOE
I'M EVEN WEARING PLATFORM SNEAKERS WITH LIFTS IN THEM.
SO IT LOOKS LIKE I'M THE SAME HEIGHT AS MY BROTHER.
AMAZING.
NOT AS CUTE AS MY REGULAR FACE, BUT THANK YOU.
NO, I MEAN THOSE ECLAIRS.
BE RIGHT BACK.
SO, THIS IS A CHANGE OF PACE.
NOW THAT WE FINISHED THAT CASE WE CAN RELAX WITH OUR FRIENDS.

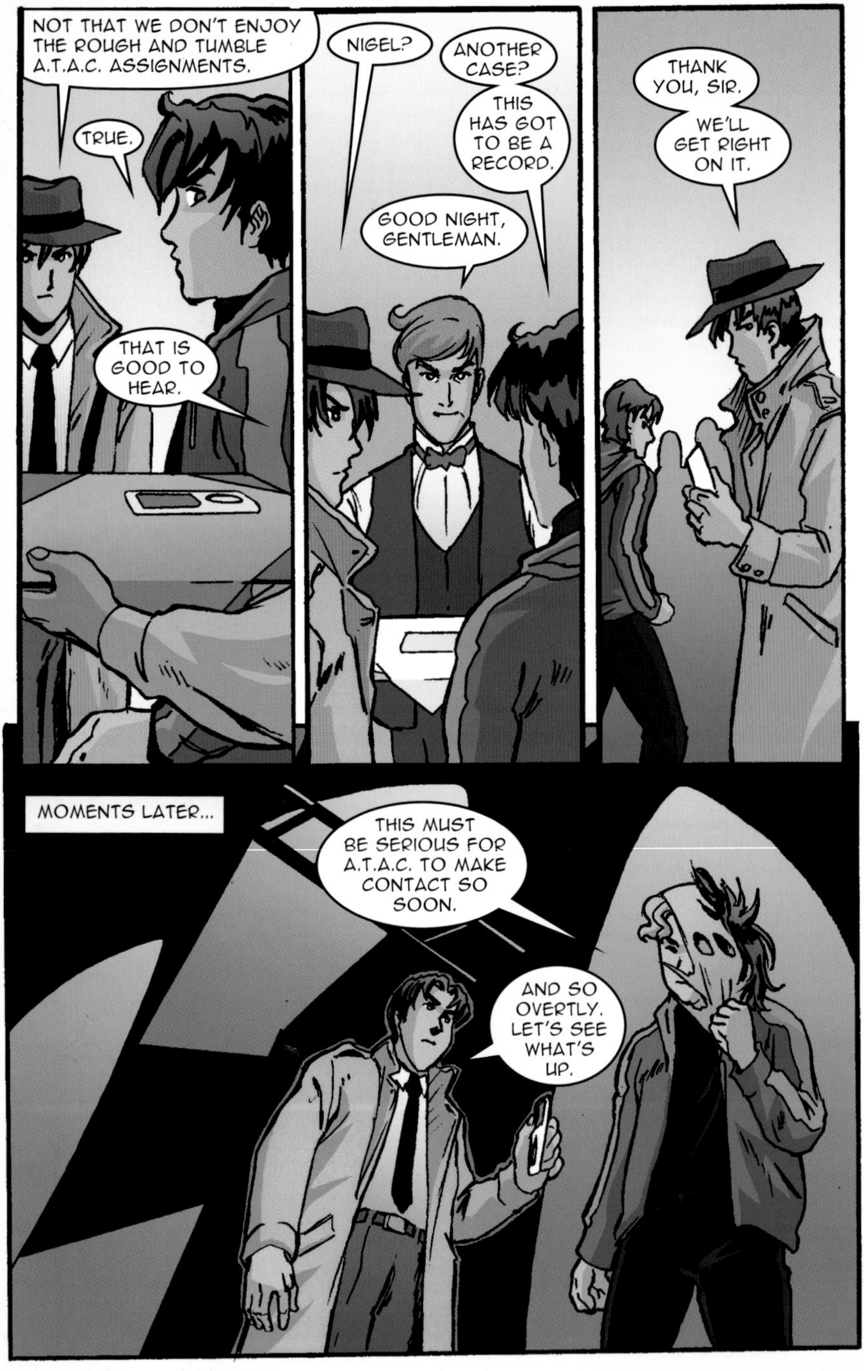
NOT THAT WE DON'T ENJOY THE ROUGH AND TUMBLE A.T.A.C. ASSIGNMENTS.
TRUE.
THAT IS GOOD TO HEAR.
NIGEL?
ANOTHER CASE?
THIS HAS GOT TO BE A RECORD.
GOOD NIGHT, GENTLEMAN.
THANK YOU, SIR.
WE'LL GET RIGHT ON IT.
MOMENTS LATER...
THIS MUST BE SERIOUS FOR A.T.A.C. TO MAKE CONTACT SO SOON.
AND SO OVERTLY. LET'S SEE WHAT'S UP.

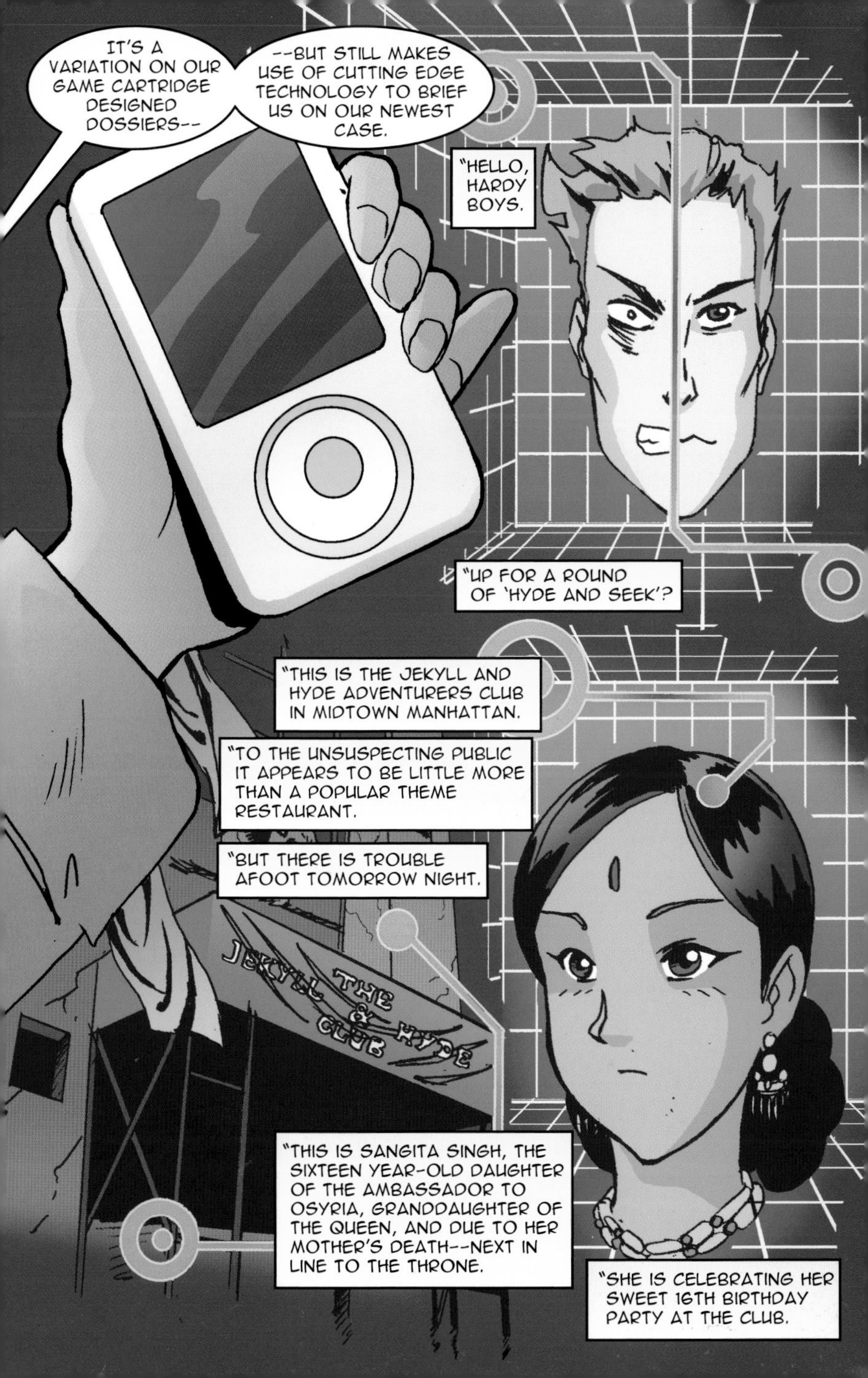
IT'S A VARIATION ON OUR GAME CARTRIDGE DESIGNED DOSSIERS--
--BUT STILL MAKES USE OF CUTTING EDGE TECHNOLOGY TO BRIEF US ON OUR NEWEST CASE.
"HELLO, HARDY BOYS.
"UP FOR A ROUND OF 'HYDE AND SEEK'?
"THIS IS THE JEKYLL AND HYDE ADVENTURERS CLUB IN MIDTOWN MANHATTAN.
"TO THE UNSUSPECTING PUBLIC IT APPEARS TO BE LITTLE MORE THAN A POPULAR THEME RESTAURANT.
"BUT THERE IS TROUBLE AFOOT TOMORROW NIGHT.
JEKYLL & THE HYDE CLUB
"THIS IS SANGITA SINGH, THE SIXTEEN YEAR-OLD DAUGHTER OF THE AMBASSADOR TO OSYRIA, GRANDDAUGHTER OF THE QUEEN, AND DUE TO HER MOTHER'S DEATH--NEXT IN LINE TO THE THRONE.
"SHE IS CELEBRATING HER SWEET 16TH BIRTHDAY PARTY AT THE CLUB.

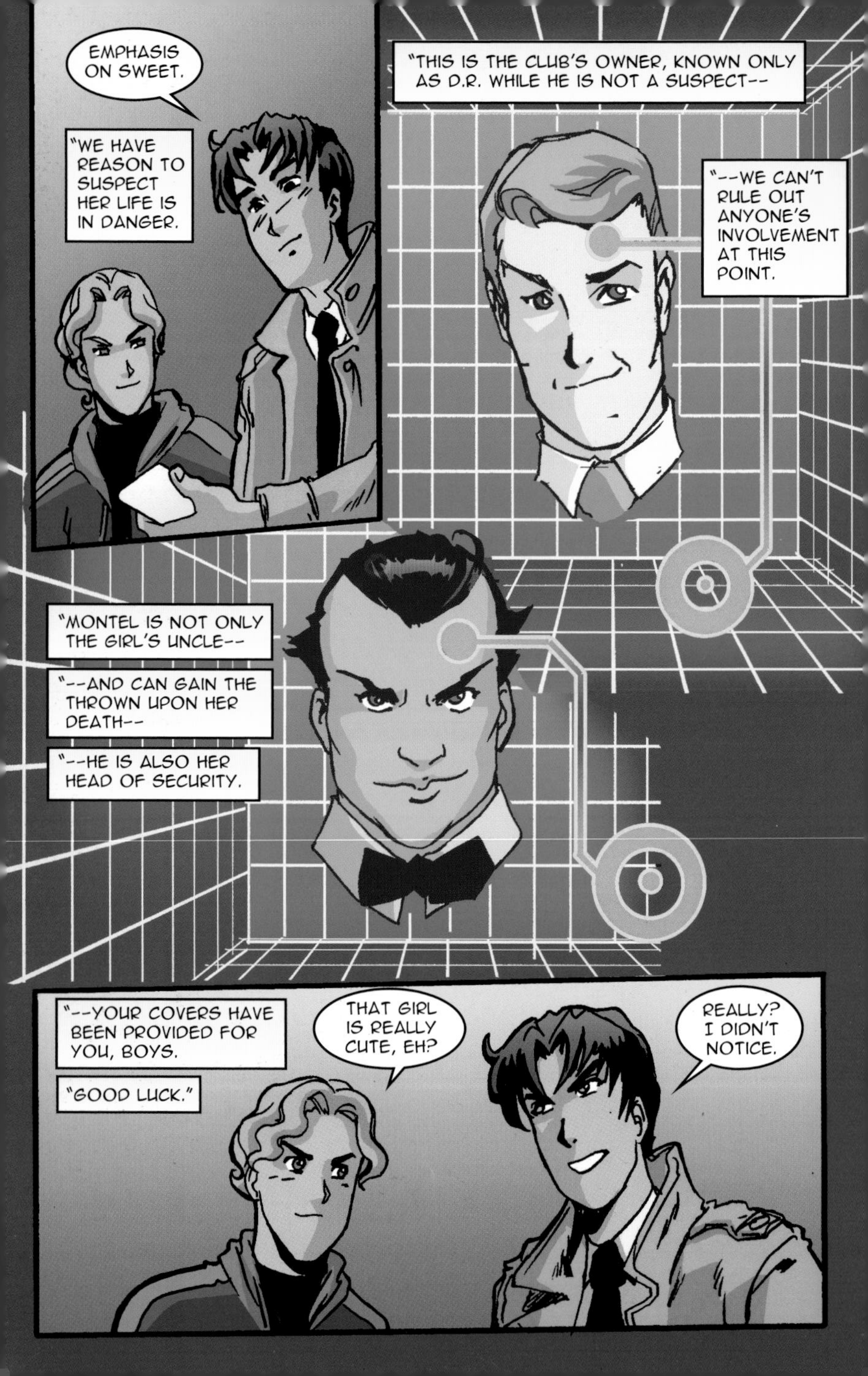

EMPHASIS ON SWEET.
"WE HAVE REASON TO SUSPECT HER LIFE IS IN DANGER.
"THIS IS THE CLUB'S OWNER, KNOWN ONLY AS D.R. WHILE HE IS NOT A SUSPECT--
"--WE CAN'T RULE OUT ANYONE'S INVOLVEMENT AT THIS POINT.
"MONTEL IS NOT ONLY THE GIRL'S UNCLE--
"--AND CAN GAIN THE THROWN UPON HER DEATH--
"--HE IS ALSO HER HEAD OF SECURITY.
"--YOUR COVERS HAVE BEEN PROVIDED FOR YOU, BOYS.
"GOOD LUCK."
THAT GIRL IS REALLY CUTE, EH?
REALLY? I DIDN'T NOTICE.

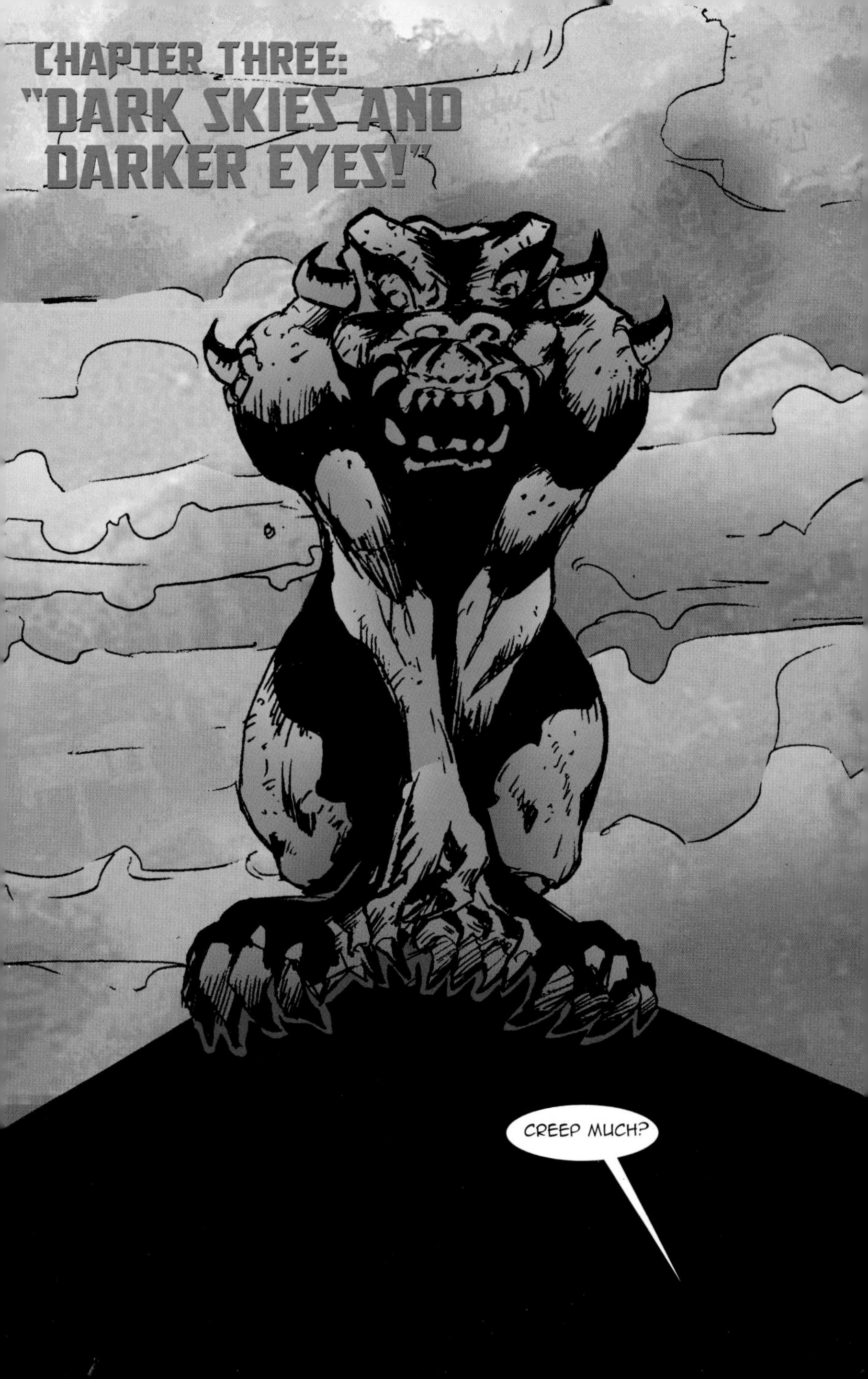
CHAPTER THREE:
"DARK SKIES AND DARKER EYES!"
CREEP MUCH?

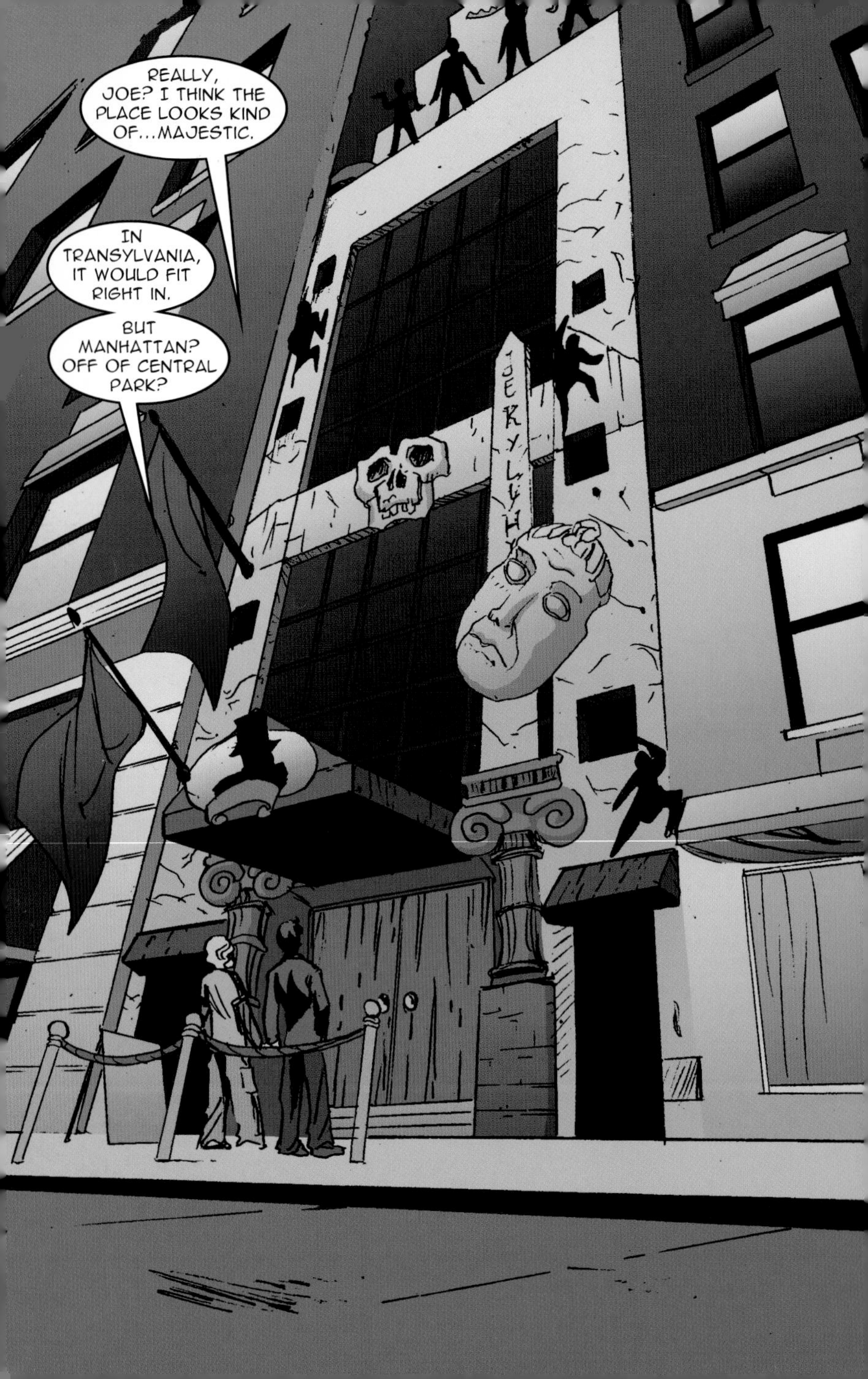
REALLY, JOE? I THINK THE PLACE LOOKS KIND OF...MAJESTIC.
IN TRANSYLVANIA, IT WOULD FIT RIGHT IN.
BUT MANHATTAN? OFF OF CENTRAL PARK?
JEKYLL HY

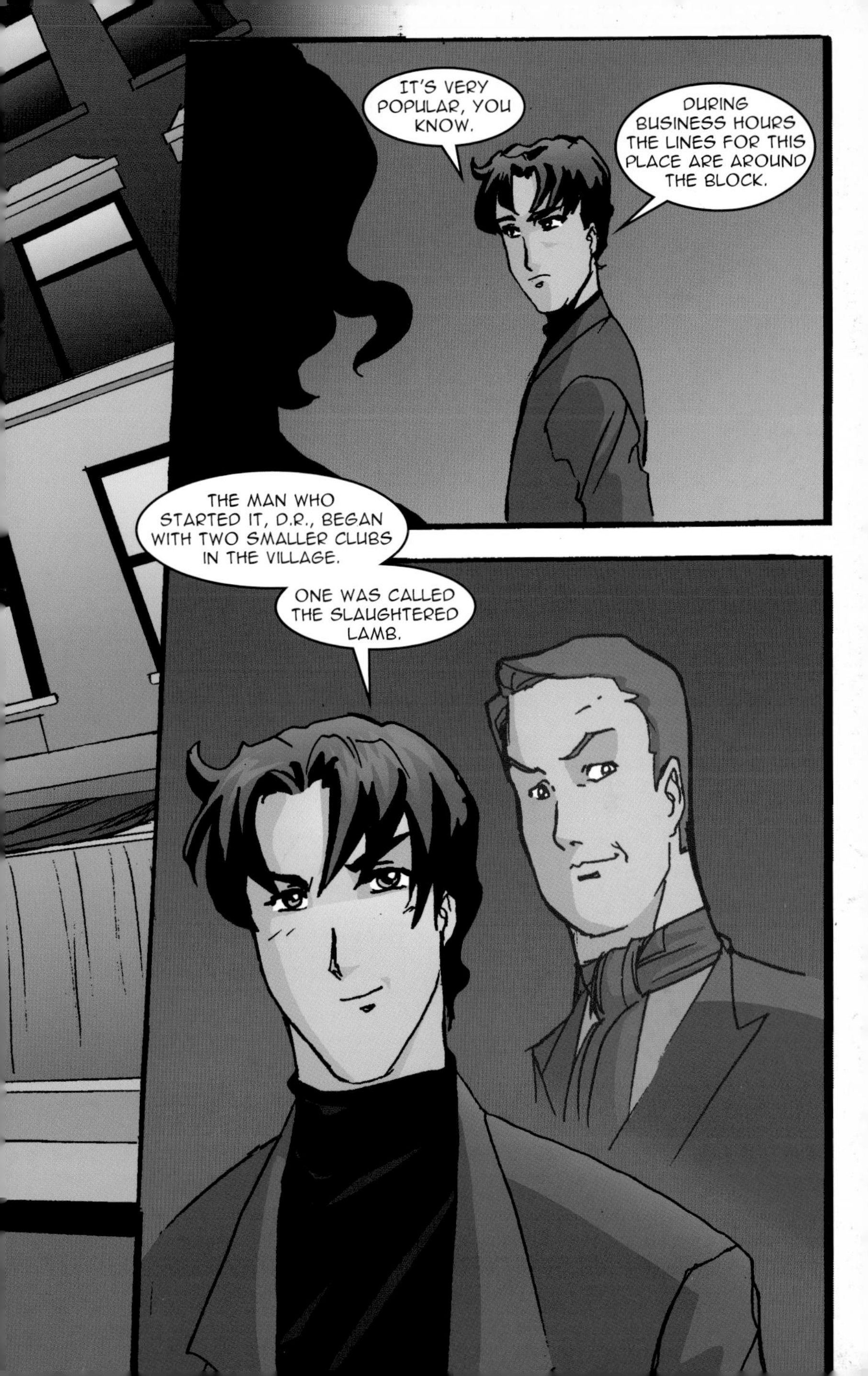
IT'S VERY POPULAR, YOU KNOW.
DURING BUSINESS HOURS THE LINES FOR THIS PLACE ARE AROUND THE BLOCK.
THE MAN WHO STARTED IT, D.R., BEGAN WITH TWO SMALLER CLUBS IN THE VILLAGE.
ONE WAS CALLED THE SLAUGHTERED LAMB.

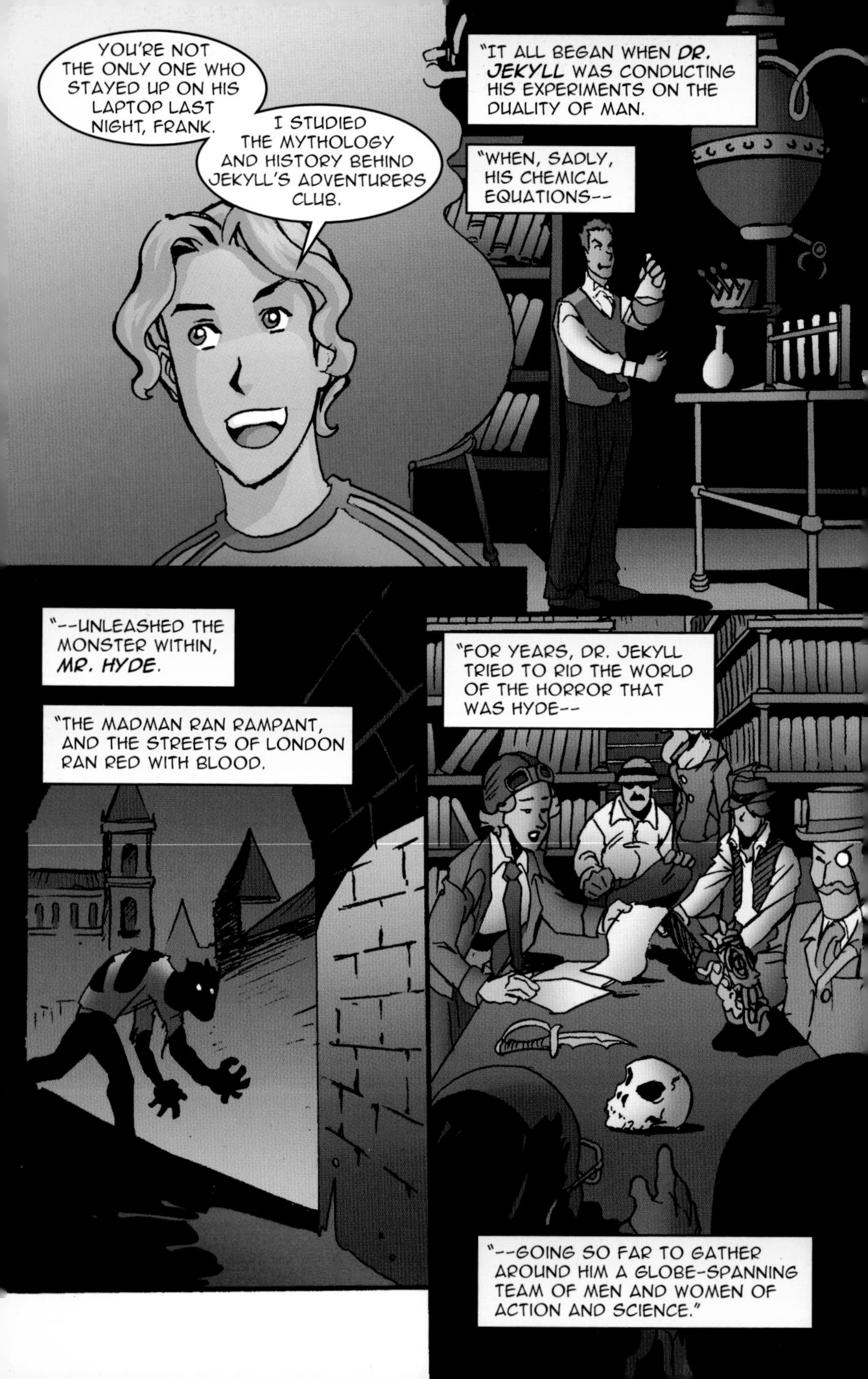
YOU'RE NOT THE ONLY ONE WHO STAYED UP ON HIS LAPTOP LAST NIGHT, FRANK.
I STUDIED THE MYTHOLOGY AND HISTORY BEHIND JEKYLL'S ADVENTURERS CLUB.
"IT ALL BEGAN WHEN DR. JEKYLL WAS CONDUCTING HIS EXPERIMENTS ON THE DUALITY OF MAN.
"WHEN, SADLY, HIS CHEMICAL EQUATIONS--
"--UNLEASHED THE MONSTER WITHIN, MR. HYDE.
"THE MADMAN RAN RAMPANT, AND THE STREETS OF LONDON RAN RED WITH BLOOD.
"FOR YEARS, DR. JEKYLL TRIED TO RID THE WORLD OF THE HORROR THAT WAS HYDE--
"--GOING SO FAR TO GATHER AROUND HIM A GLOBE-SPANNING TEAM OF MEN AND WOMEN OF ACTION AND SCIENCE."

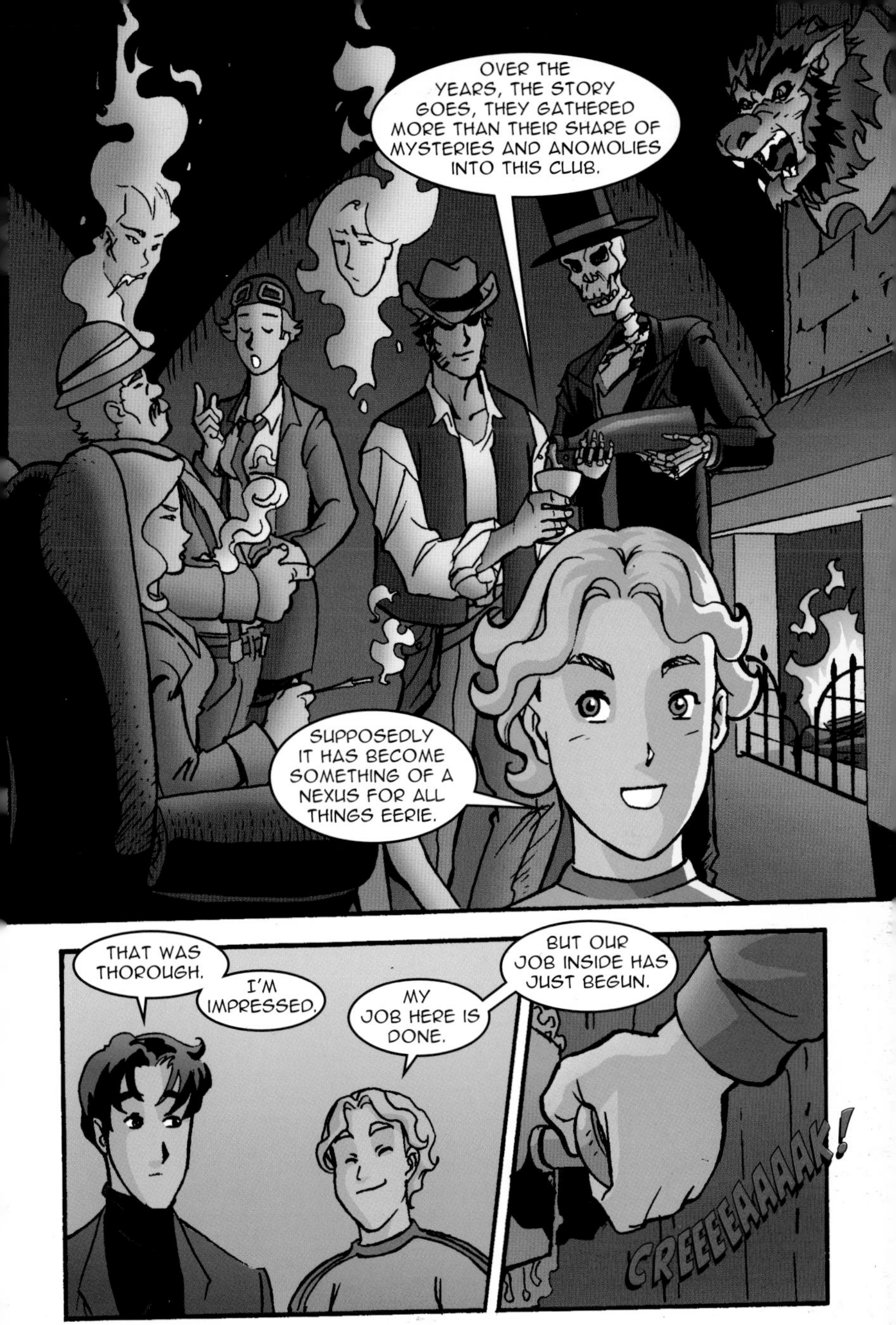
OVER THE YEARS, THE STORY GOES, THEY GATHERED MORE THAN THEIR SHARE OF MYSTERIES AND ANOMOLIES INTO THIS CLUB.
SUPPOSEDLY IT HAS BECOME SOMETHING OF A NEXUS FOR ALL THINGS EERIE.
THAT WAS THOROUGH.
I'M IMPRESSED.
MY JOB HERE IS DONE.
BUT OUR JOB INSIDE HAS JUST BEGUN.
CREEEEAAAAK!

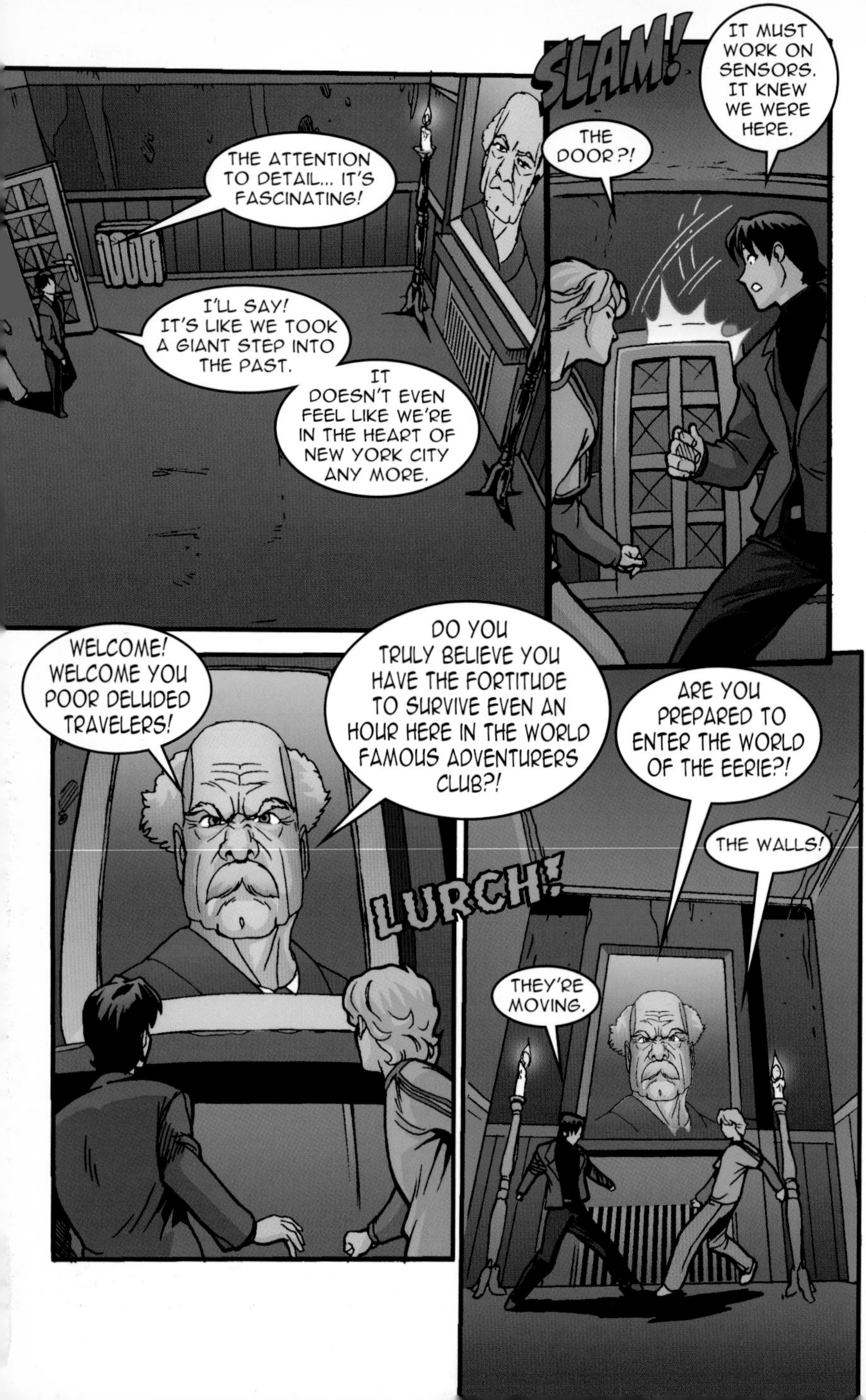
THE ATTENTION TO DETAIL... IT'S FASCINATING!
I'LL SAY! IT'S LIKE WE TOOK A GIANT STEP INTO THE PAST.
IT DOESN'T EVEN FEEL LIKE WE'RE IN THE HEART OF NEW YORK CITY ANY MORE.
SLAM!
THE DOOR?!
IT MUST WORK ON SENSORS. IT KNEW WE WERE HERE.
WELCOME! WELCOME YOU POOR DELUDED TRAVELERS!
DO YOU TRULY BELIEVE YOU HAVE THE FORTITUDE TO SURVIVE EVEN AN HOUR HERE IN THE WORLD FAMOUS ADVENTURERS CLUB?!
ARE YOU PREPARED TO ENTER THE WORLD OF THE EERIE?!
LURCH!
THE WALLS!
THEY'RE MOVING.

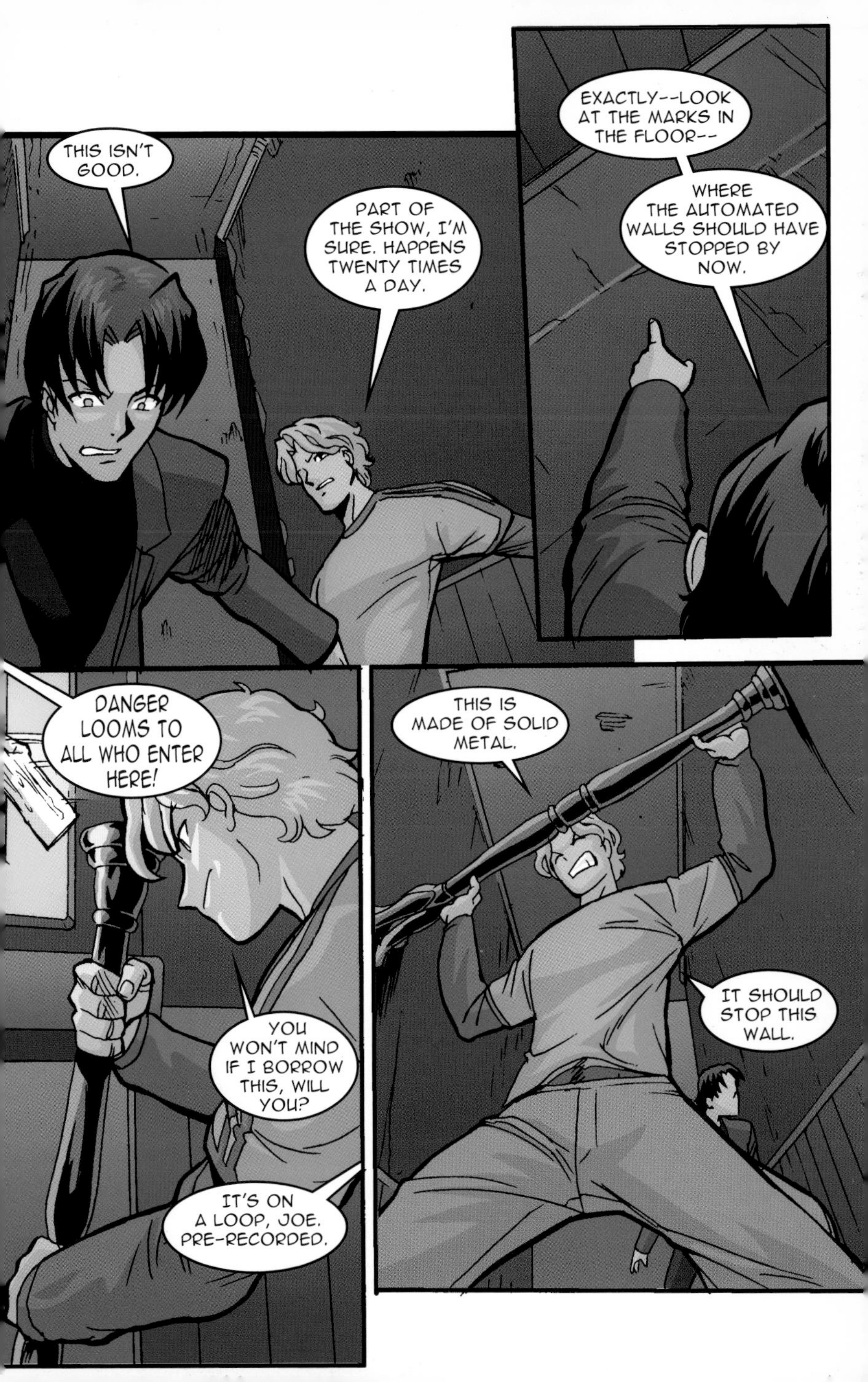
THIS ISN'T GOOD.
PART OF THE SHOW, I'M SURE. HAPPENS TWENTY TIMES A DAY.
EXACTLY--LOOK AT THE MARKS IN THE FLOOR--
WHERE THE AUTOMATED WALLS SHOULD HAVE STOPPED BY NOW.
DANGER LOOMS TO ALL WHO ENTER HERE!
YOU WON'T MIND IF I BORROW THIS, WILL YOU?
IT'S ON A LOOP, JOE. PRE-RECORDED.
THIS IS MADE OF SOLID METAL.
IT SHOULD STOP THIS WALL.

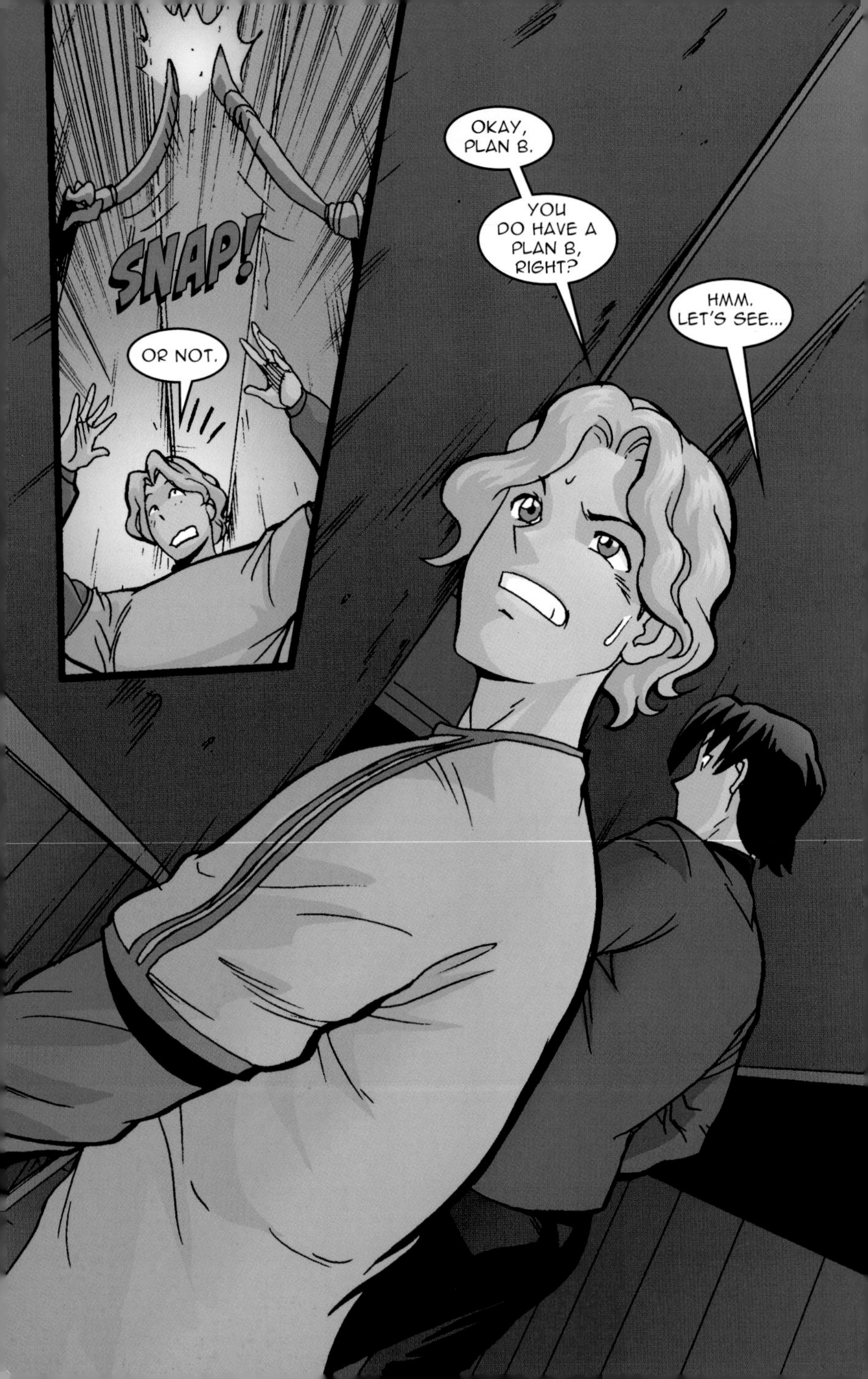
SNAP!
OR NOT.
OKAY, PLAN B.
YOU DO HAVE A PLAN B, RIGHT?
HMM. LET'S SEE...

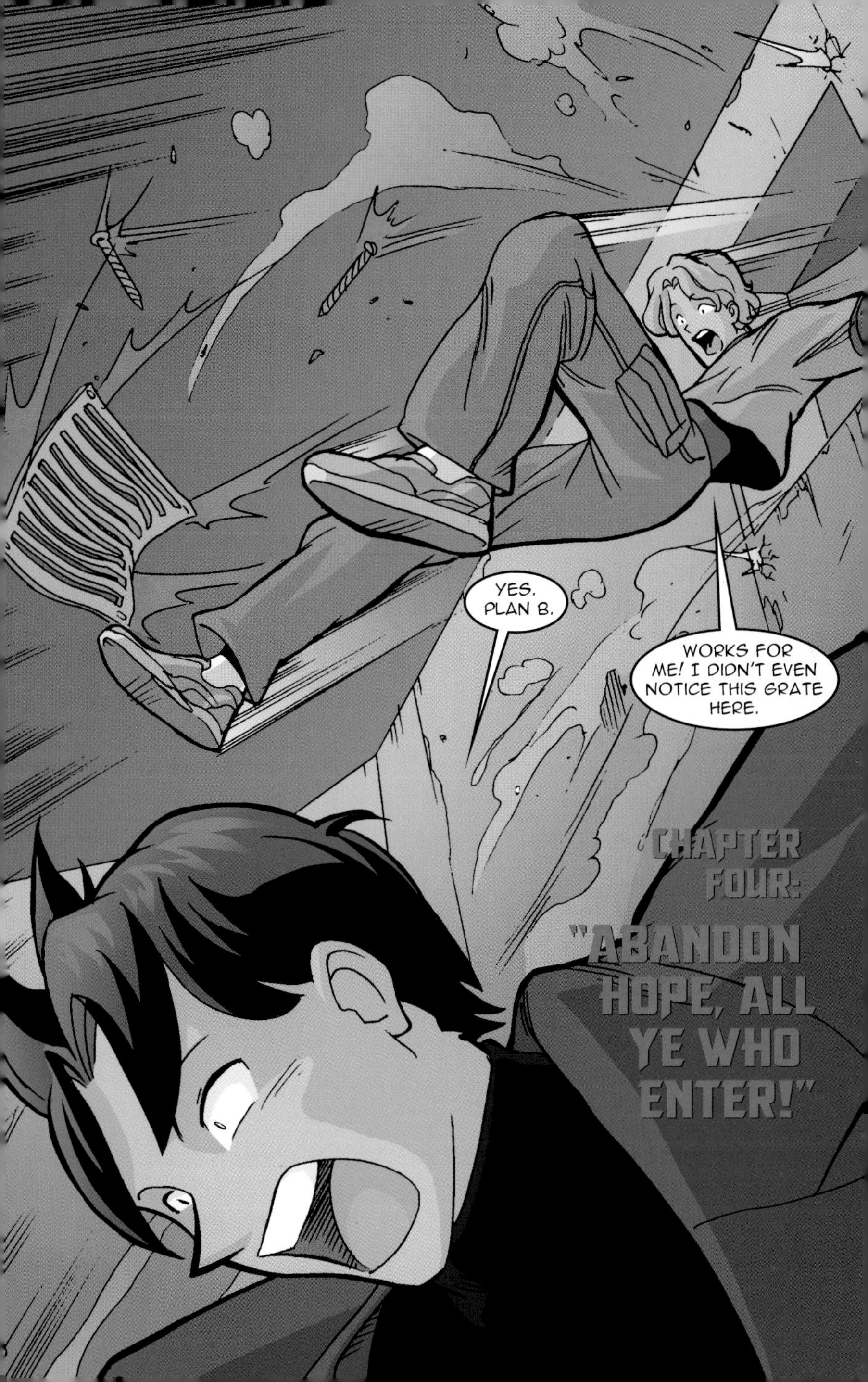
YES. PLAN B.
WORKS FOR ME! I DIDN'T EVEN NOTICE THIS GRATE HERE.
CHAPTER FOUR:
"ABANDON HOPE, ALL YE WHO ENTER!"

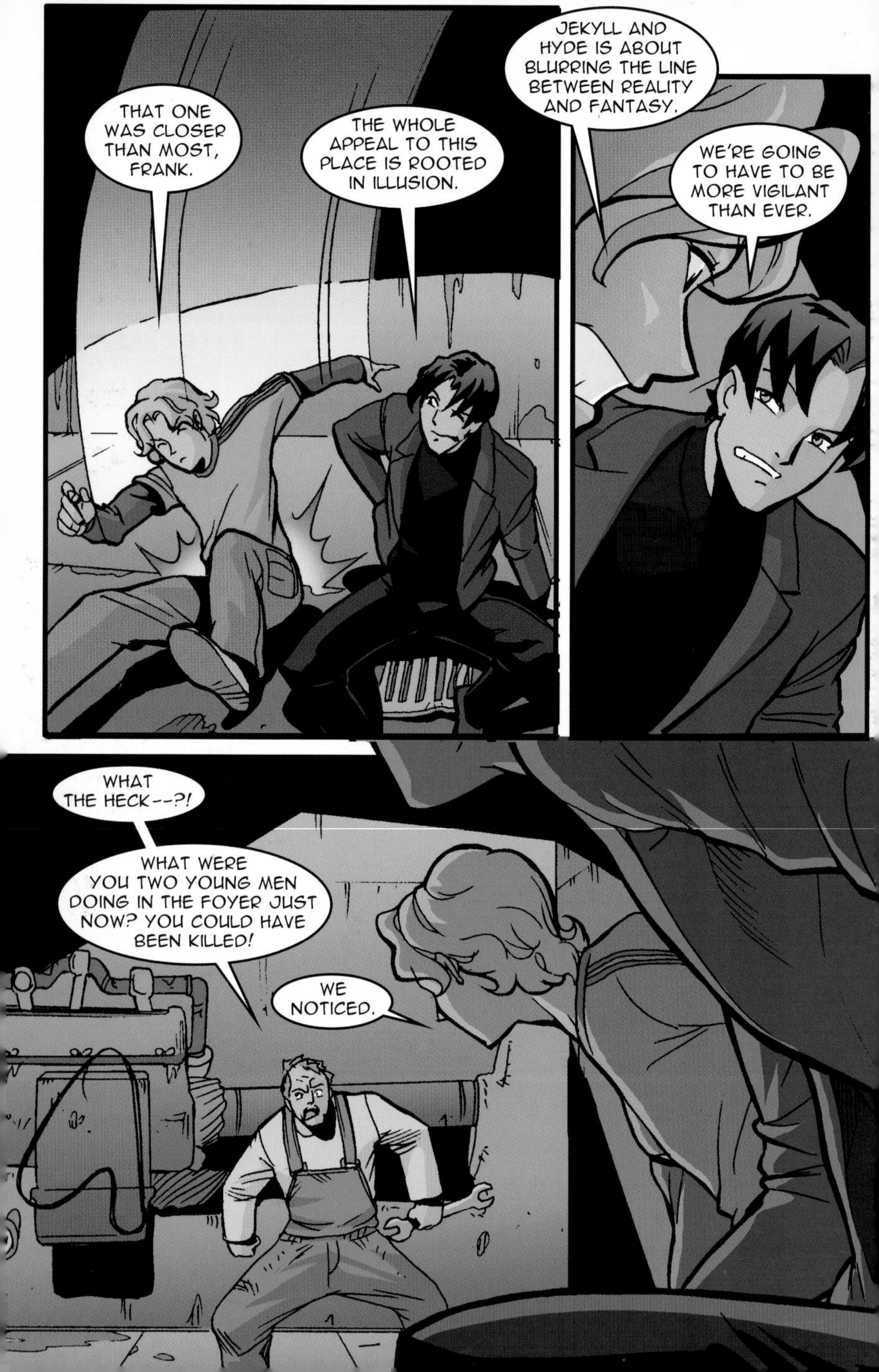
THAT ONE WAS CLOSER THAN MOST, FRANK.
THE WHOLE APPEAL TO THIS PLACE IS ROOTED IN ILLUSION.
JEKYLL AND HYDE IS ABOUT BLURRING THE LINE BETWEEN REALITY AND FANTASY.
WE'RE GOING TO HAVE TO BE MORE VIGILANT THAN EVER.
WHAT THE HECK--?!
WHAT WERE YOU TWO YOUNG MEN DOING IN THE FOYER JUST NOW? YOU COULD HAVE BEEN KILLED!
WE NOTICED.

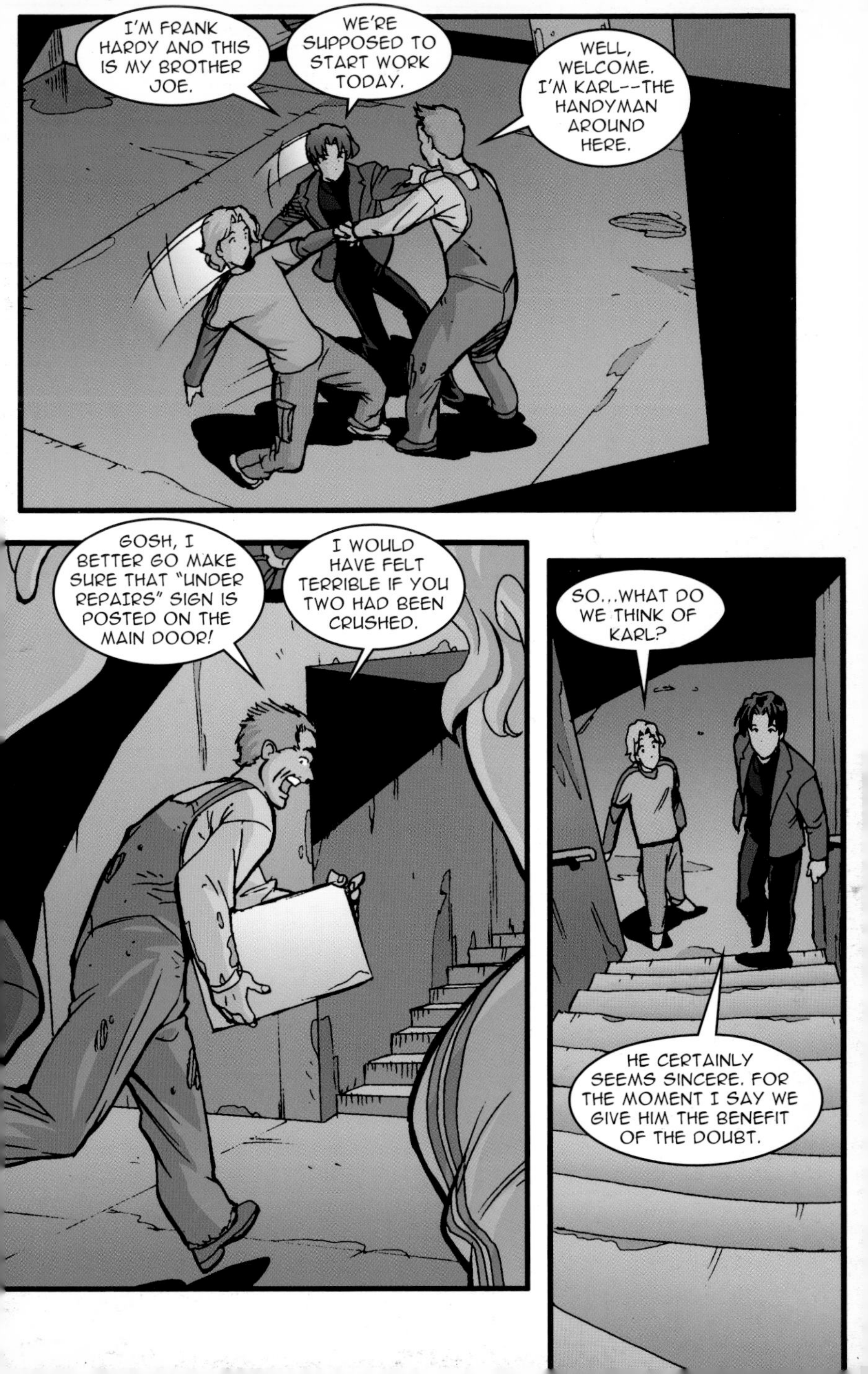
I'M FRANK HARDY AND THIS IS MY BROTHER JOE.
WE'RE SUPPOSED TO START WORK TODAY.
WELL, WELCOME. I'M KARL--THE HANDYMAN AROUND HERE.
GOSH, I BETTER GO MAKE SURE THAT "UNDER REPAIRS" SIGN IS POSTED ON THE MAIN DOOR!
I WOULD HAVE FELT TERRIBLE IF YOU TWO HAD BEEN CRUSHED.
SO...WHAT DO WE THINK OF KARL?
HE CERTAINLY SEEMS SINCERE. FOR THE MOMENT I SAY WE GIVE HIM THE BENEFIT OF THE DOUBT.

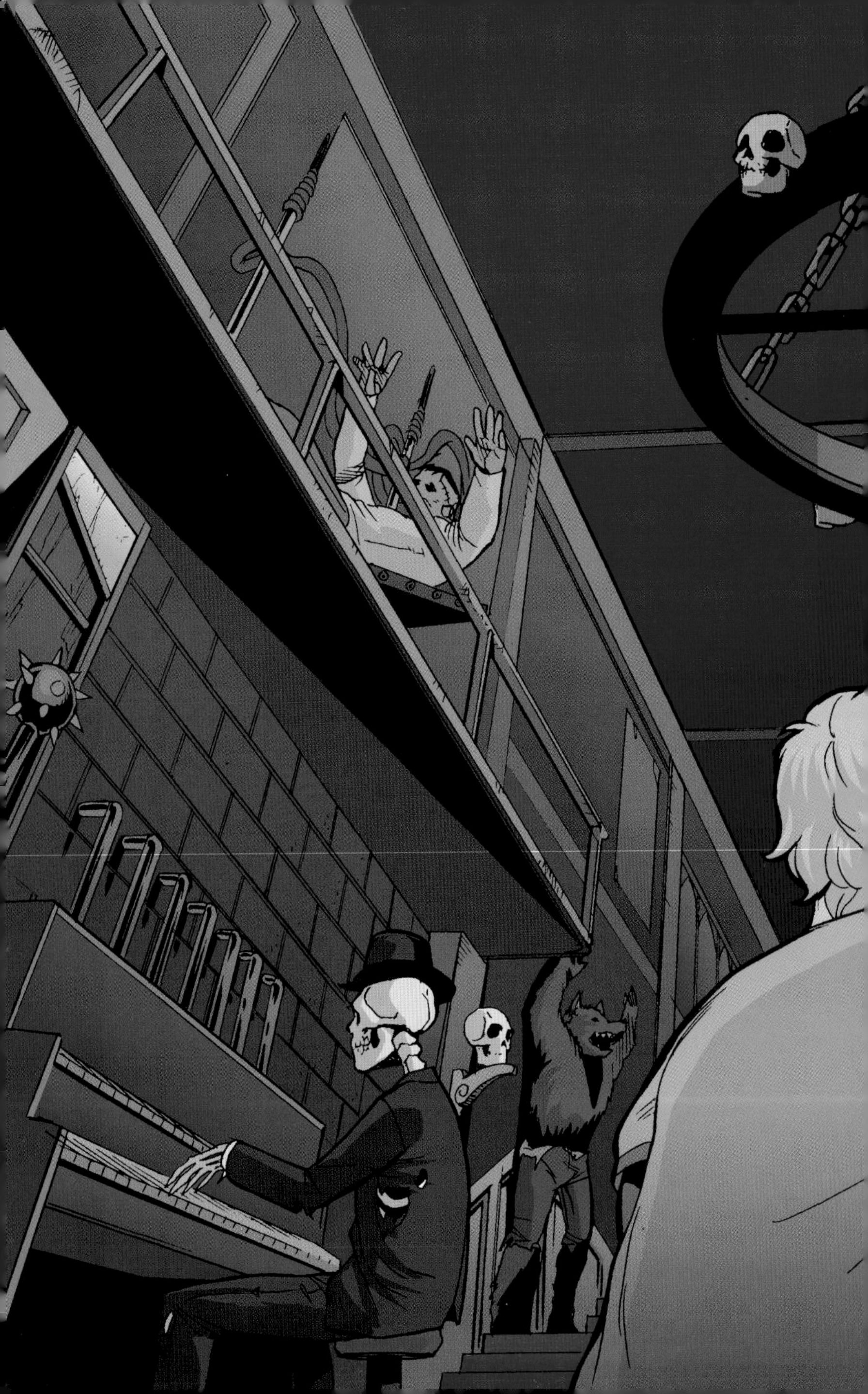

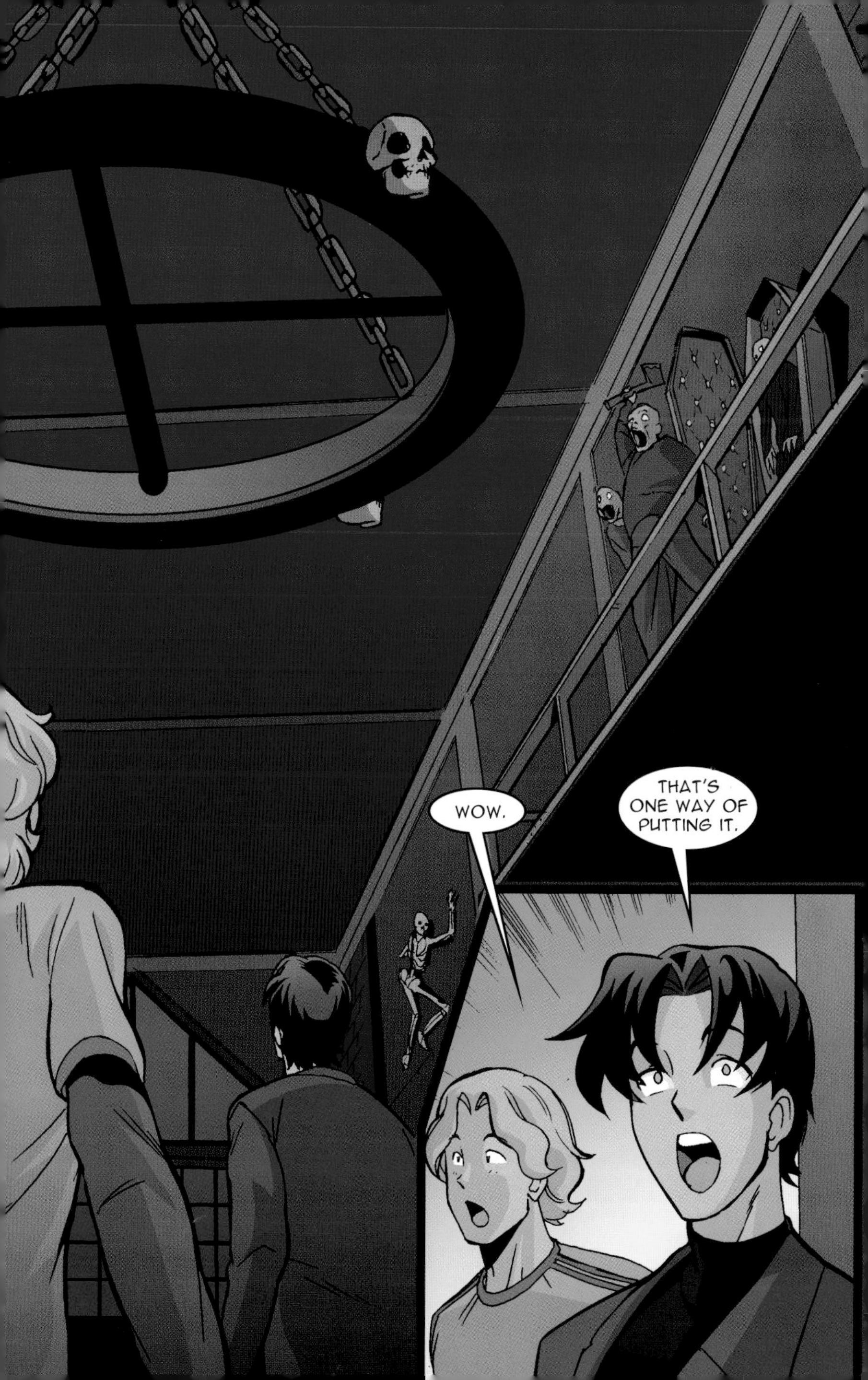
WOW.
THAT'S ONE WAY OF PUTTING IT.

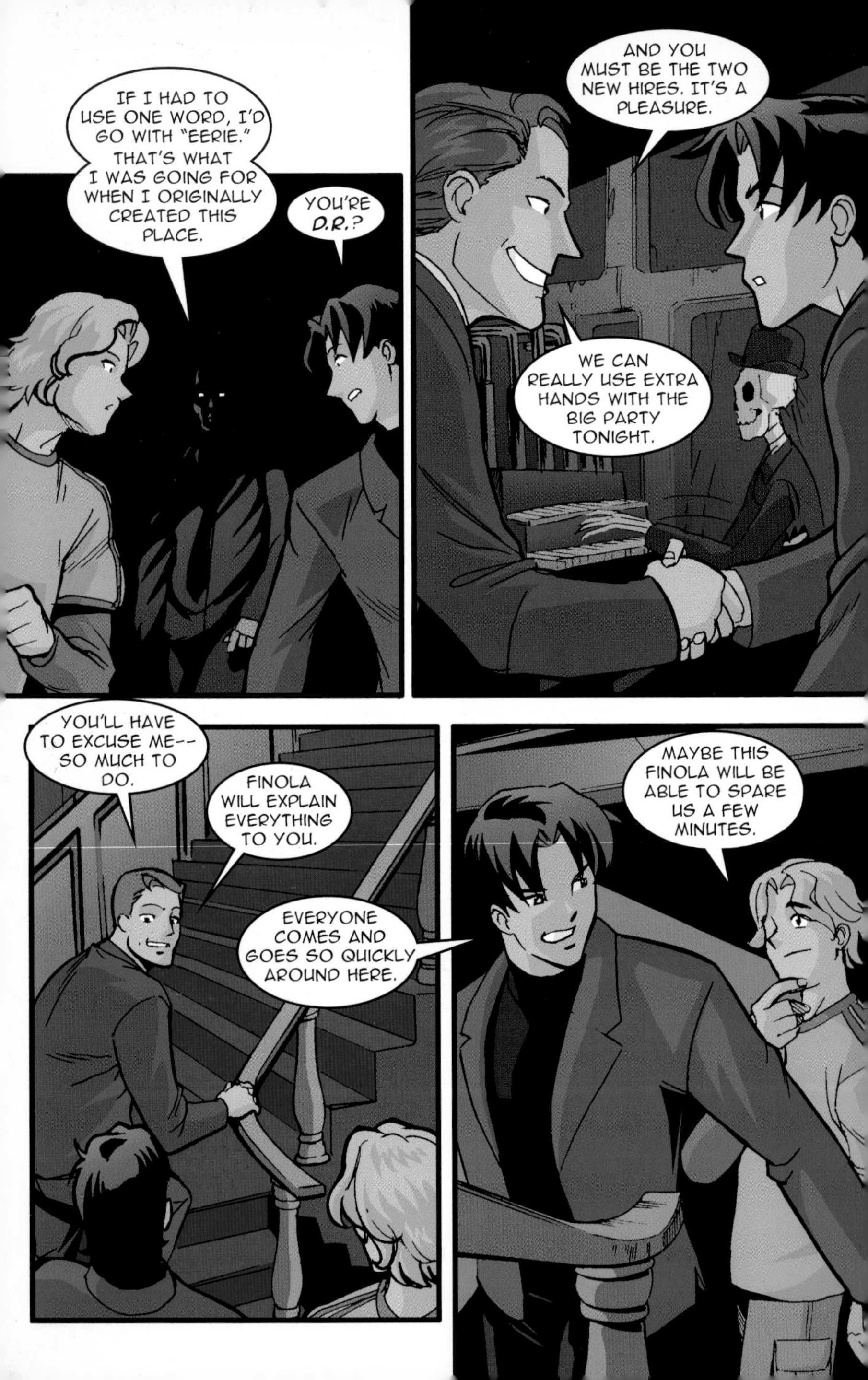
IF I HAD TO USE ONE WORD, I'D GO WITH "EERIE."
THAT'S WHAT I WAS GOING FOR WHEN I ORIGINALLY CREATED THIS PLACE.
YOU'RE *D.R.*?
AND YOU MUST BE THE TWO NEW HIRES. IT'S A PLEASURE.
WE CAN REALLY USE EXTRA HANDS WITH THE BIG PARTY TONIGHT.
YOU'LL HAVE TO EXCUSE ME-- SO MUCH TO DO.
FINOLA WILL EXPLAIN EVERYTHING TO YOU.
EVERYONE COMES AND GOES SO QUICKLY AROUND HERE.
MAYBE THIS FINOLA WILL BE ABLE TO SPARE US A FEW MINUTES.

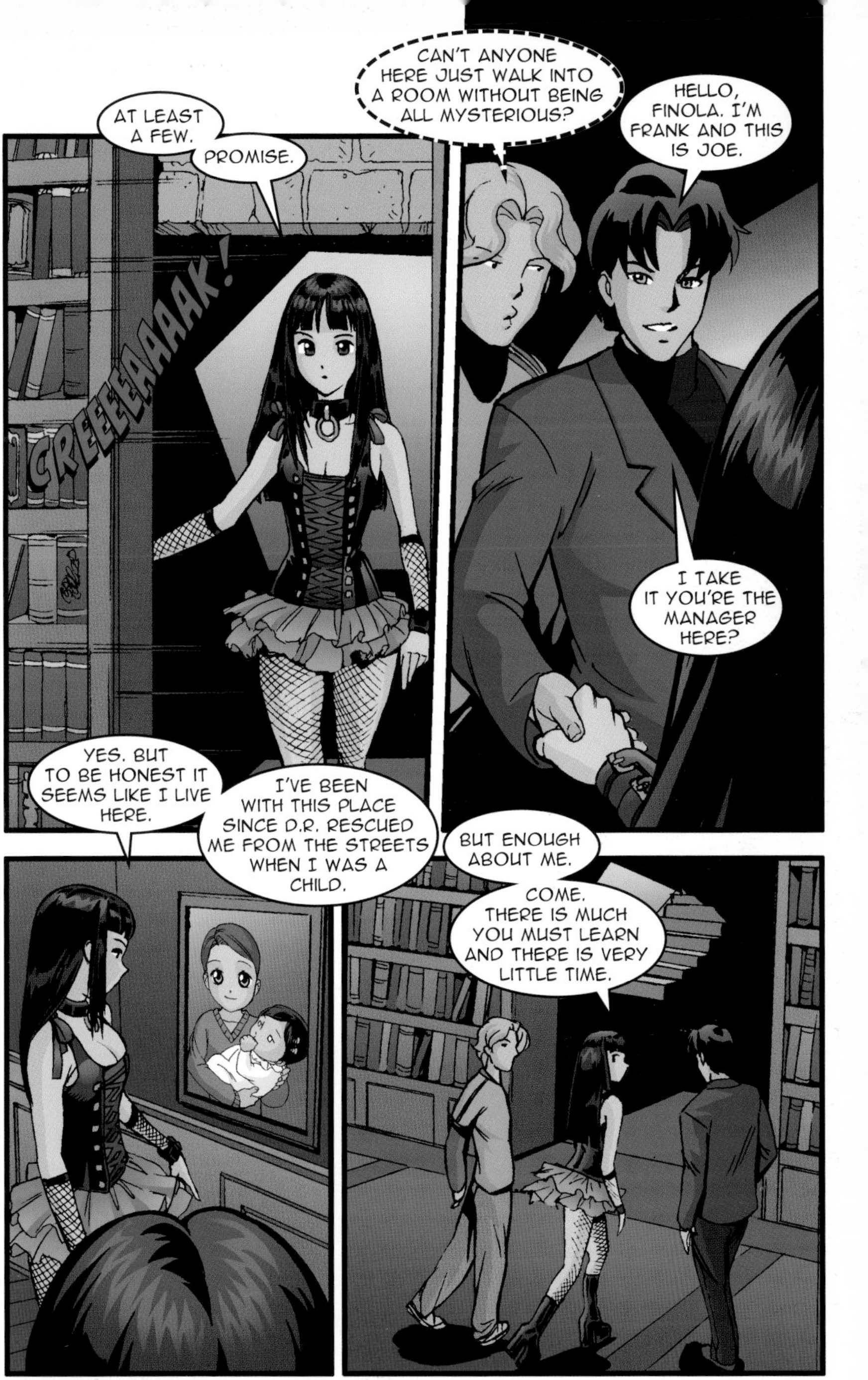
AT LEAST A FEW.
PROMISE.
CREEEEAAAAK!
CAN'T ANYONE HERE JUST WALK INTO A ROOM WITHOUT BEING ALL MYSTERIOUS?
HELLO, FINOLA. I'M FRANK AND THIS IS JOE.
I TAKE IT YOU'RE THE MANAGER HERE?
YES. BUT TO BE HONEST IT SEEMS LIKE I LIVE HERE.
I'VE BEEN WITH THIS PLACE SINCE D.R. RESCUED ME FROM THE STREETS WHEN I WAS A CHILD.
BUT ENOUGH ABOUT ME.
COME. THERE IS MUCH YOU MUST LEARN AND THERE IS VERY LITTLE TIME.

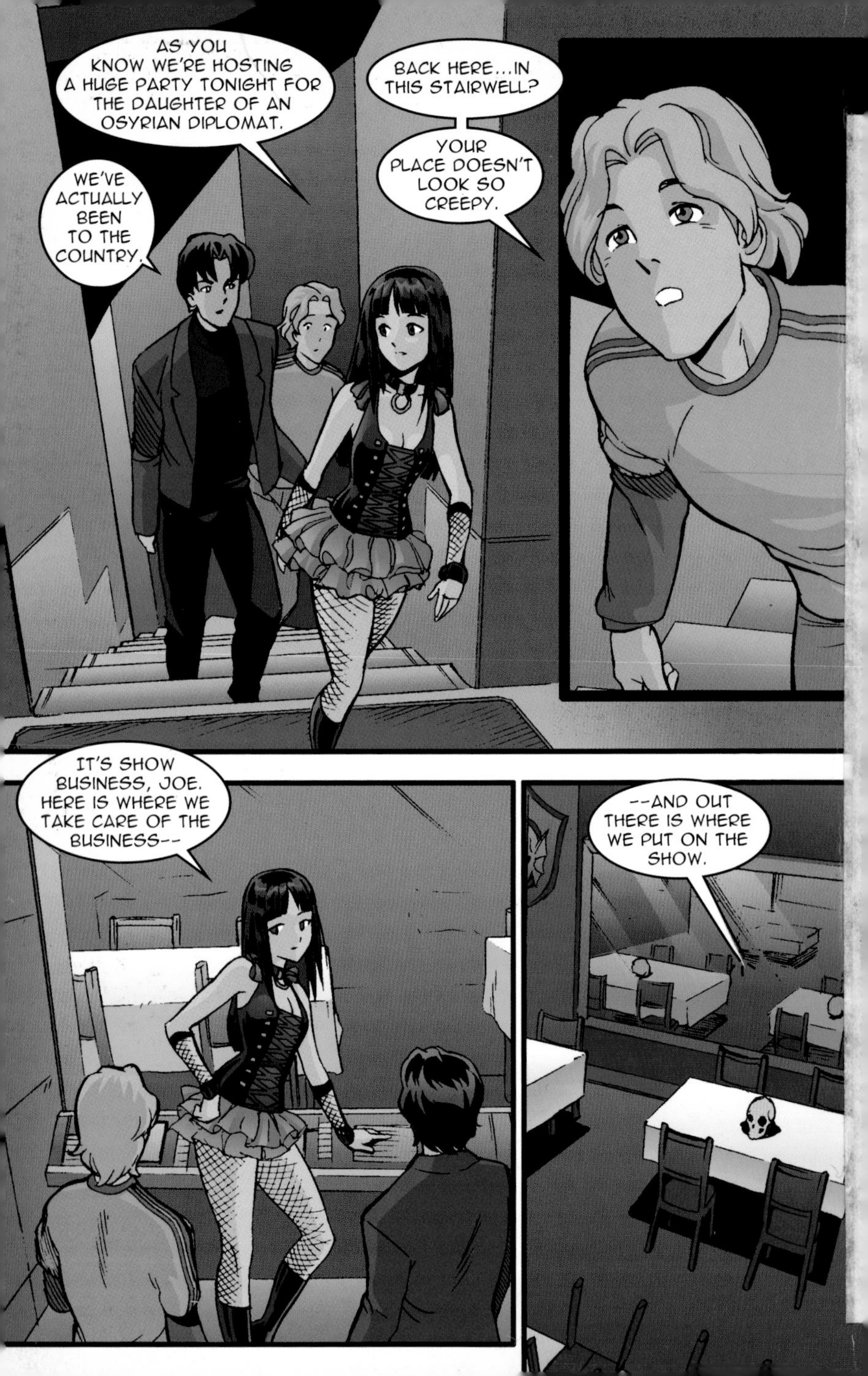

AS YOU KNOW WE'RE HOSTING A HUGE PARTY TONIGHT FOR THE DAUGHTER OF AN OSYRIAN DIPLOMAT.
WE'VE ACTUALLY BEEN TO THE COUNTRY.
BACK HERE...IN THIS STAIRWELL?
YOUR PLACE DOESN'T LOOK SO CREEPY.
IT'S SHOW BUSINESS, JOE. HERE IS WHERE WE TAKE CARE OF THE BUSINESS--
--AND OUT THERE IS WHERE WE PUT ON THE SHOW.

THIS IS THE PREP ROOM, WHERE THE ADVENTURERS WHO WANDER THE FLOOR SLIP FROM THEIR DAY-TO-DAY CLOTHES.

FRANK, YOU'VE BEEN ASSIGNED THE ROLE OF AN INTERNATIONAL PARANORMAL HUNTER.

NOT EXACTLY MY FORTE, TO BE HONEST.

I'M MORE OF A "FACTS" GUY, BUT I'LL DO MY BEST.

I HAVE EVERY CONFIDENCE.

JOE, IF YOU'LL COME WITH ME?

I DON'T GET A COSTUME?

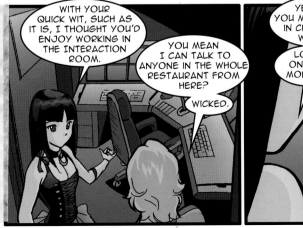

WITH YOUR QUICK WIT, SUCH AS IT IS, I THOUGHT YOU'D ENJOY WORKING IN THE INTERACTION ROOM.

YOU MEAN I CAN TALK TO ANYONE IN THE WHOLE RESTAURANT FROM HERE?

WICKED.

YES, BUT YOU MUST REMAIN IN CHARACTER WHEN--

LOOK! ON THAT MONITOR!

HELP ME! SOMEONE, PLEASE!

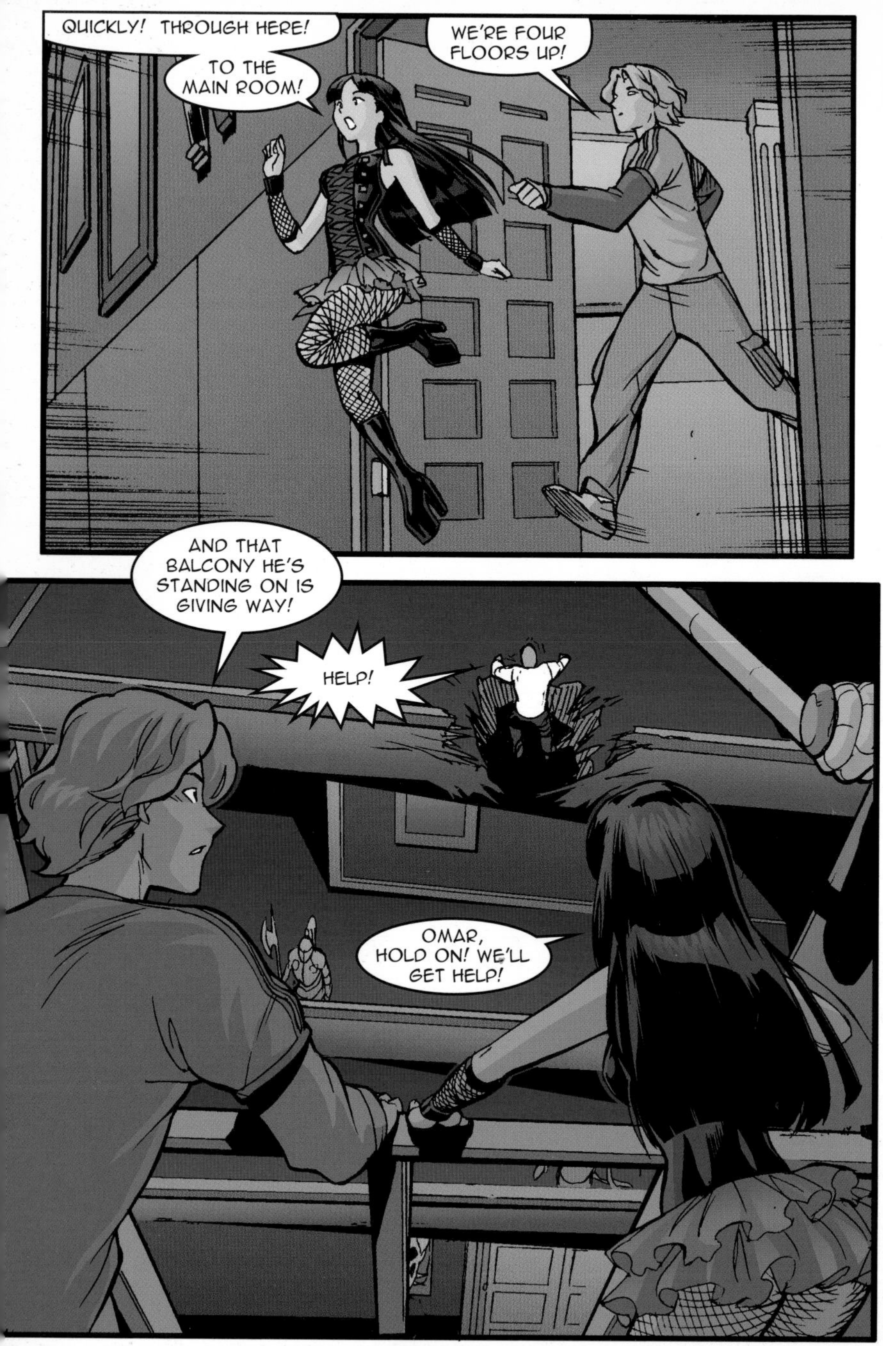
QUICKLY! THROUGH HERE!
TO THE MAIN ROOM!
WE'RE FOUR FLOORS UP!
AND THAT BALCONY HE'S STANDING ON IS GIVING WAY!
HELP!
OMAR, HOLD ON! WE'LL GET HELP!

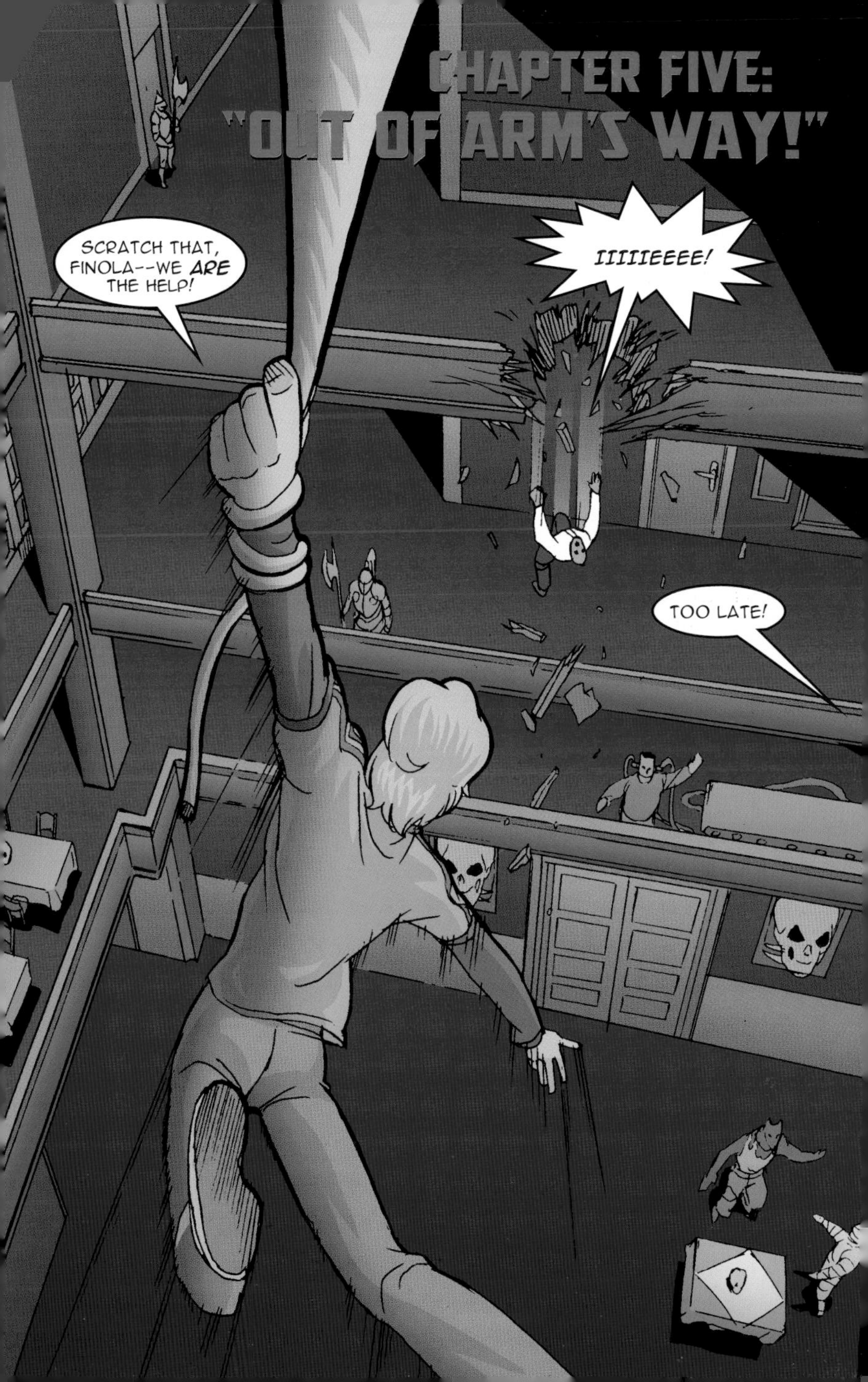
CHAPTER FIVE:
"OUT OF ARM'S WAY!"
SCRATCH THAT, FINOLA--WE ARE THE HELP!
IIIIIEEEE!
TOO LATE!

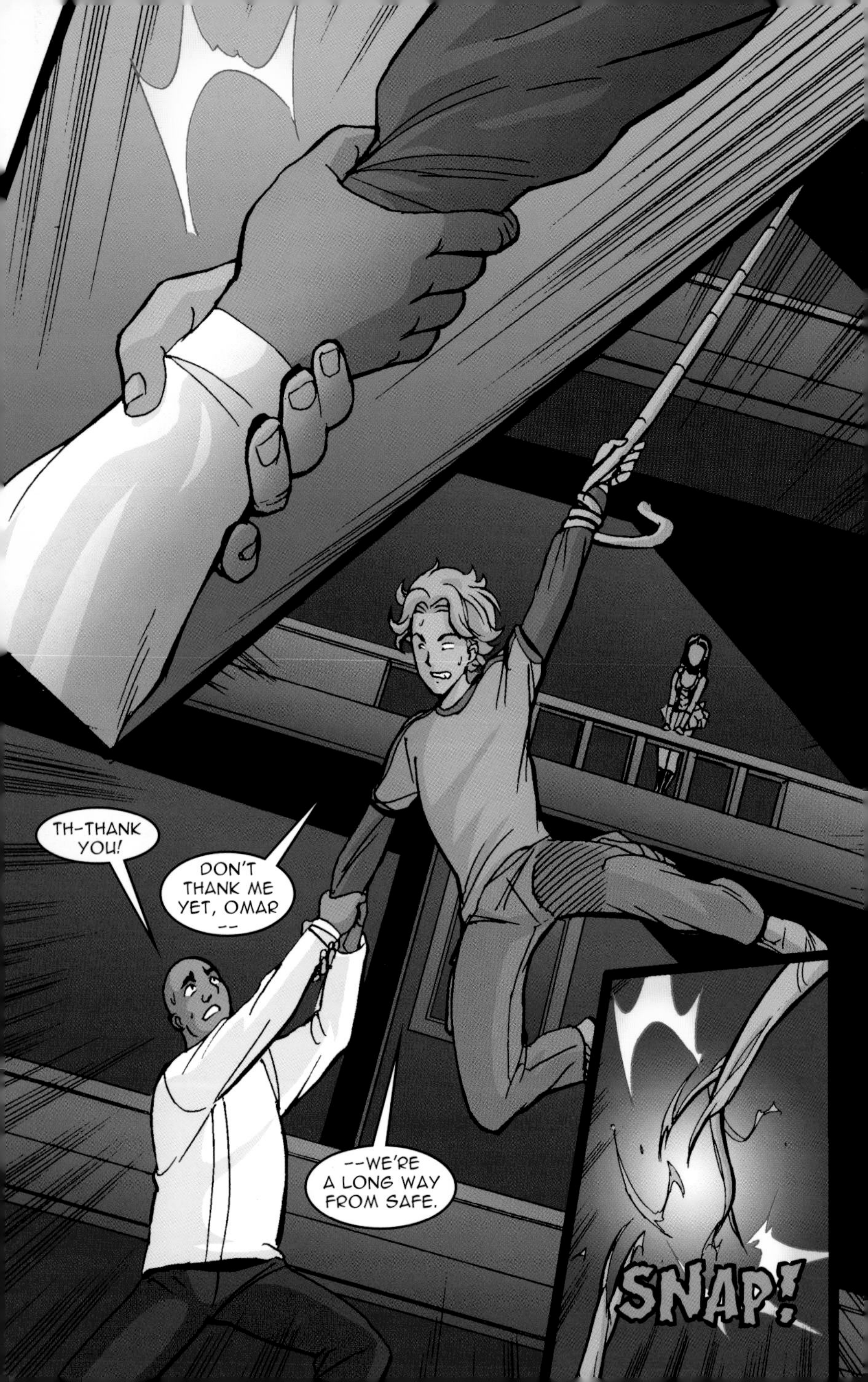
TH-THANK YOU!
DON'T THANK ME YET, OMAR --
--WE'RE A LONG WAY FROM SAFE.
SNAP!

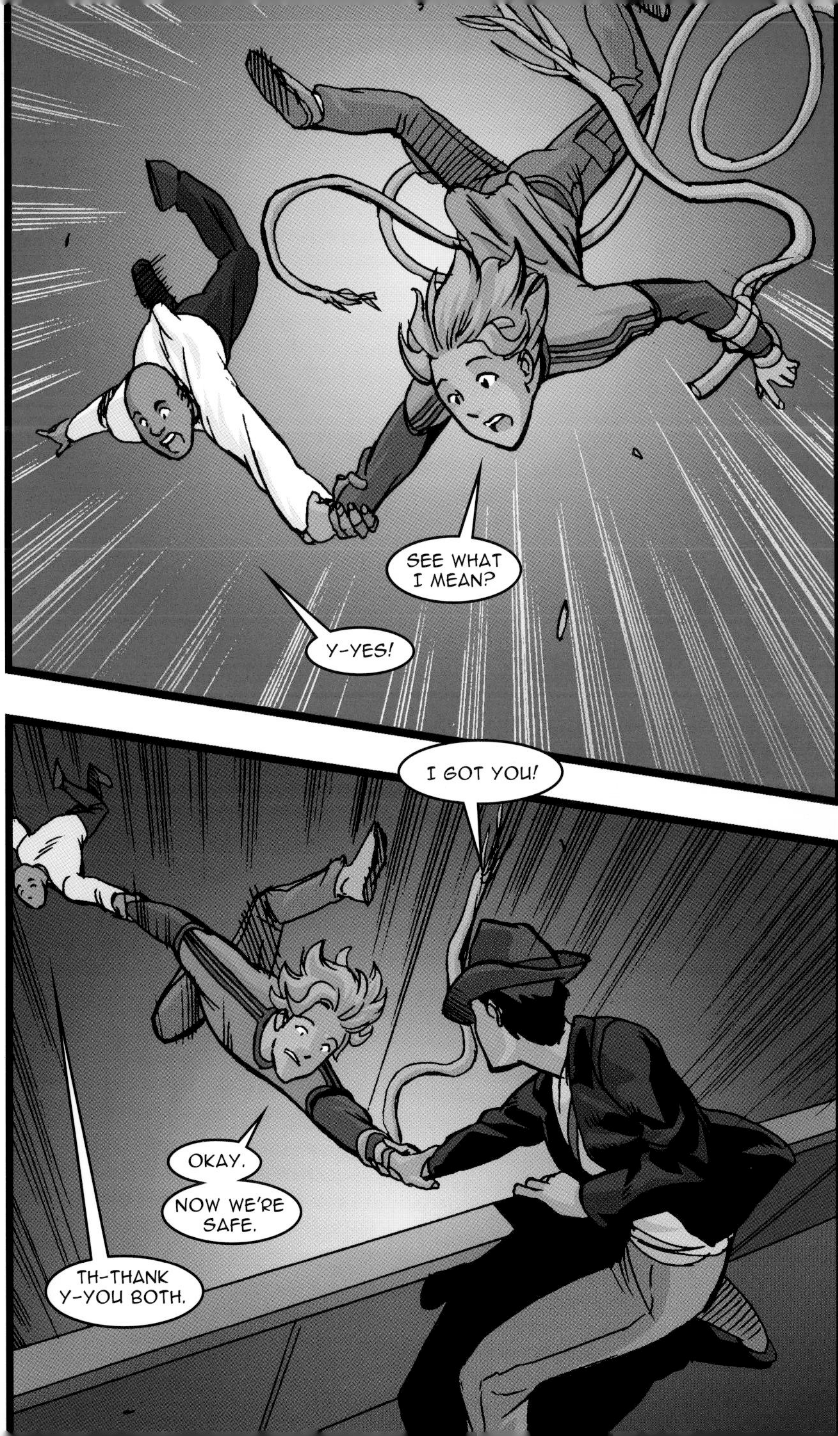
SEE WHAT I MEAN?
Y-YES!
I GOT YOU!
OKAY.
NOW WE'RE SAFE.
TH-THANK Y-YOU BOTH.

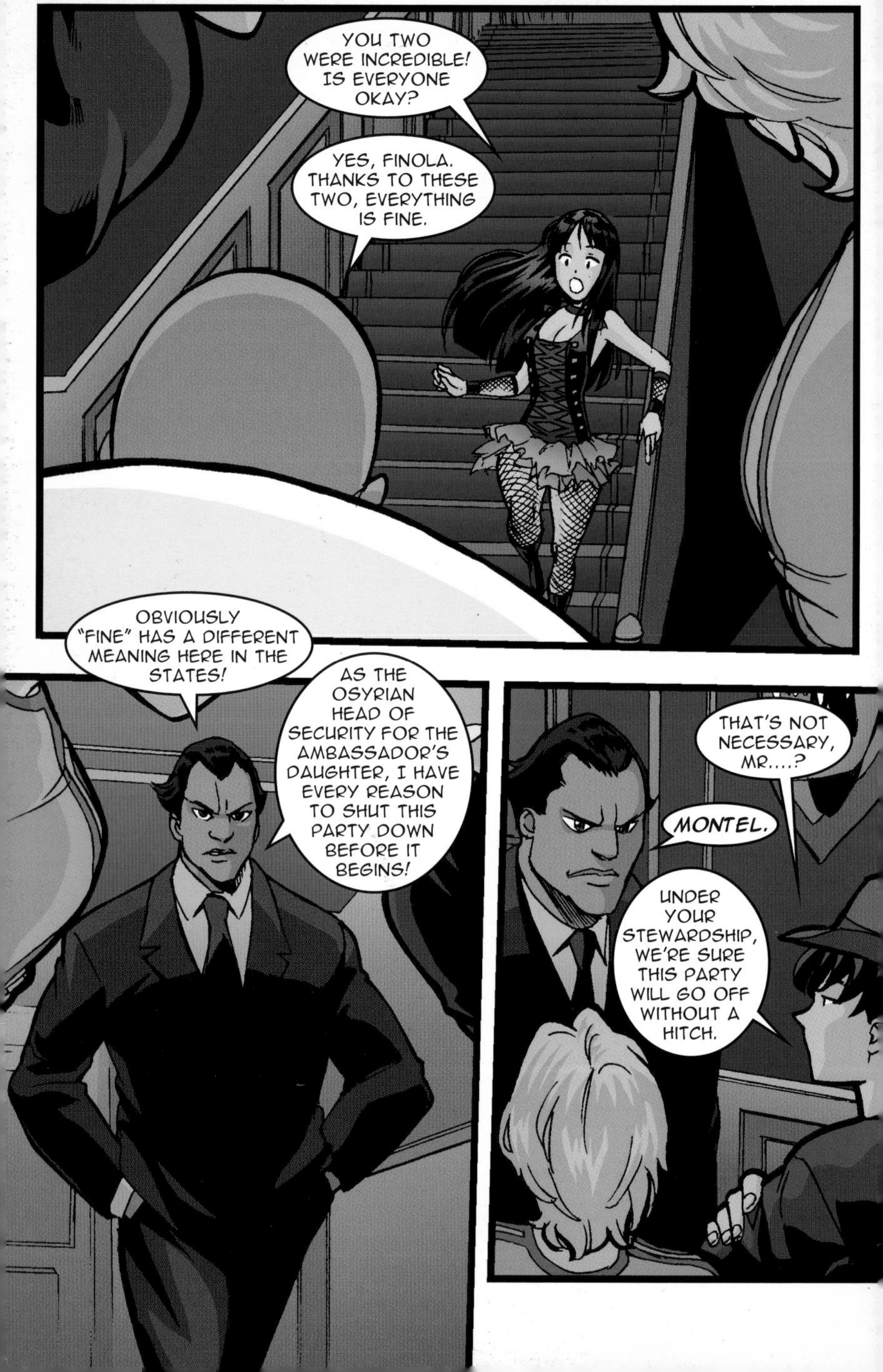
YOU TWO WERE INCREDIBLE! IS EVERYONE OKAY?
YES, FINOLA. THANKS TO THESE TWO, EVERYTHING IS FINE.
OBVIOUSLY "FINE" HAS A DIFFERENT MEANING HERE IN THE STATES!
AS THE OSYRIAN HEAD OF SECURITY FOR THE AMBASSADOR'S DAUGHTER, I HAVE EVERY REASON TO SHUT THIS PARTY DOWN BEFORE IT BEGINS!
THAT'S NOT NECESSARY, MR....?
MONTEL.
UNDER YOUR STEWARDSHIP, WE'RE SURE THIS PARTY WILL GO OFF WITHOUT A HITCH.

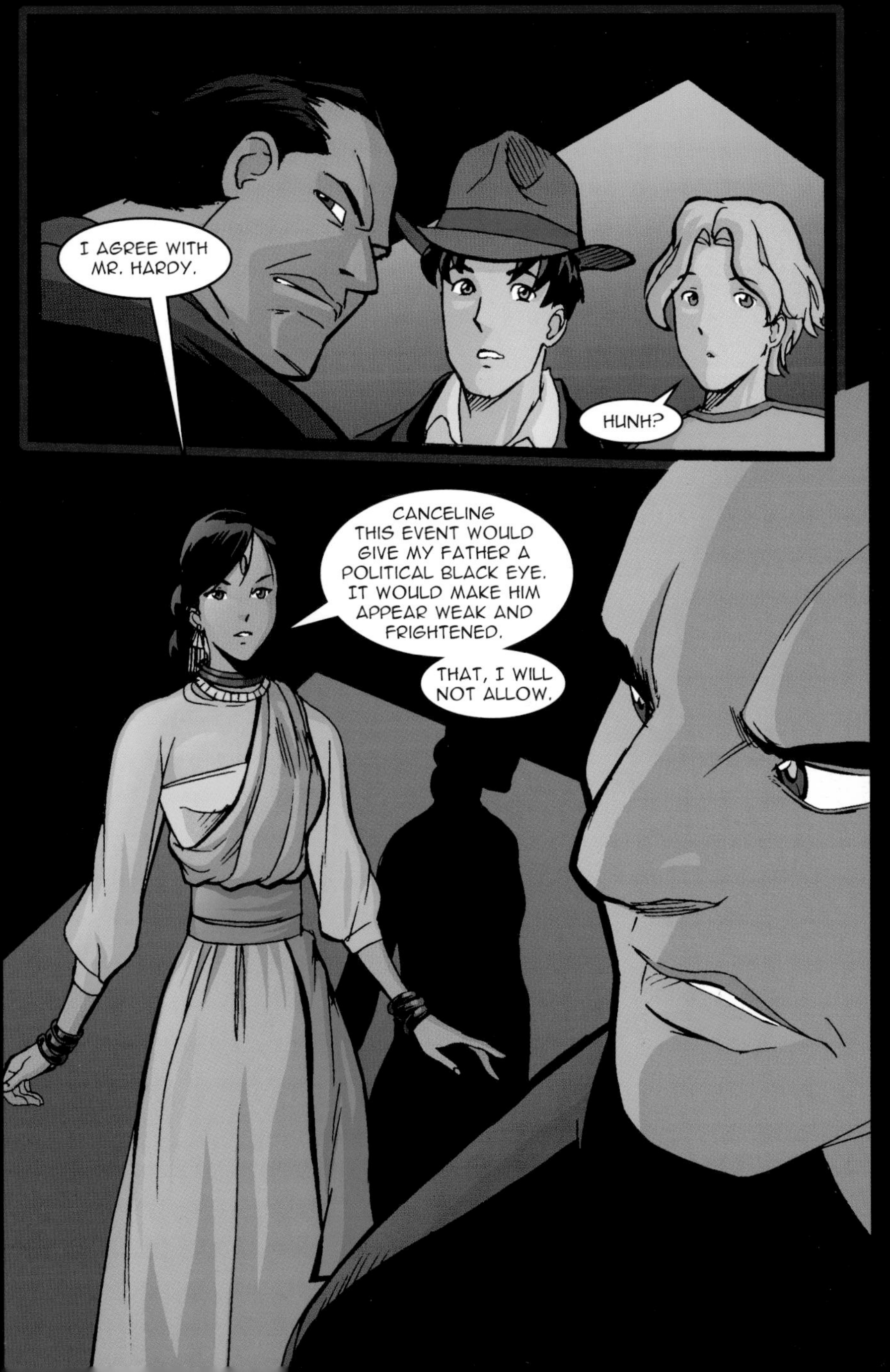
I AGREE WITH MR. HARDY.
HUNH?
CANCELING THIS EVENT WOULD GIVE MY FATHER A POLITICAL BLACK EYE. IT WOULD MAKE HIM APPEAR WEAK AND FRIGHTENED.
THAT, I WILL NOT ALLOW.

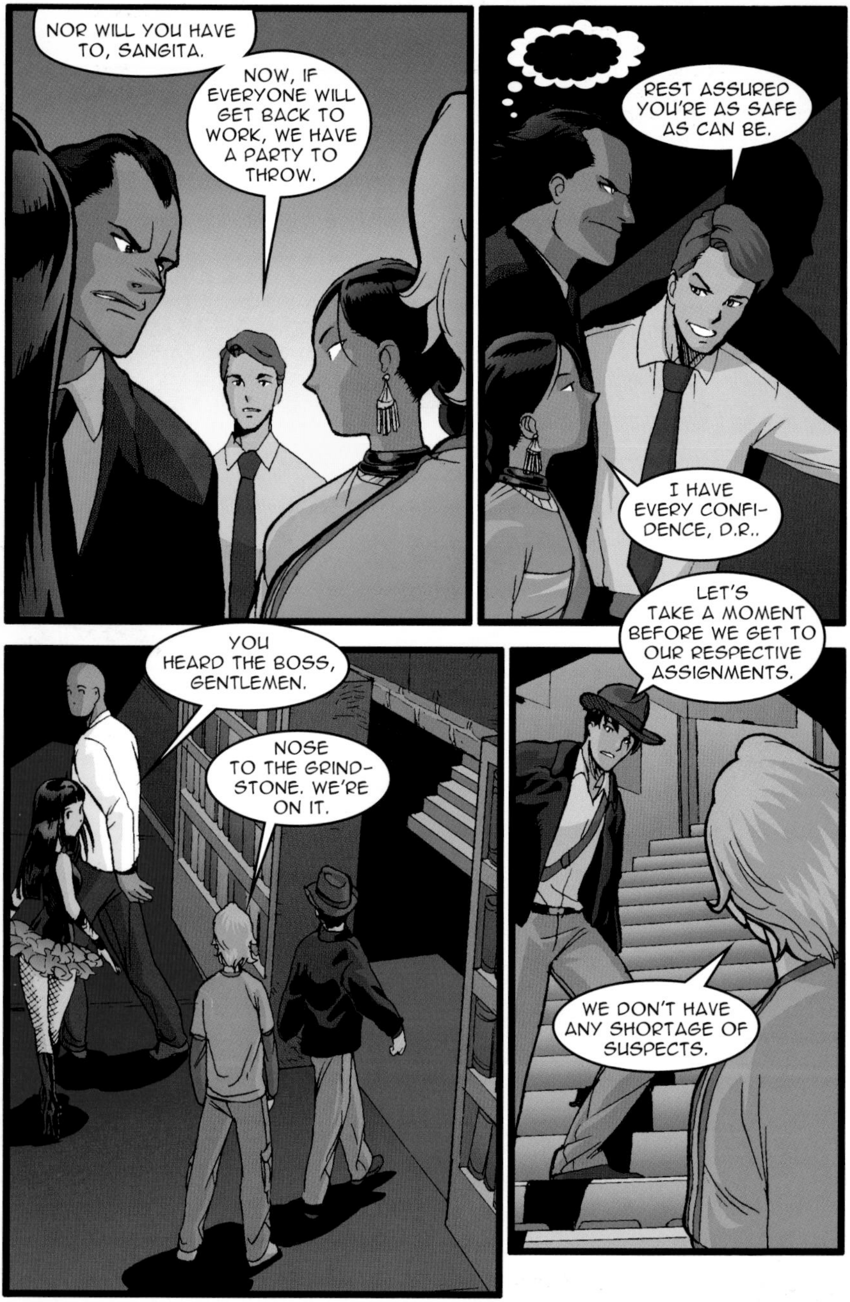
NOR WILL YOU HAVE TO, SANGITA.
NOW, IF EVERYONE WILL GET BACK TO WORK, WE HAVE A PARTY TO THROW.
REST ASSURED YOU'RE AS SAFE AS CAN BE.
I HAVE EVERY CONFI-DENCE, D.R..
YOU HEARD THE BOSS, GENTLEMEN.
NOSE TO THE GRIND-STONE. WE'RE ON IT.
LET'S TAKE A MOMENT BEFORE WE GET TO OUR RESPECTIVE ASSIGNMENTS.
WE DON'T HAVE ANY SHORTAGE OF SUSPECTS.

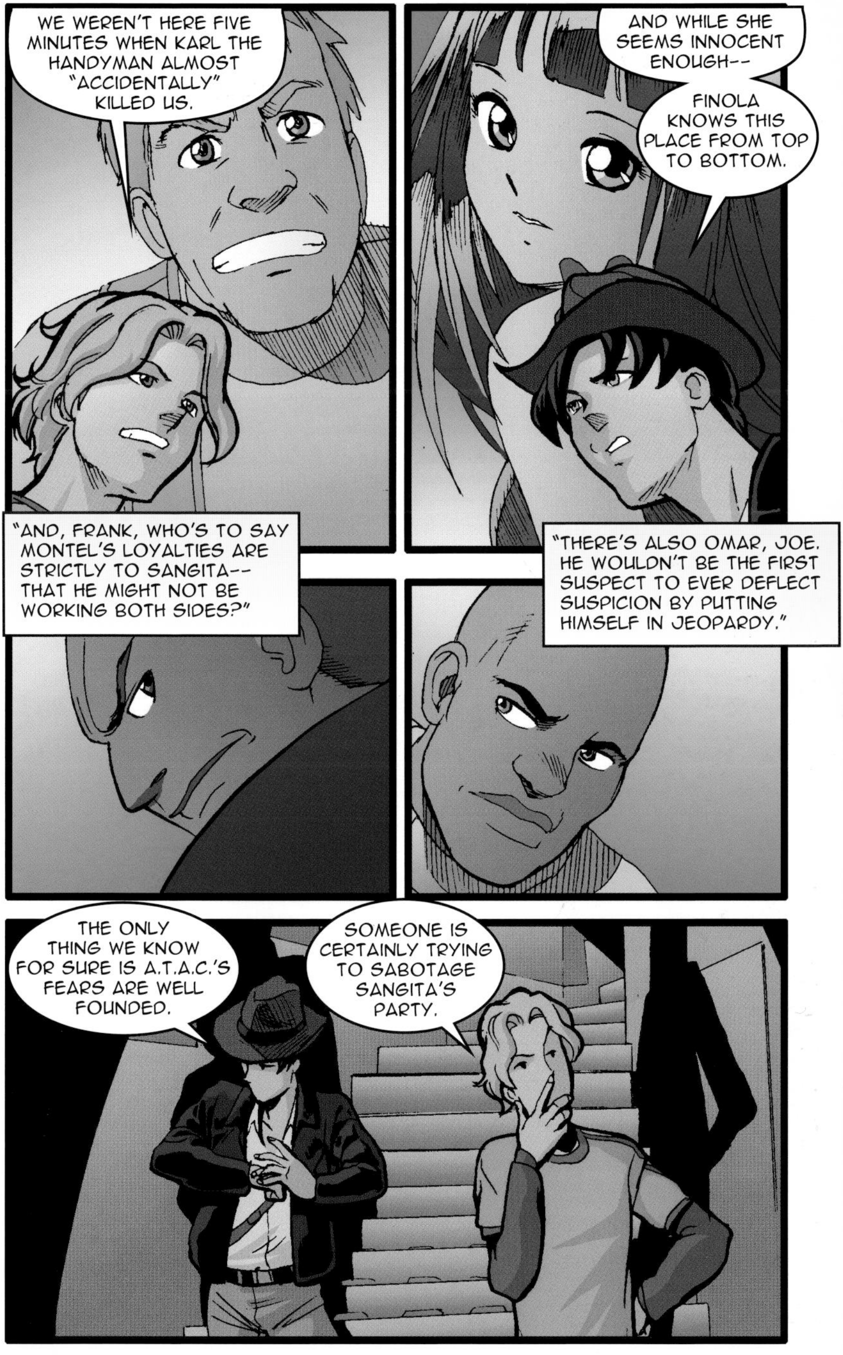
WE WEREN'T HERE FIVE MINUTES WHEN KARL THE HANDYMAN ALMOST "ACCIDENTALLY" KILLED US.
AND WHILE SHE SEEMS INNOCENT ENOUGH--
FINOLA KNOWS THIS PLACE FROM TOP TO BOTTOM.
"AND, FRANK, WHO'S TO SAY MONTEL'S LOYALTIES ARE STRICTLY TO SANGITA-- THAT HE MIGHT NOT BE WORKING BOTH SIDES?"
"THERE'S ALSO OMAR, JOE. HE WOULDN'T BE THE FIRST SUSPECT TO EVER DEFLECT SUSPICION BY PUTTING HIMSELF IN JEOPARDY."
THE ONLY THING WE KNOW FOR SURE IS A.T.A.C.'S FEARS ARE WELL FOUNDED.
SOMEONE IS CERTAINLY TRYING TO SABOTAGE SANGITA'S PARTY.

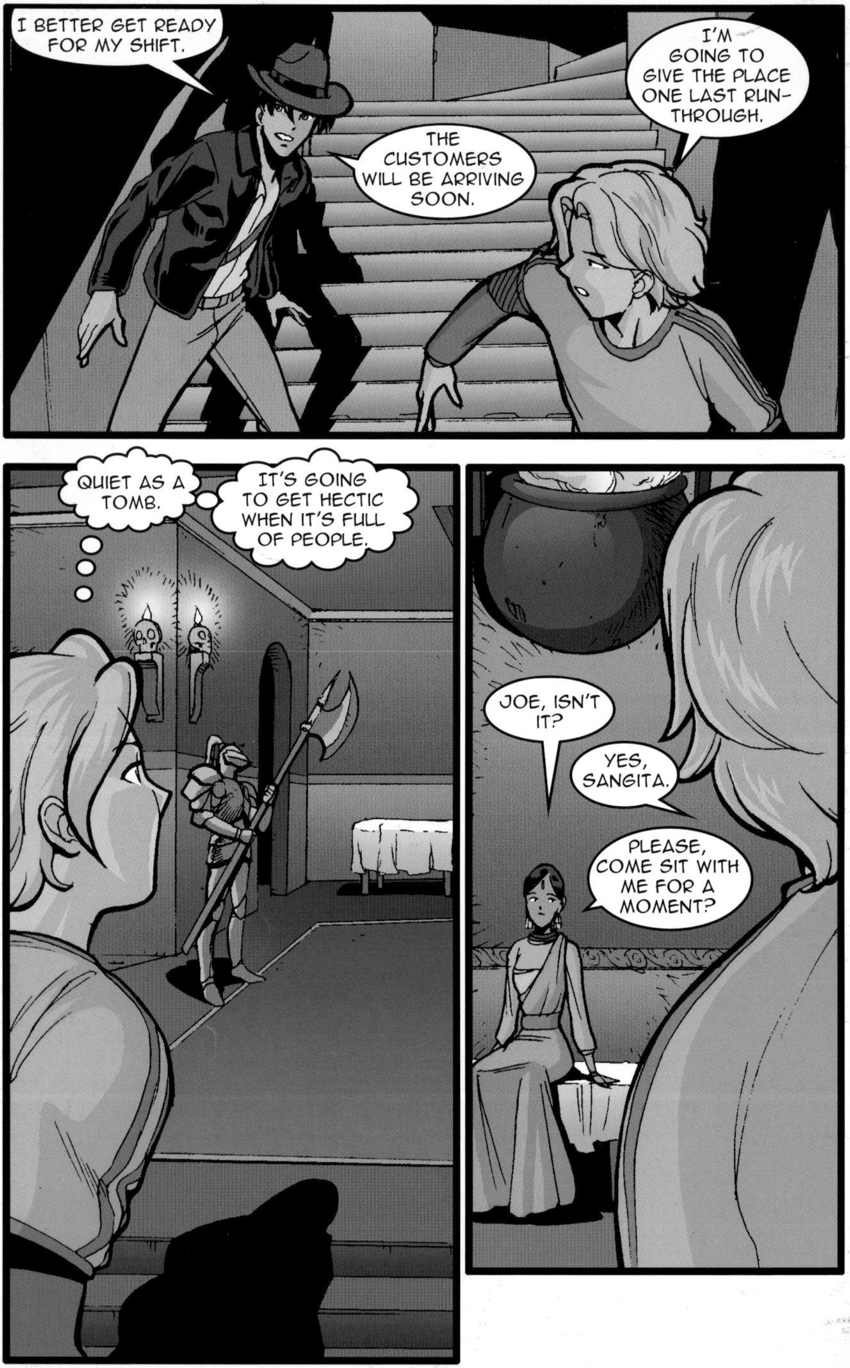
I BETTER GET READY FOR MY SHIFT.
THE CUSTOMERS WILL BE ARRIVING SOON.
I'M GOING TO GIVE THE PLACE ONE LAST RUN-THROUGH.
QUIET AS A TOMB.
IT'S GOING TO GET HECTIC WHEN IT'S FULL OF PEOPLE.
JOE, ISN'T IT?
YES, SANGITA.
PLEASE, COME SIT WITH ME FOR A MOMENT?

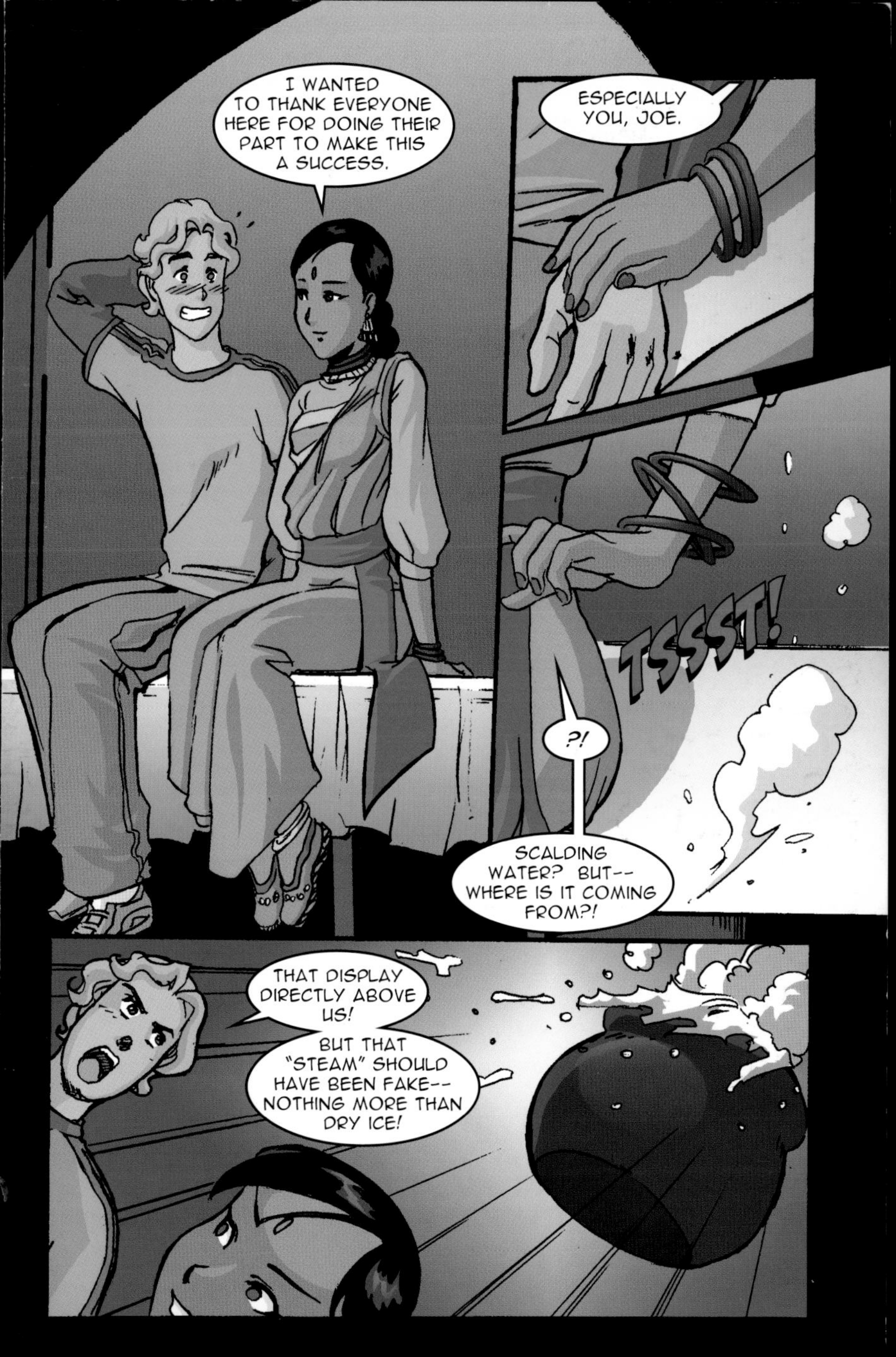
I WANTED TO THANK EVERYONE HERE FOR DOING THEIR PART TO MAKE THIS A SUCCESS.
ESPECIALLY YOU, JOE.
TSSST!
?!
SCALDING WATER? BUT-- WHERE IS IT COMING FROM?!
THAT DISPLAY DIRECTLY ABOVE US!
BUT THAT "STEAM" SHOULD HAVE BEEN FAKE-- NOTHING MORE THAN DRY ICE!

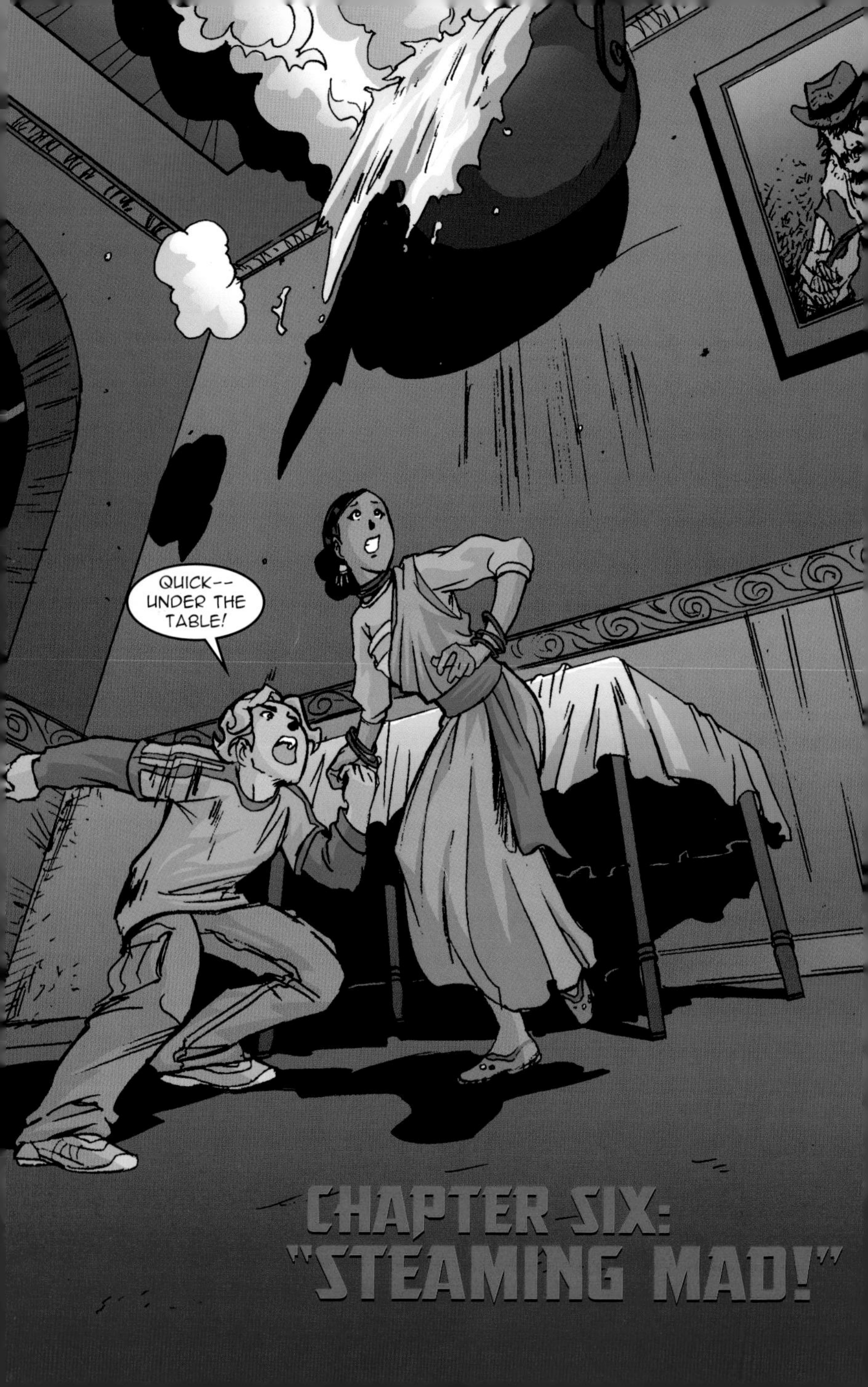
QUICK-- UNDER THE TABLE!
CHAPTER SIX: "STEAMING MAD!"

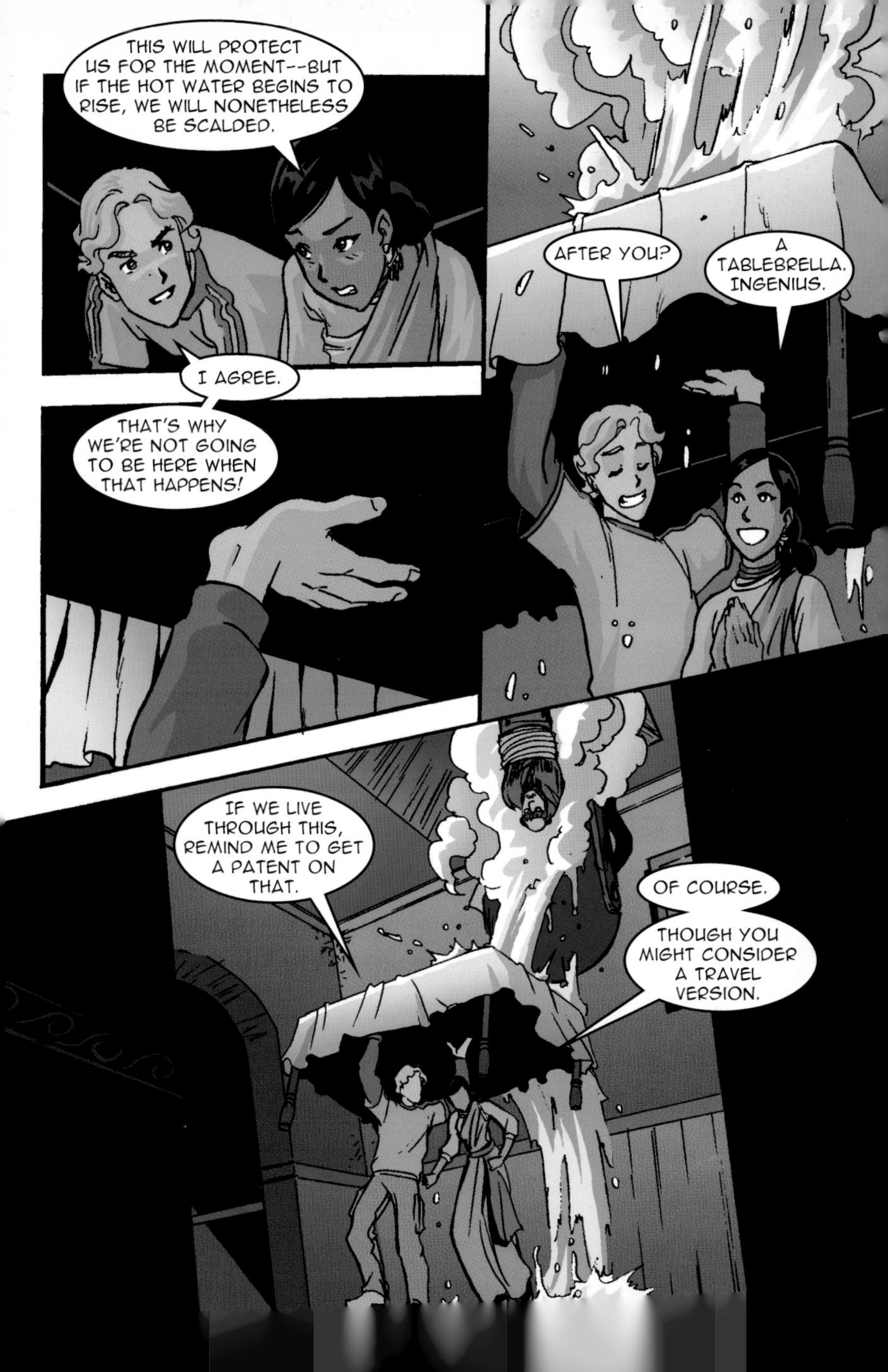
THIS WILL PROTECT US FOR THE MOMENT--BUT IF THE HOT WATER BEGINS TO RISE, WE WILL NONETHELESS BE SCALDED.
I AGREE.
THAT'S WHY WE'RE NOT GOING TO BE HERE WHEN THAT HAPPENS!
AFTER YOU?
A TABLEBRELLA. INGENIUS.
IF WE LIVE THROUGH THIS, REMIND ME TO GET A PATENT ON THAT.
OF COURSE.
THOUGH YOU MIGHT CONSIDER A TRAVEL VERSION.

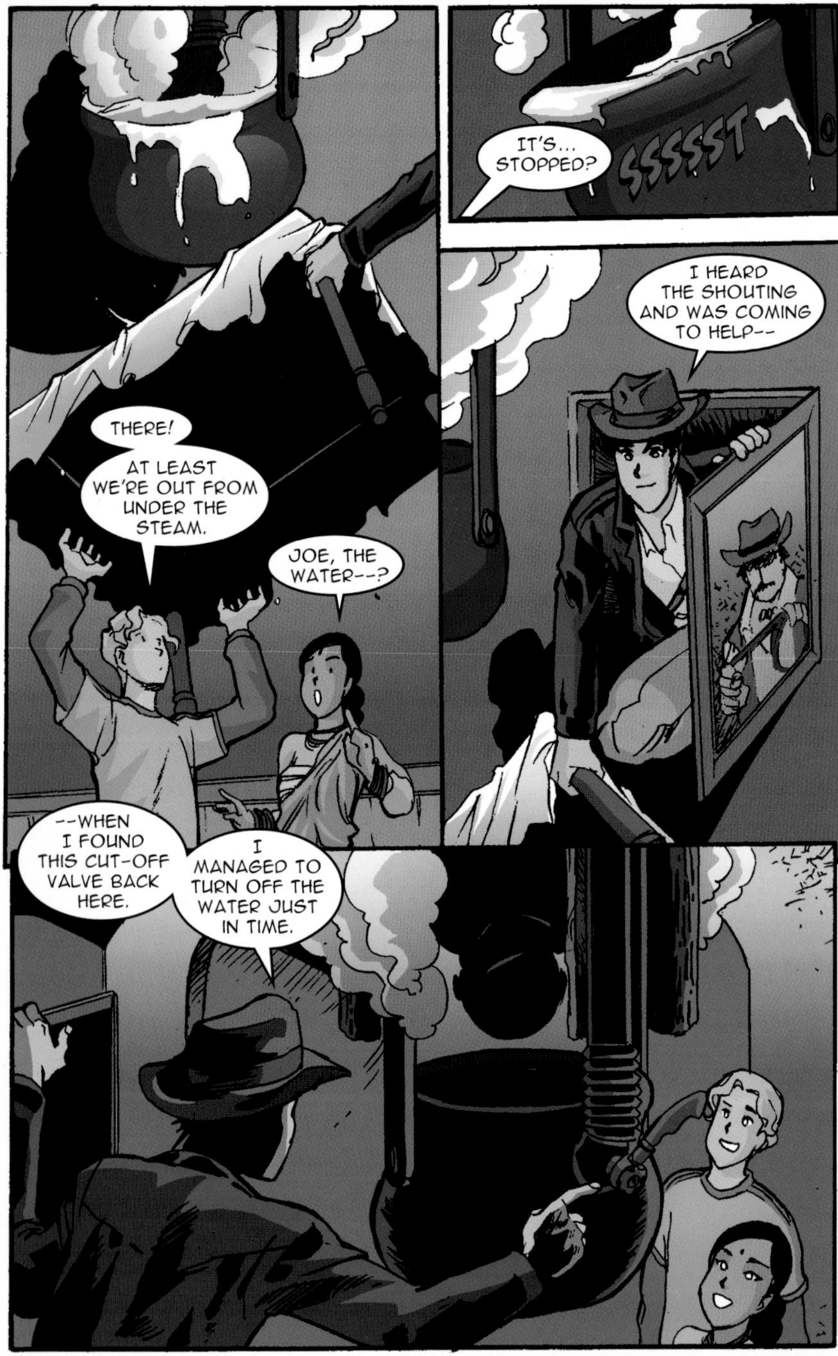
IT'S... STOPPED?
SSSSST
THERE!
AT LEAST WE'RE OUT FROM UNDER THE STEAM.
JOE, THE WATER--?
I HEARD THE SHOUTING AND WAS COMING TO HELP--
--WHEN I FOUND THIS CUT-OFF VALVE BACK HERE.
I MANAGED TO TURN OFF THE WATER JUST IN TIME.

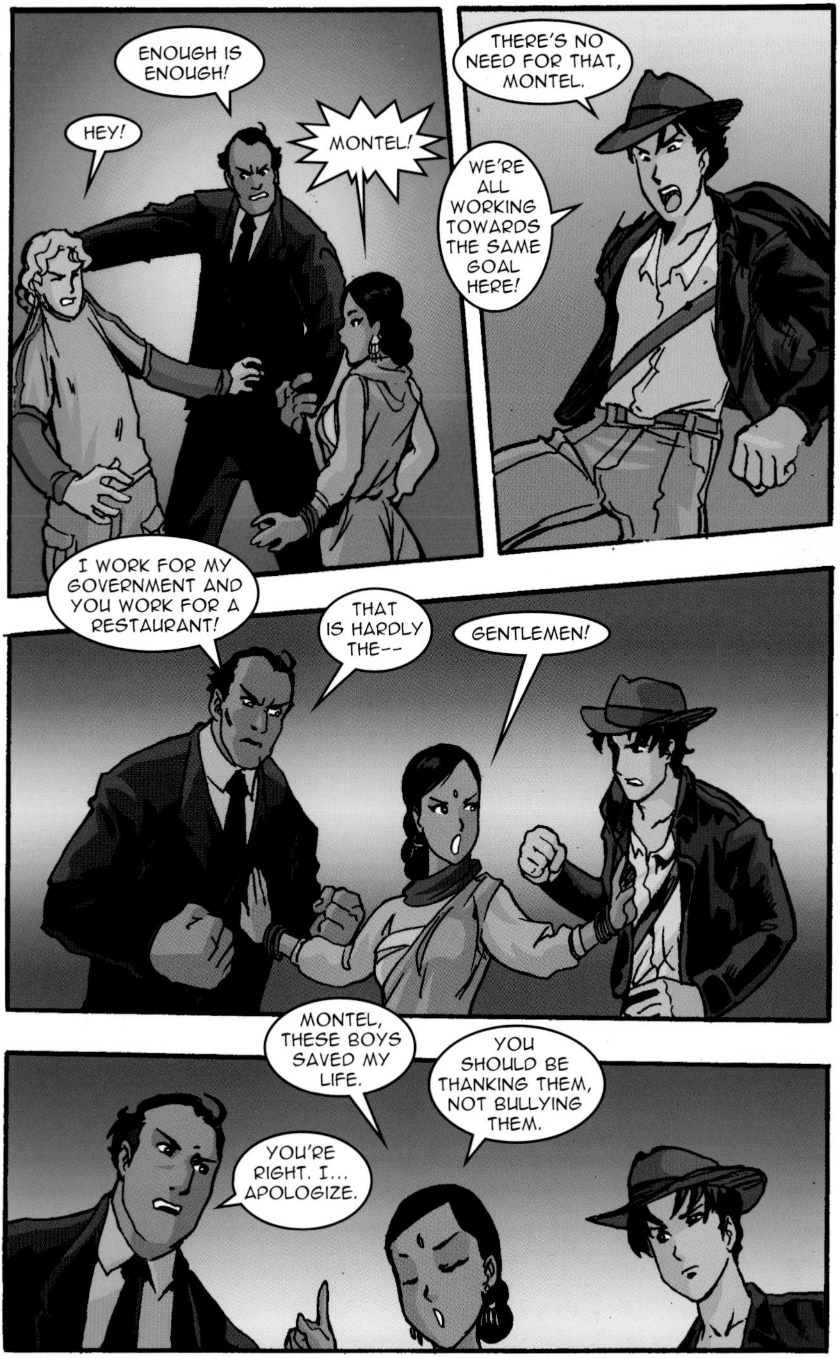
ENOUGH IS ENOUGH!
HEY!
MONTEL!
THERE'S NO NEED FOR THAT, MONTEL.
WE'RE ALL WORKING TOWARDS THE SAME GOAL HERE!
I WORK FOR MY GOVERNMENT AND YOU WORK FOR A RESTAURANT!
THAT IS HARDLY THE--
GENTLEMEN!
MONTEL, THESE BOYS SAVED MY LIFE.
YOU SHOULD BE THANKING THEM, NOT BULLYING THEM.
YOU'RE RIGHT. I... APOLOGIZE.

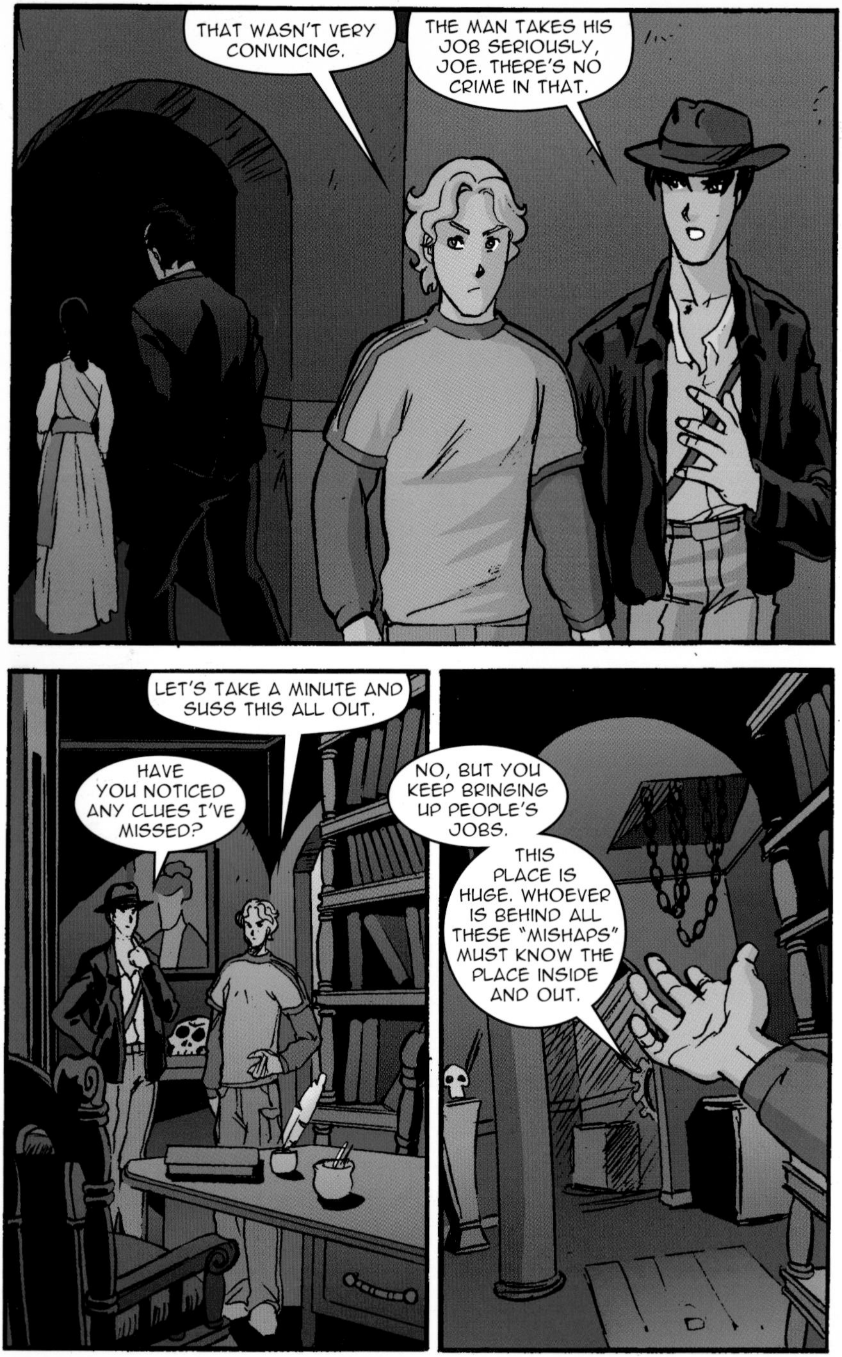
THAT WASN'T VERY CONVINCING.
THE MAN TAKES HIS JOB SERIOUSLY, JOE. THERE'S NO CRIME IN THAT.
LET'S TAKE A MINUTE AND SUSS THIS ALL OUT.
HAVE YOU NOTICED ANY CLUES I'VE MISSED?
NO, BUT YOU KEEP BRINGING UP PEOPLE'S JOBS.
THIS PLACE IS HUGE. WHOEVER IS BEHIND ALL THESE "MISHAPS" MUST KNOW THE PLACE INSIDE AND OUT.

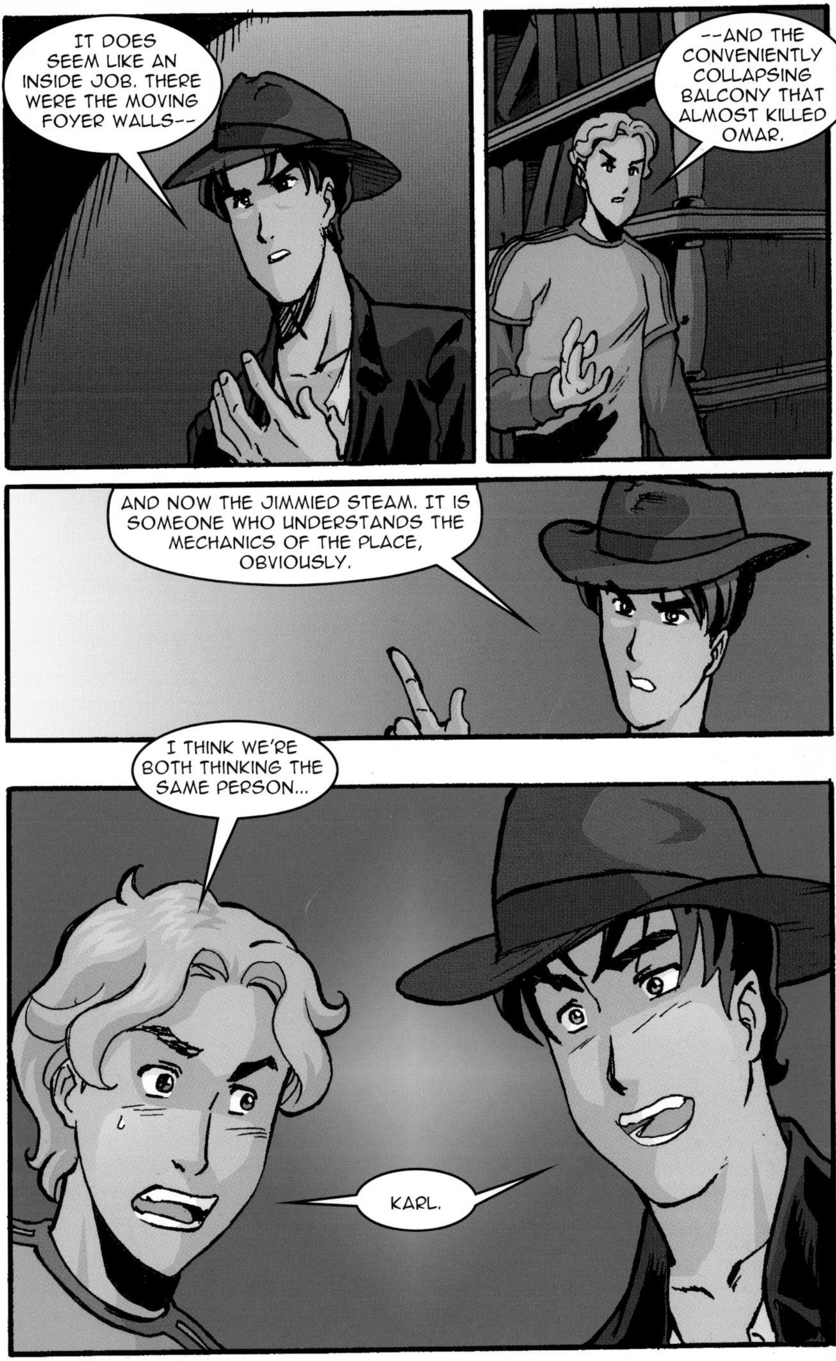
IT DOES SEEM LIKE AN INSIDE JOB. THERE WERE THE MOVING FOYER WALLS--
--AND THE CONVENIENTLY COLLAPSING BALCONY THAT ALMOST KILLED OMAR.
AND NOW THE JIMMIED STEAM. IT IS SOMEONE WHO UNDERSTANDS THE MECHANICS OF THE PLACE, OBVIOUSLY.
I THINK WE'RE BOTH THINKING THE SAME PERSON...
KARL.

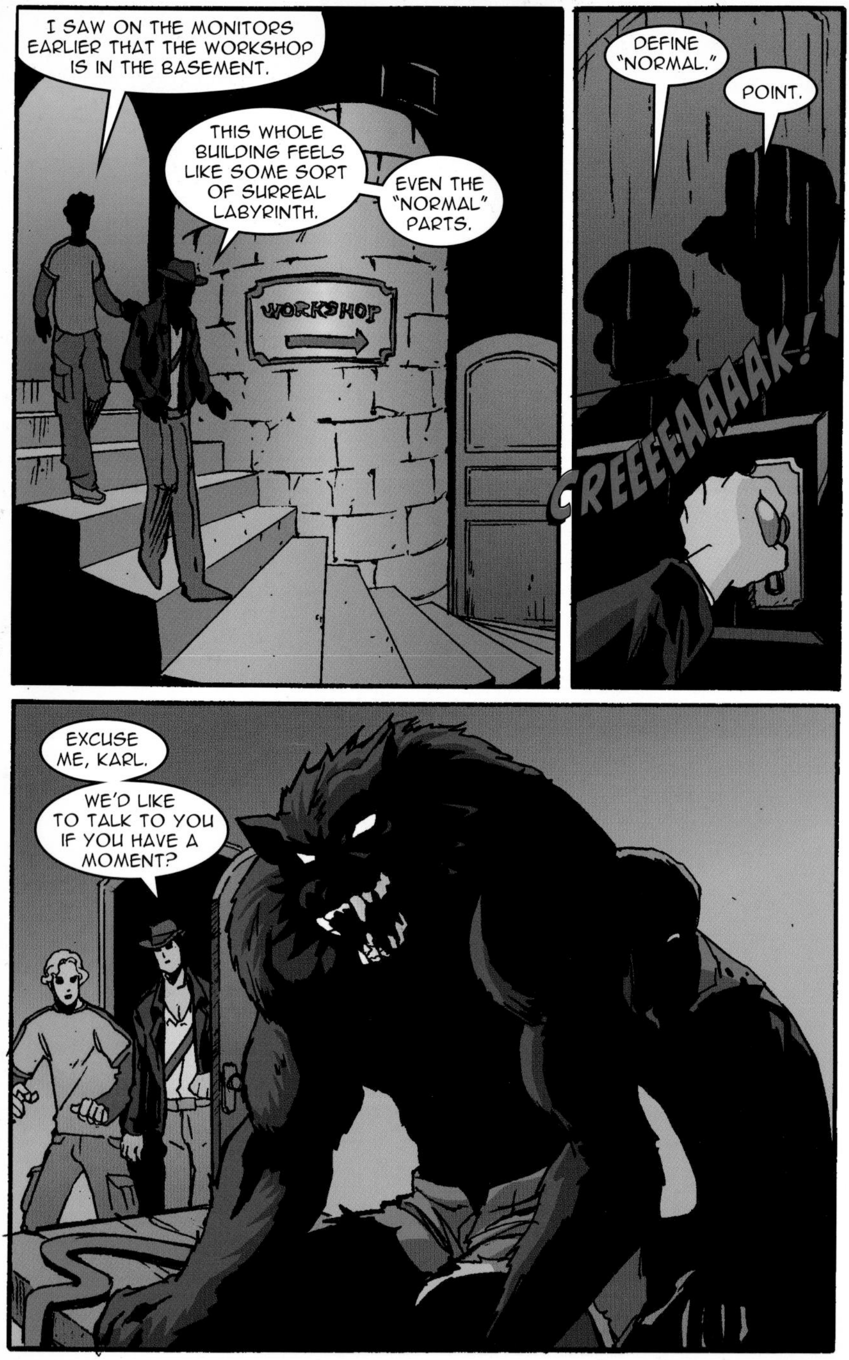
I SAW ON THE MONITORS EARLIER THAT THE WORKSHOP IS IN THE BASEMENT.
THIS WHOLE BUILDING FEELS LIKE SOME SORT OF SURREAL LABYRINTH.
EVEN THE "NORMAL" PARTS.
WORKSHOP
DEFINE "NORMAL."
POINT.
CREEEEAAAAK!
EXCUSE ME, KARL.
WE'D LIKE TO TALK TO YOU IF YOU HAVE A MOMENT?

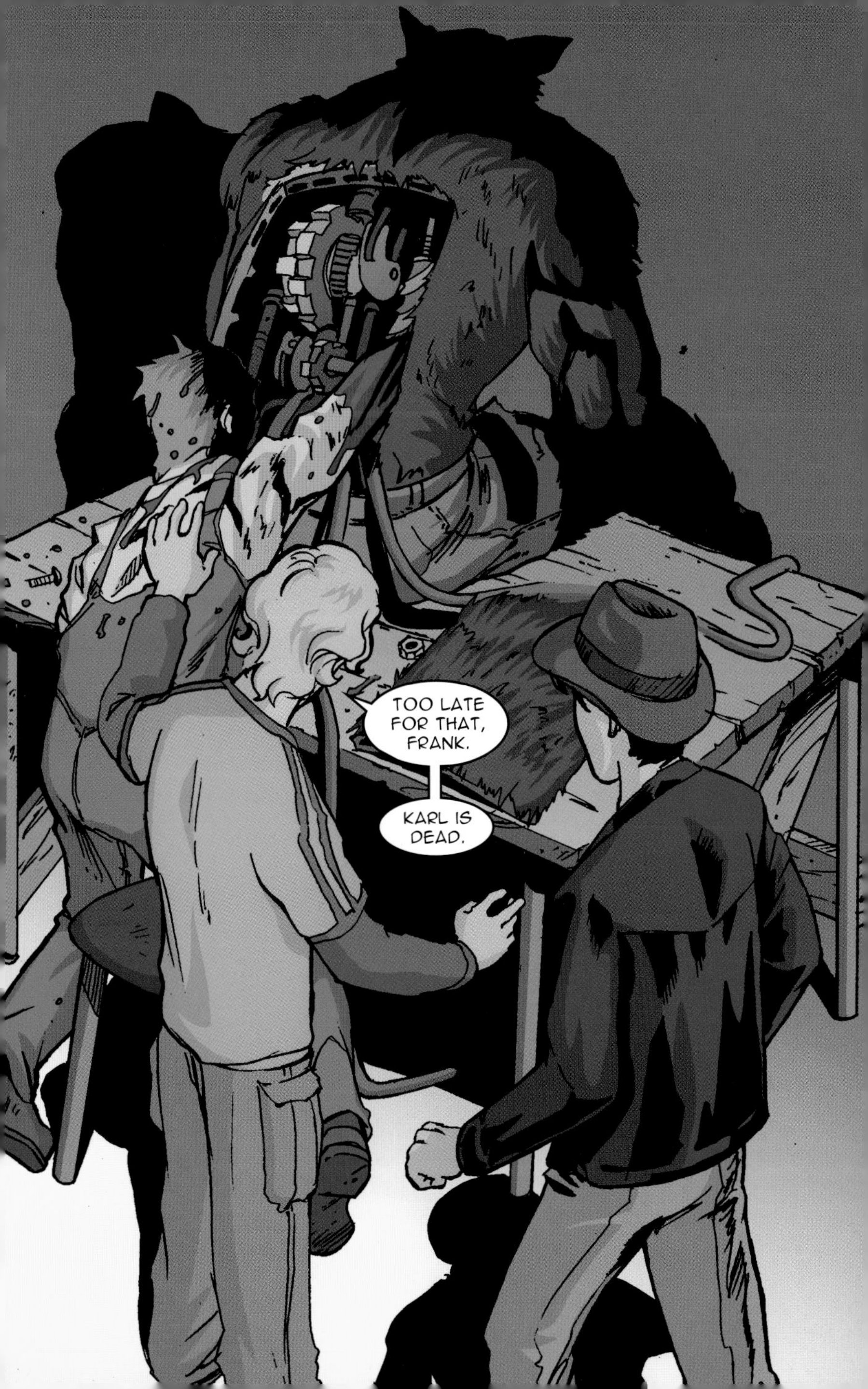
TOO LATE FOR THAT, FRANK.
KARL IS DEAD.

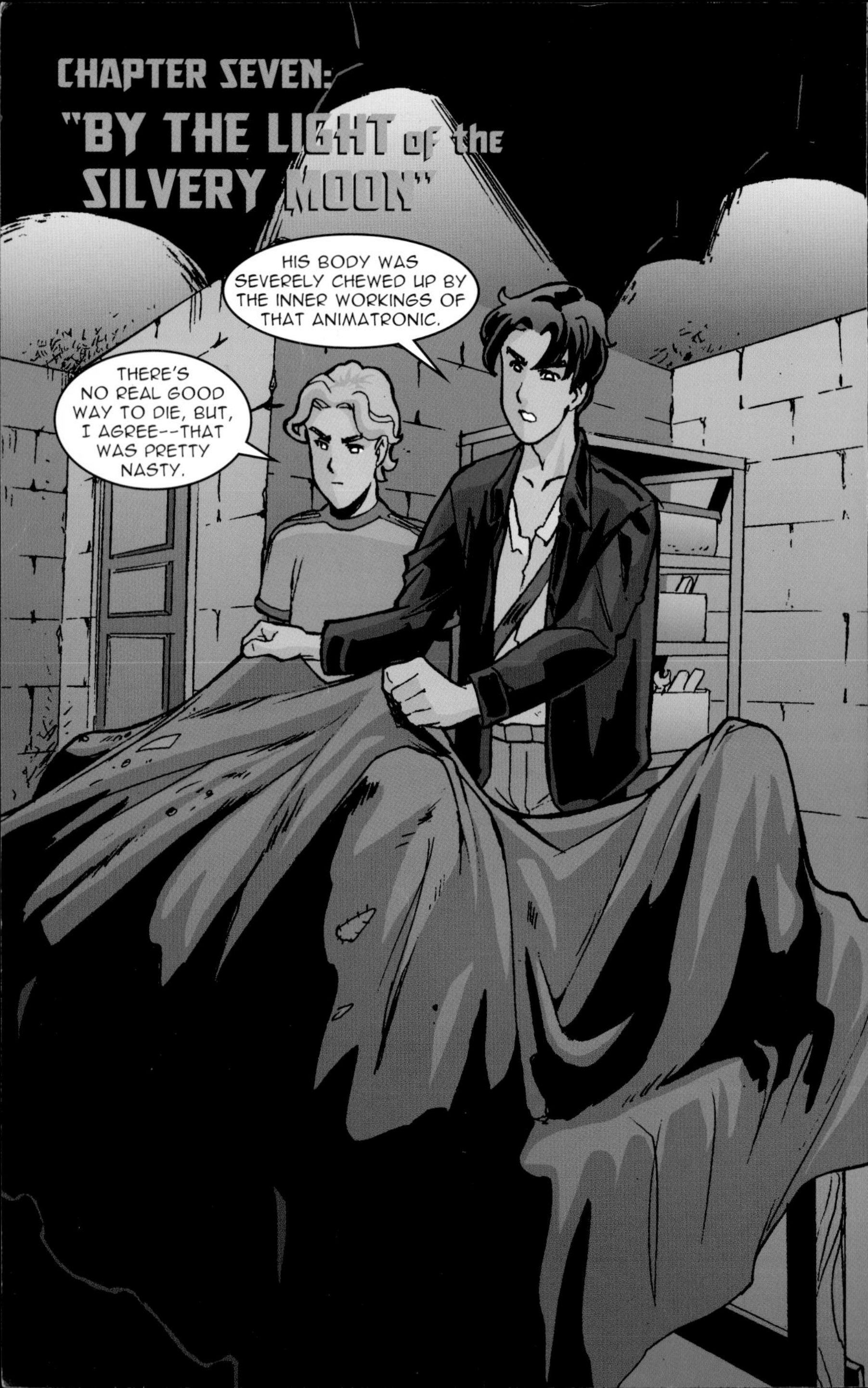
CHAPTER SEVEN:
"BY THE LIGHT of the SILVERY MOON"
HIS BODY WAS SEVERELY CHEWED UP BY THE INNER WORKINGS OF THAT ANIMATRONIC.
THERE'S NO REAL GOOD WAY TO DIE, BUT, I AGREE--THAT WAS PRETTY NASTY.

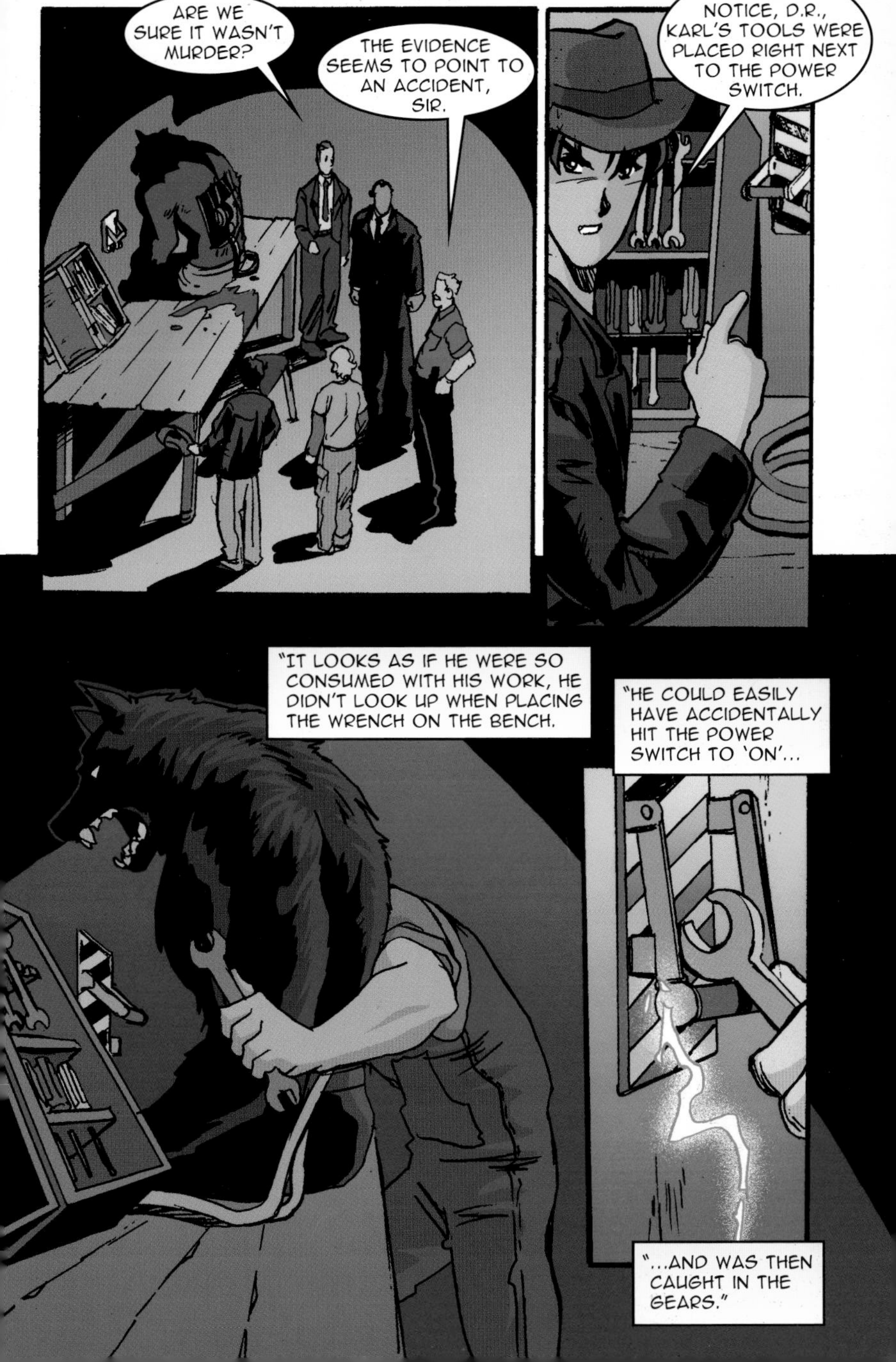
ARE WE SURE IT WASN'T MURDER?
THE EVIDENCE SEEMS TO POINT TO AN ACCIDENT, SIR.
IF YOU'LL NOTICE, D.R., KARL'S TOOLS WERE PLACED RIGHT NEXT TO THE POWER SWITCH.
"IT LOOKS AS IF HE WERE SO CONSUMED WITH HIS WORK, HE DIDN'T LOOK UP WHEN PLACING THE WRENCH ON THE BENCH.
"HE COULD EASILY HAVE ACCIDENTALLY HIT THE POWER SWITCH TO 'ON'...
"...AND WAS THEN CAUGHT IN THE GEARS."

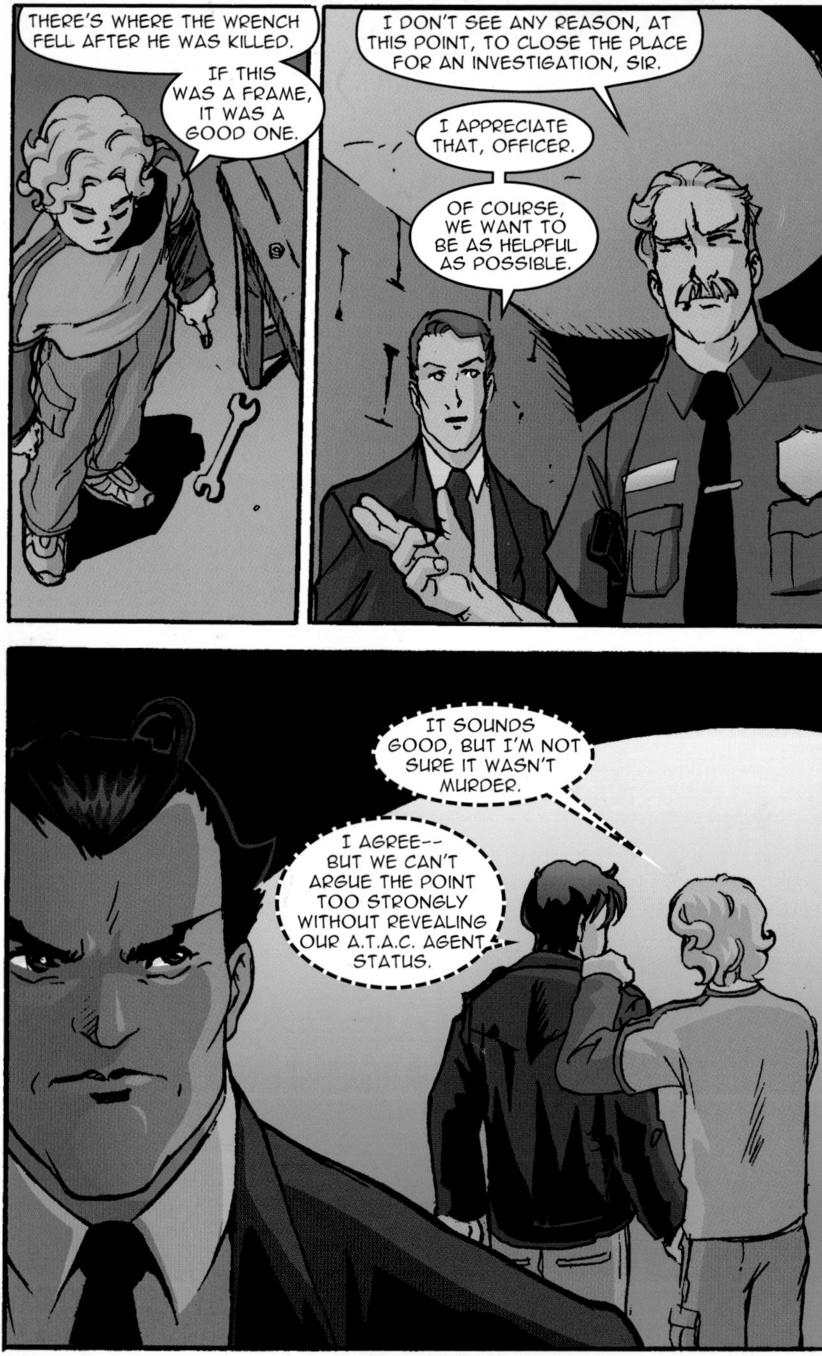
THERE'S WHERE THE WRENCH FELL AFTER HE WAS KILLED.
IF THIS WAS A FRAME, IT WAS A GOOD ONE.
I DON'T SEE ANY REASON, AT THIS POINT, TO CLOSE THE PLACE FOR AN INVESTIGATION, SIR.
I APPRECIATE THAT, OFFICER.
OF COURSE, WE WANT TO BE AS HELPFUL AS POSSIBLE.
IT SOUNDS GOOD, BUT I'M NOT SURE IT WASN'T MURDER.
I AGREE-- BUT WE CAN'T ARGUE THE POINT TOO STRONGLY WITHOUT REVEALING OUR A.T.A.C. AGENT STATUS.

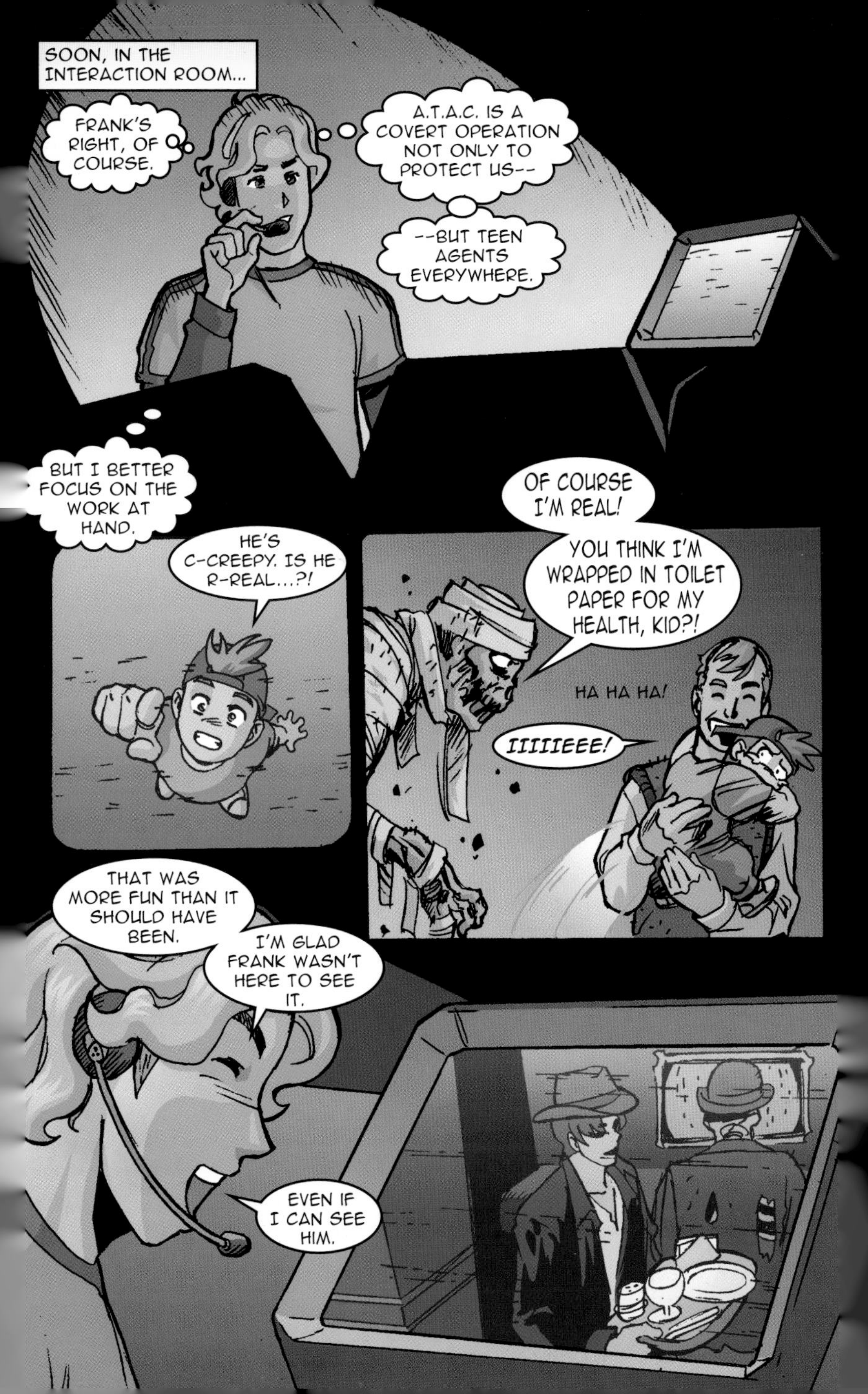
SOON, IN THE INTERACTION ROOM...
FRANK'S RIGHT, OF COURSE.
A.T.A.C. IS A COVERT OPERATION NOT ONLY TO PROTECT US--
--BUT TEEN AGENTS EVERYWHERE.
BUT I BETTER FOCUS ON THE WORK AT HAND.
HE'S C-CREEPY. IS HE R-REAL...?!
OF COURSE I'M REAL!
YOU THINK I'M WRAPPED IN TOILET PAPER FOR MY HEALTH, KID?!
HA HA HA!
IIIIIEEE!
THAT WAS MORE FUN THAN IT SHOULD HAVE BEEN.
I'M GLAD FRANK WASN'T HERE TO SEE IT.
EVEN IF I CAN SEE HIM.

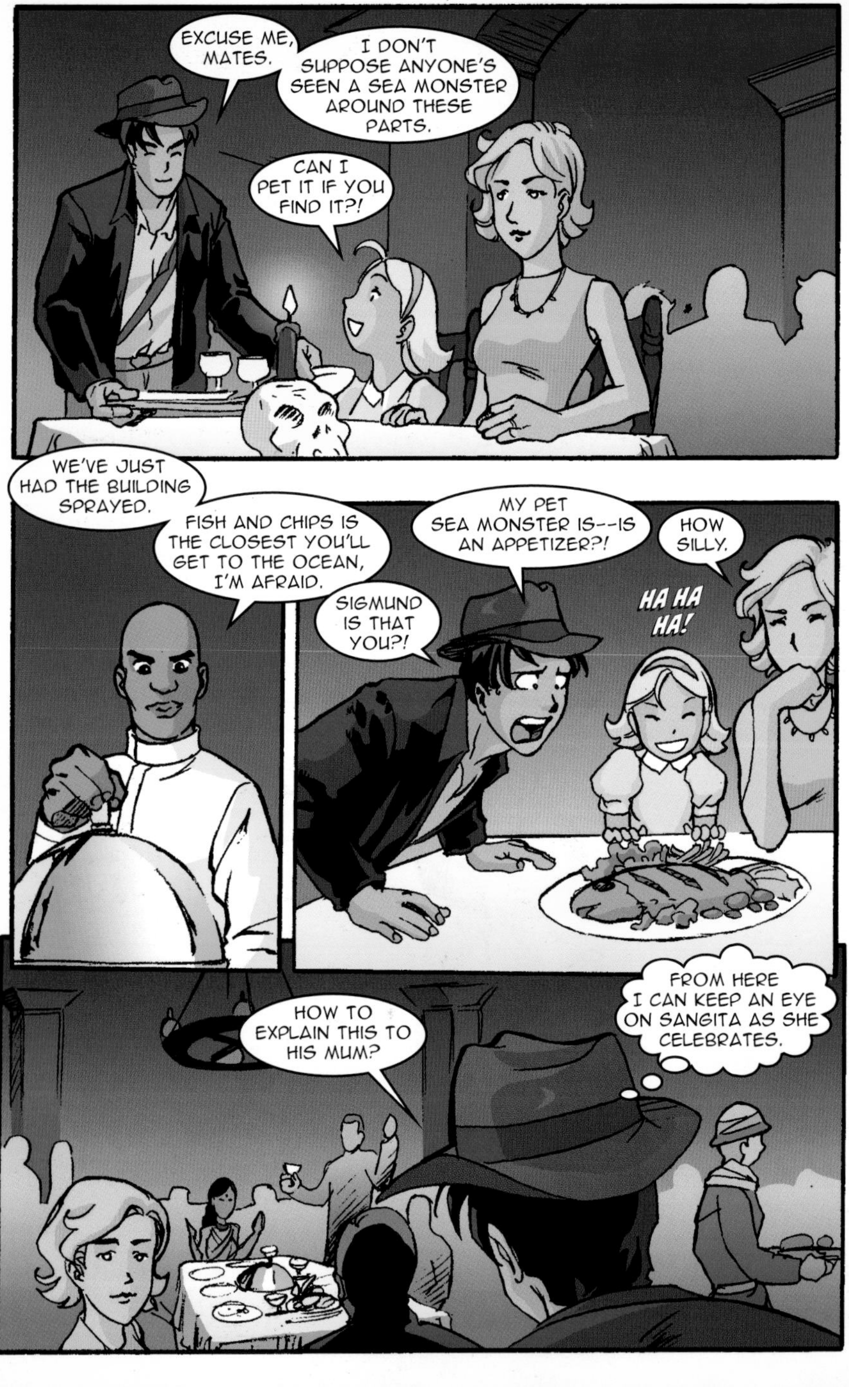
EXCUSE ME, MATES.
I DON'T SUPPOSE ANYONE'S SEEN A SEA MONSTER AROUND THESE PARTS.
CAN I PET IT IF YOU FIND IT?!
WE'VE JUST HAD THE BUILDING SPRAYED.
FISH AND CHIPS IS THE CLOSEST YOU'LL GET TO THE OCEAN, I'M AFRAID.
MY PET SEA MONSTER IS--IS AN APPETIZER?!
SIGMUND IS THAT YOU?!
HOW SILLY.
HA HA HA!
HOW TO EXPLAIN THIS TO HIS MUM?
FROM HERE I CAN KEEP AN EYE ON SANGITA AS SHE CELEBRATES.

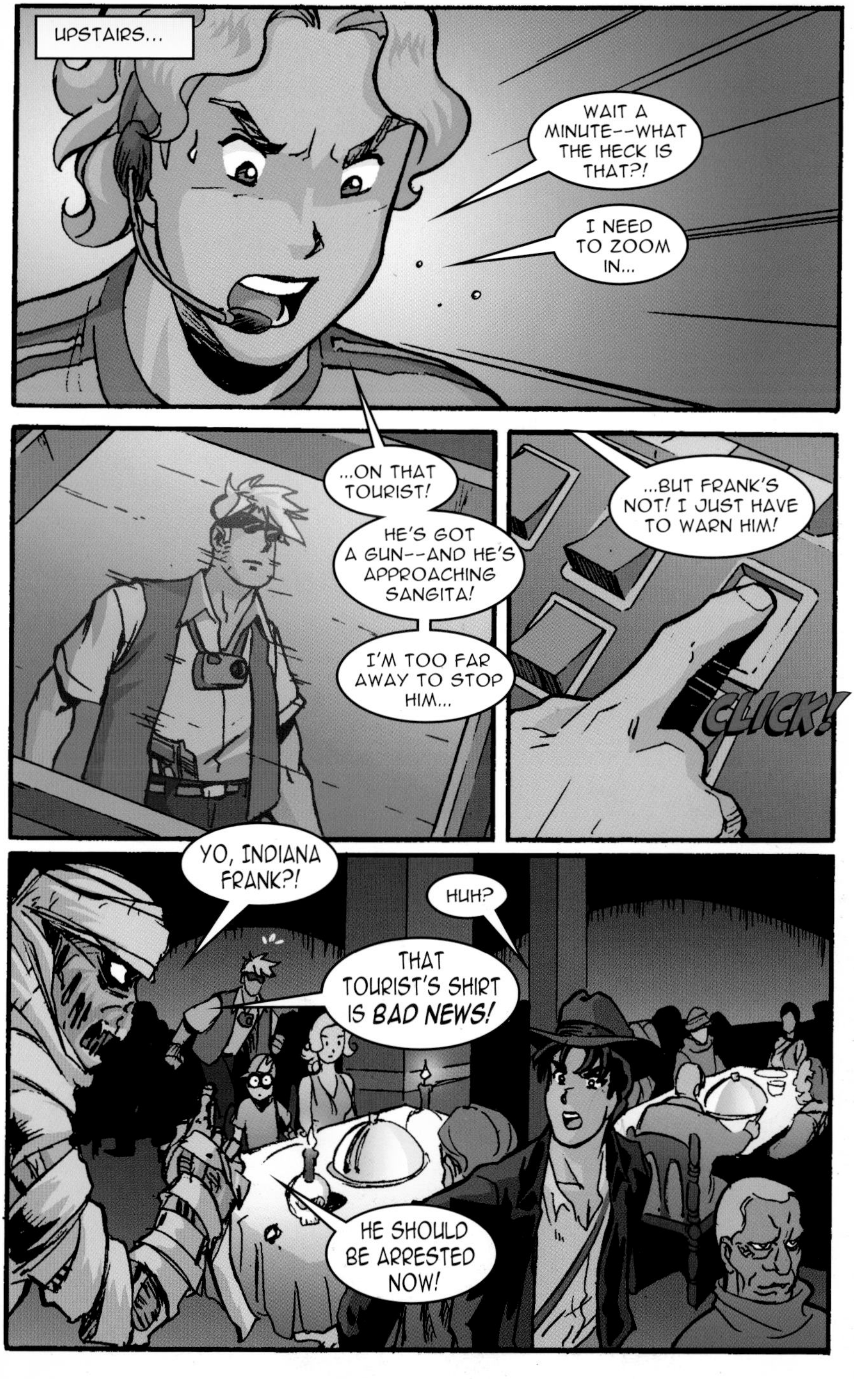
UPSTAIRS...
WAIT A MINUTE--WHAT THE HECK IS THAT?!
I NEED TO ZOOM IN...
...ON THAT TOURIST!
HE'S GOT A GUN--AND HE'S APPROACHING SANGITA!
I'M TOO FAR AWAY TO STOP HIM...
...BUT FRANK'S NOT! I JUST HAVE TO WARN HIM!
CLICK!
YO, INDIANA FRANK?!
HUH?
THAT TOURIST'S SHIRT IS BAD NEWS!
HE SHOULD BE ARRESTED NOW!

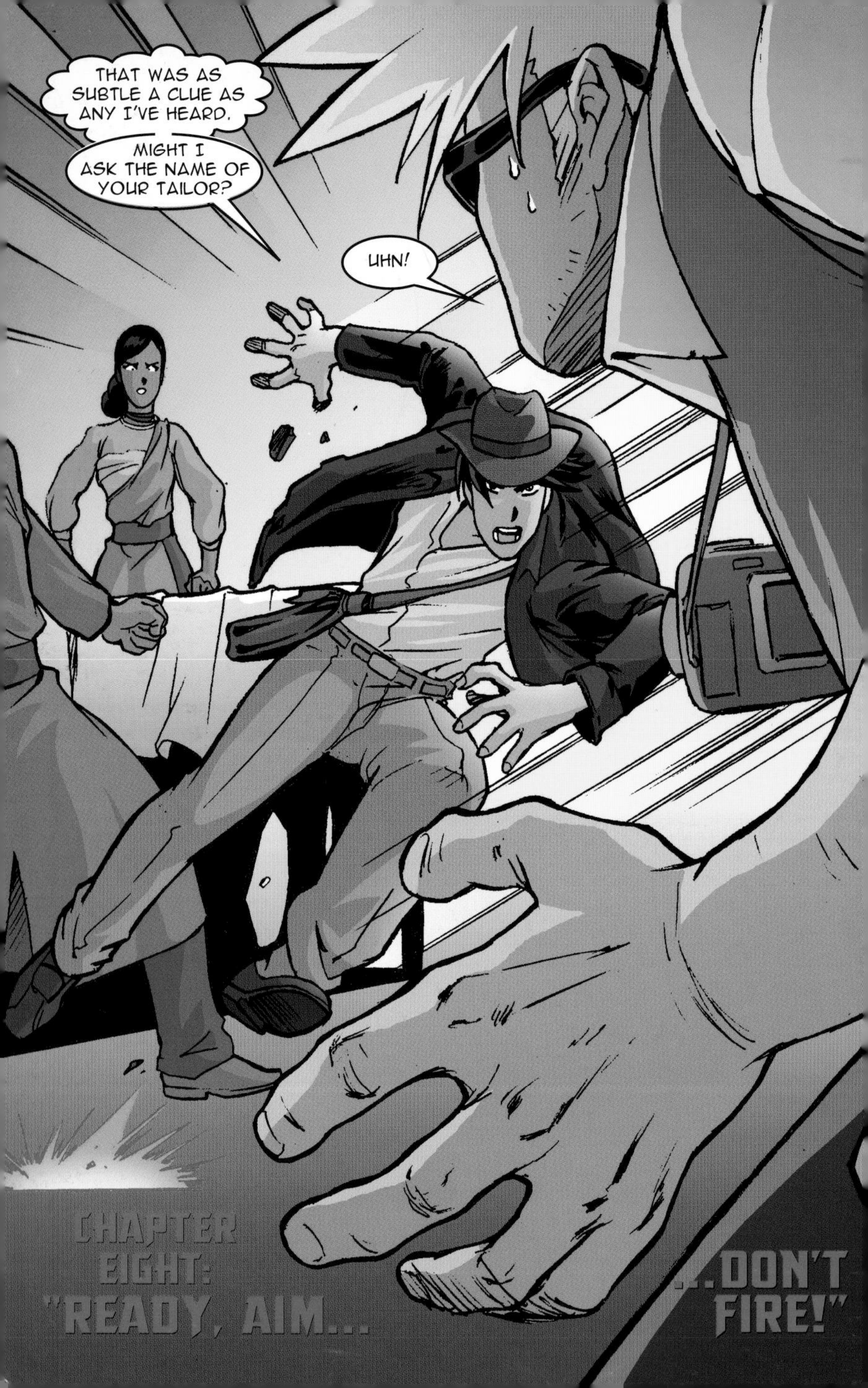

THAT WAS AS SUBTLE A CLUE AS ANY I'VE HEARD.
MIGHT I ASK THE NAME OF YOUR TAILOR?
UHN!
CHAPTER EIGHT: "READY, AIM...
...DON'T FIRE!"

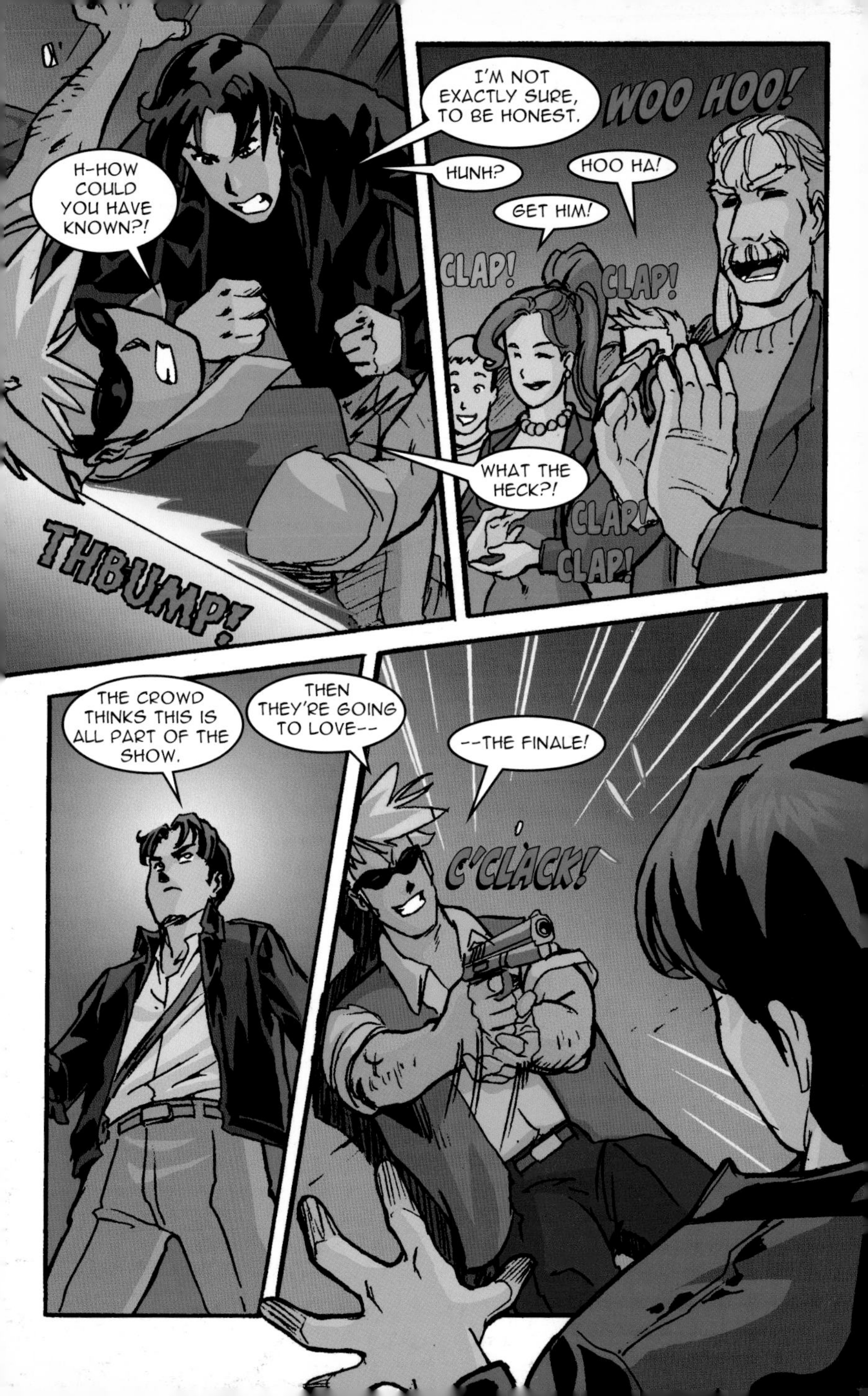
H-HOW COULD YOU HAVE KNOWN?!
I'M NOT EXACTLY SURE, TO BE HONEST.
THBUMP!
HUNH?
WOO HOO!
HOO HA!
GET HIM!
CLAP!
CLAP!
WHAT THE HECK?!
CLAP!
CLAP!
THE CROWD THINKS THIS IS ALL PART OF THE SHOW.
THEN THEY'RE GOING TO LOVE--
--THE FINALE!
C'CLACK!

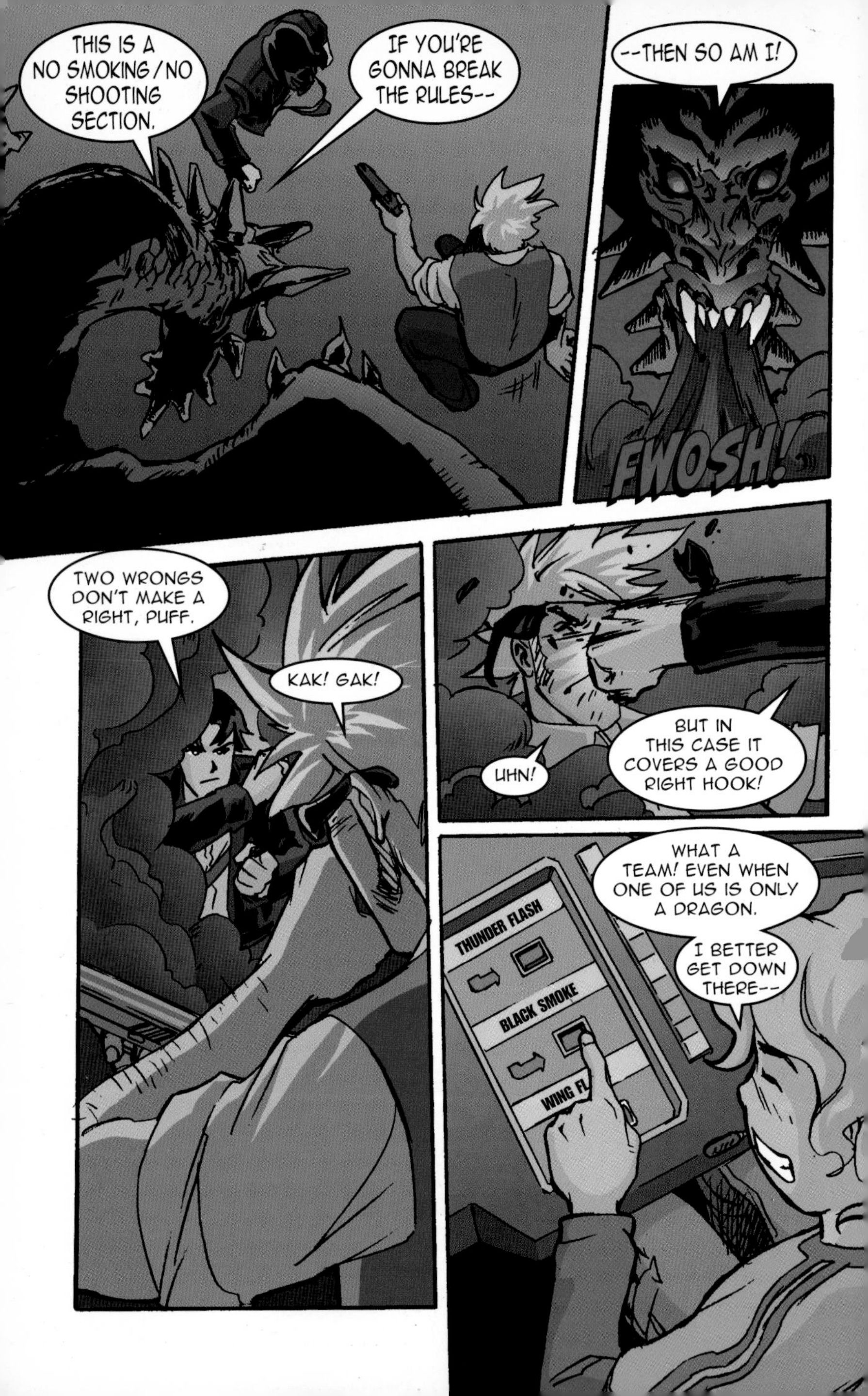
THIS IS A NO SMOKING/NO SHOOTING SECTION.
IF YOU'RE GONNA BREAK THE RULES--
--THEN SO AM I!
FWOSH!
TWO WRONGS DON'T MAKE A RIGHT, PUFF.
KAK! GAK!
UHN!
BUT IN THIS CASE IT COVERS A GOOD RIGHT HOOK!
WHAT A TEAM! EVEN WHEN ONE OF US IS ONLY A DRAGON.
I BETTER GET DOWN THERE--
THUNDER FLASH
BLACK SMOKE
WING FL

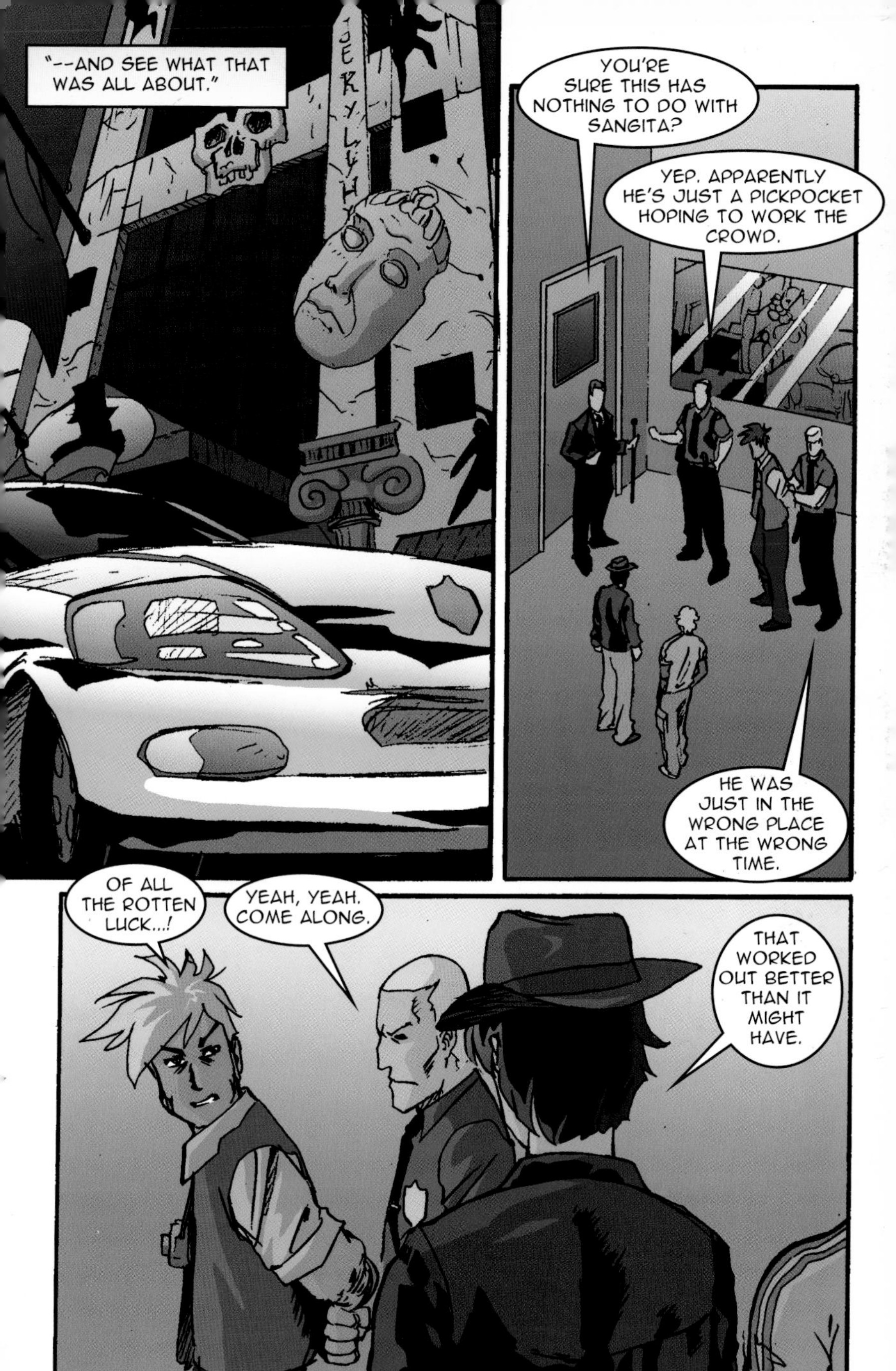
"--AND SEE WHAT THAT WAS ALL ABOUT."
YOU'RE SURE THIS HAS NOTHING TO DO WITH SANGITA?
YEP. APPARENTLY HE'S JUST A PICKPOCKET HOPING TO WORK THE CROWD.
HE WAS JUST IN THE WRONG PLACE AT THE WRONG TIME.
OF ALL THE ROTTEN LUCK...!
YEAH, YEAH. COME ALONG.
THAT WORKED OUT BETTER THAN IT MIGHT HAVE.

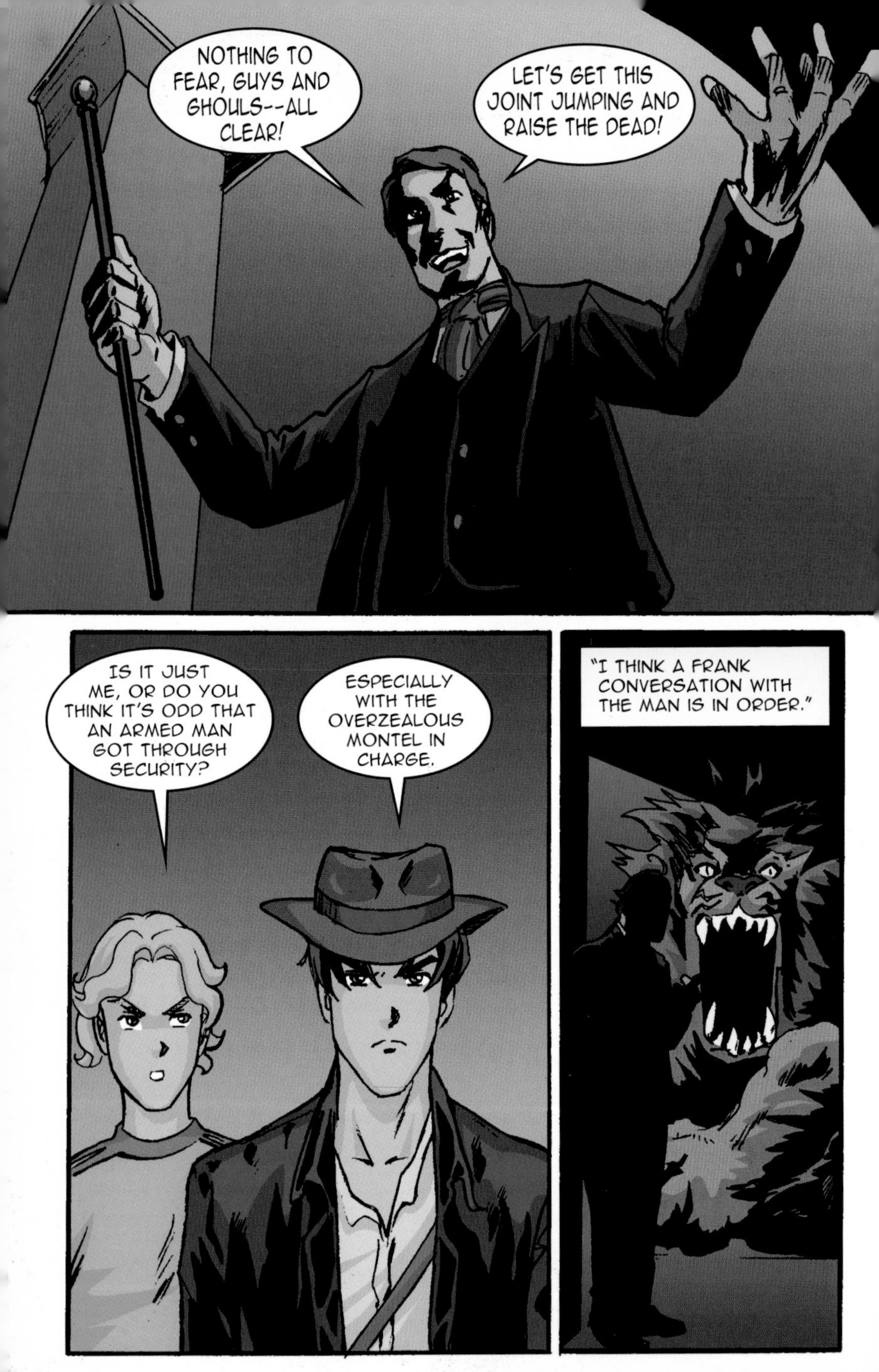
NOTHING TO FEAR, GUYS AND GHOULS--ALL CLEAR!
LET'S GET THIS JOINT JUMPING AND RAISE THE DEAD!
IS IT JUST ME, OR DO YOU THINK IT'S ODD THAT AN ARMED MAN GOT THROUGH SECURITY?
ESPECIALLY WITH THE OVERZEALOUS MONTEL IN CHARGE.
"I THINK A FRANK CONVERSATION WITH THE MAN IS IN ORDER."

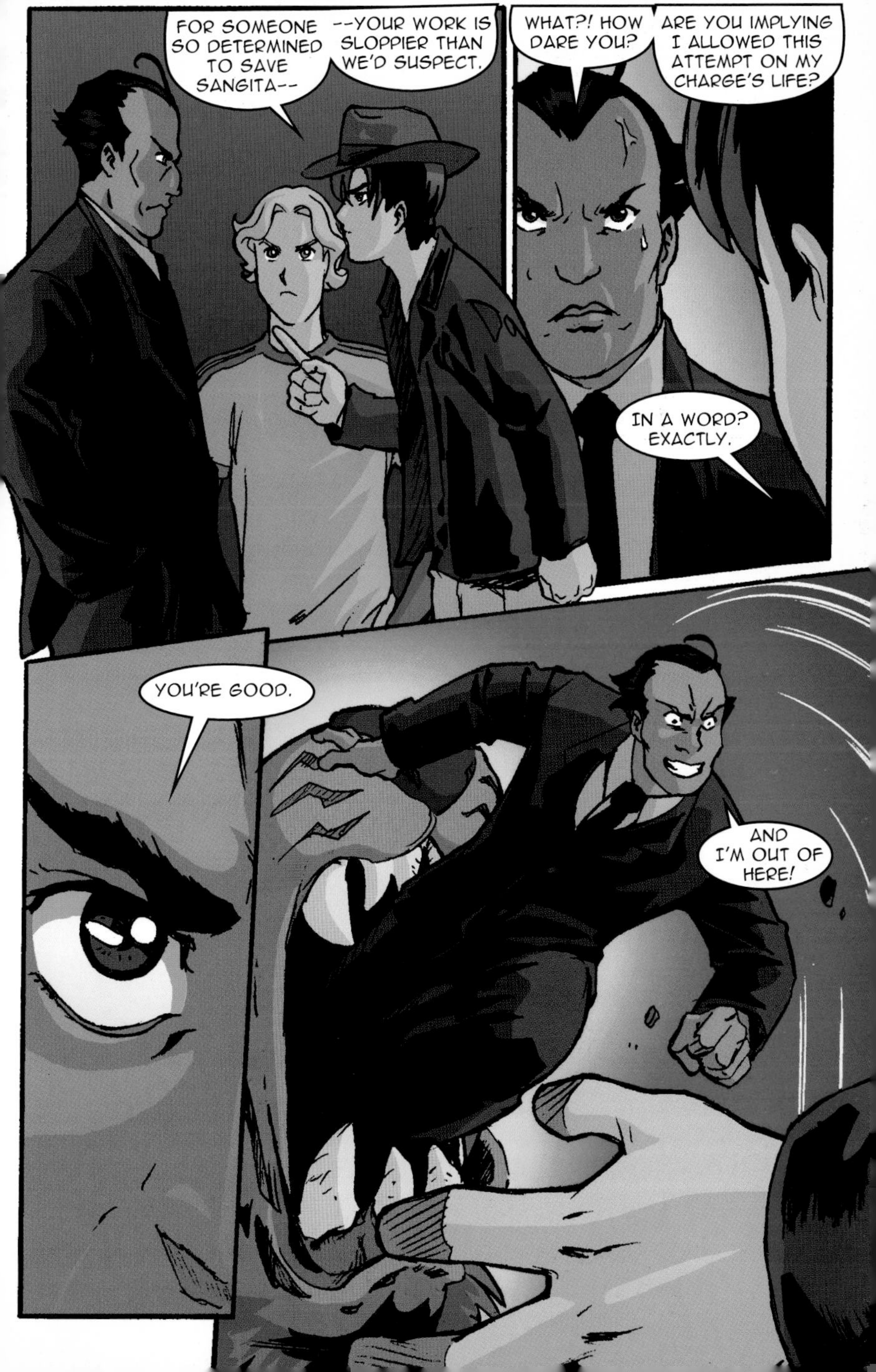
FOR SOMEONE SO DETERMINED TO SAVE SANGITA--
--YOUR WORK IS SLOPPIER THAN WE'D SUSPECT.
WHAT?! HOW DARE YOU?
ARE YOU IMPLYING I ALLOWED THIS ATTEMPT ON MY CHARGE'S LIFE?
IN A WORD? EXACTLY.
YOU'RE GOOD.
AND I'M OUT OF HERE!

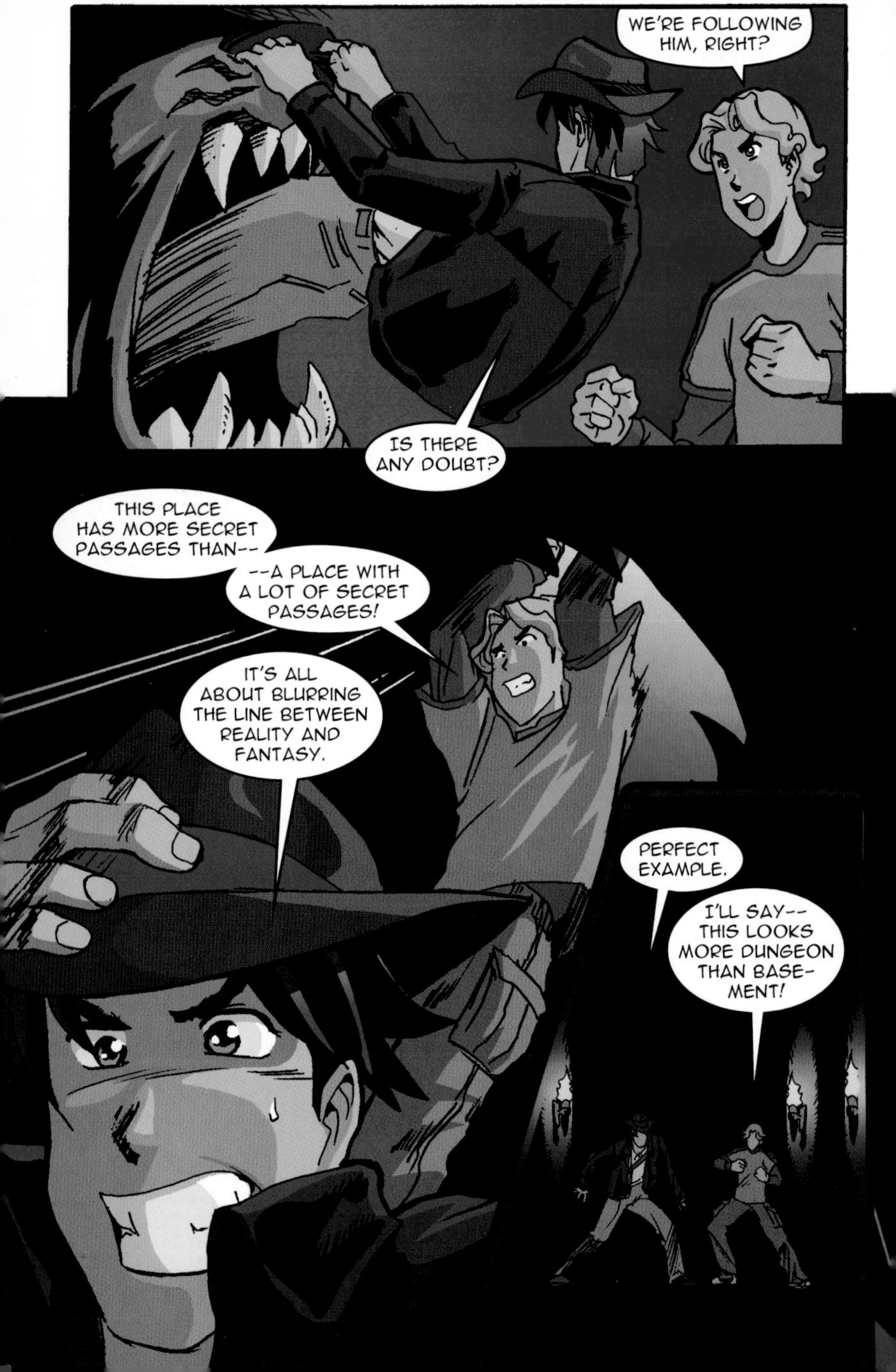
WE'RE FOLLOWING HIM, RIGHT?
IS THERE ANY DOUBT?
THIS PLACE HAS MORE SECRET PASSAGES THAN--
--A PLACE WITH A LOT OF SECRET PASSAGES!
IT'S ALL ABOUT BLURRING THE LINE BETWEEN REALITY AND FANTASY.
PERFECT EXAMPLE.
I'LL SAY-- THIS LOOKS MORE DUNGEON THAN BASE- MENT!

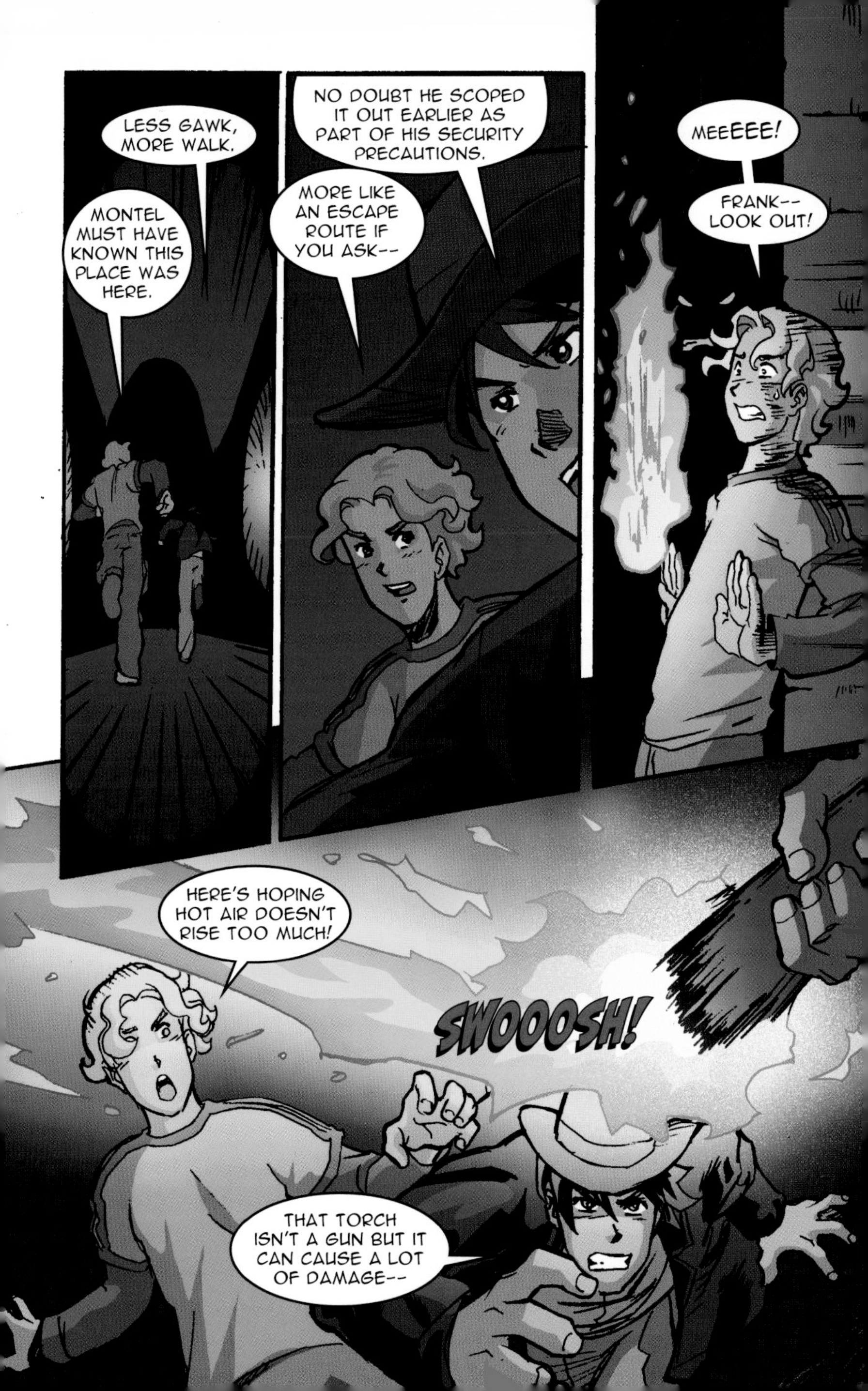

LESS GAWK, MORE WALK.
MONTEL MUST HAVE KNOWN THIS PLACE WAS HERE.
NO DOUBT HE SCOPED IT OUT EARLIER AS PART OF HIS SECURITY PRECAUTIONS.
MORE LIKE AN ESCAPE ROUTE IF YOU ASK--
MEEEEE!
FRANK-- LOOK OUT!
HERE'S HOPING HOT AIR DOESN'T RISE TOO MUCH!
SWOOOSH!
THAT TORCH ISN'T A GUN BUT IT CAN CAUSE A LOT OF DAMAGE--

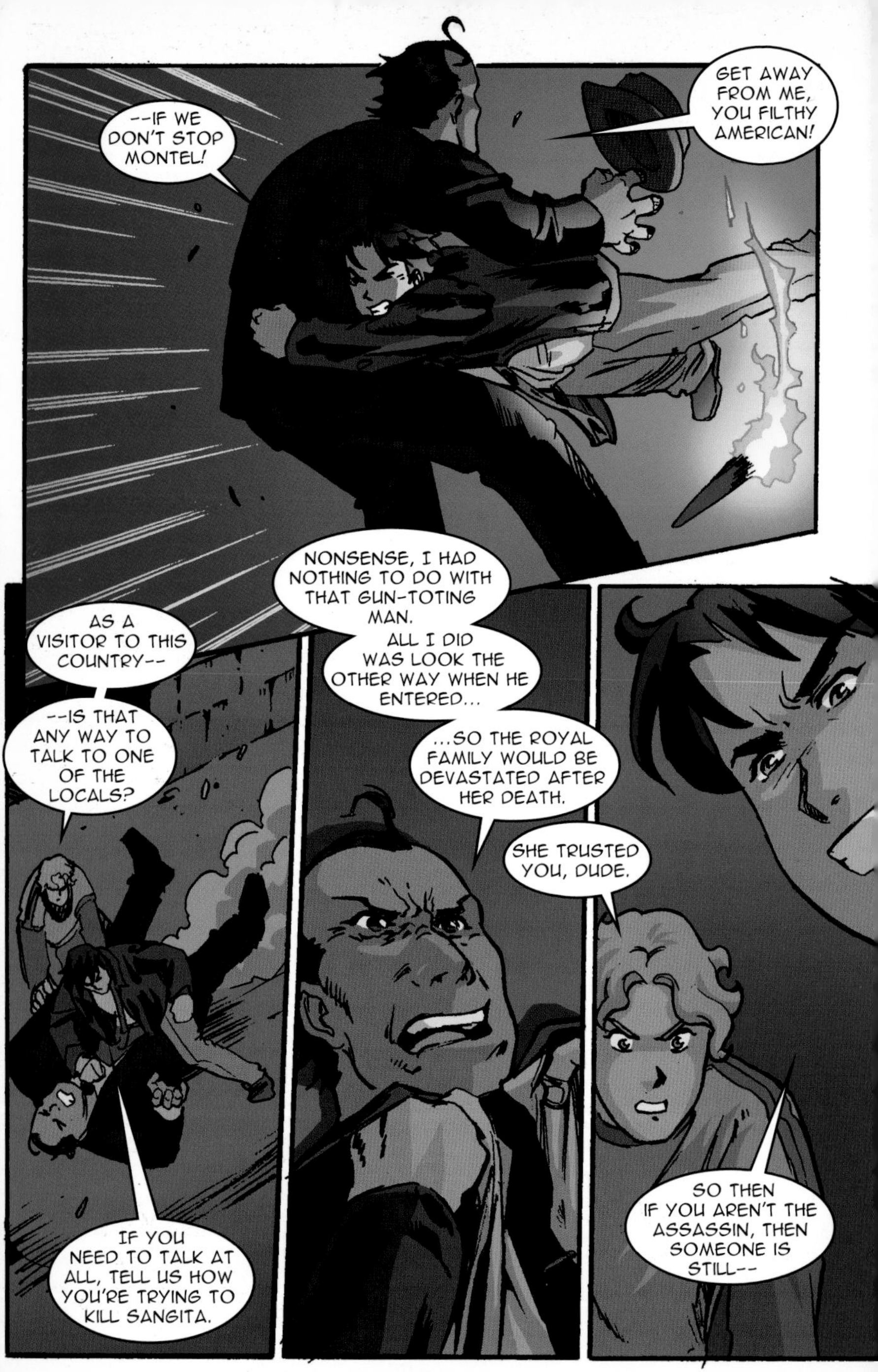
--IF WE DON'T STOP MONTEL!
GET AWAY FROM ME, YOU FILTHY AMERICAN!
AS A VISITOR TO THIS COUNTRY--
--IS THAT ANY WAY TO TALK TO ONE OF THE LOCALS?
IF YOU NEED TO TALK AT ALL, TELL US HOW YOU'RE TRYING TO KILL SANGITA.
NONSENSE, I HAD NOTHING TO DO WITH THAT GUN-TOTING MAN.
ALL I DID WAS LOOK THE OTHER WAY WHEN HE ENTERED...
...SO THE ROYAL FAMILY WOULD BE DEVASTATED AFTER HER DEATH.
SHE TRUSTED YOU, DUDE.
SO THEN IF YOU AREN'T THE ASSASSIN, THEN SOMEONE IS STILL--

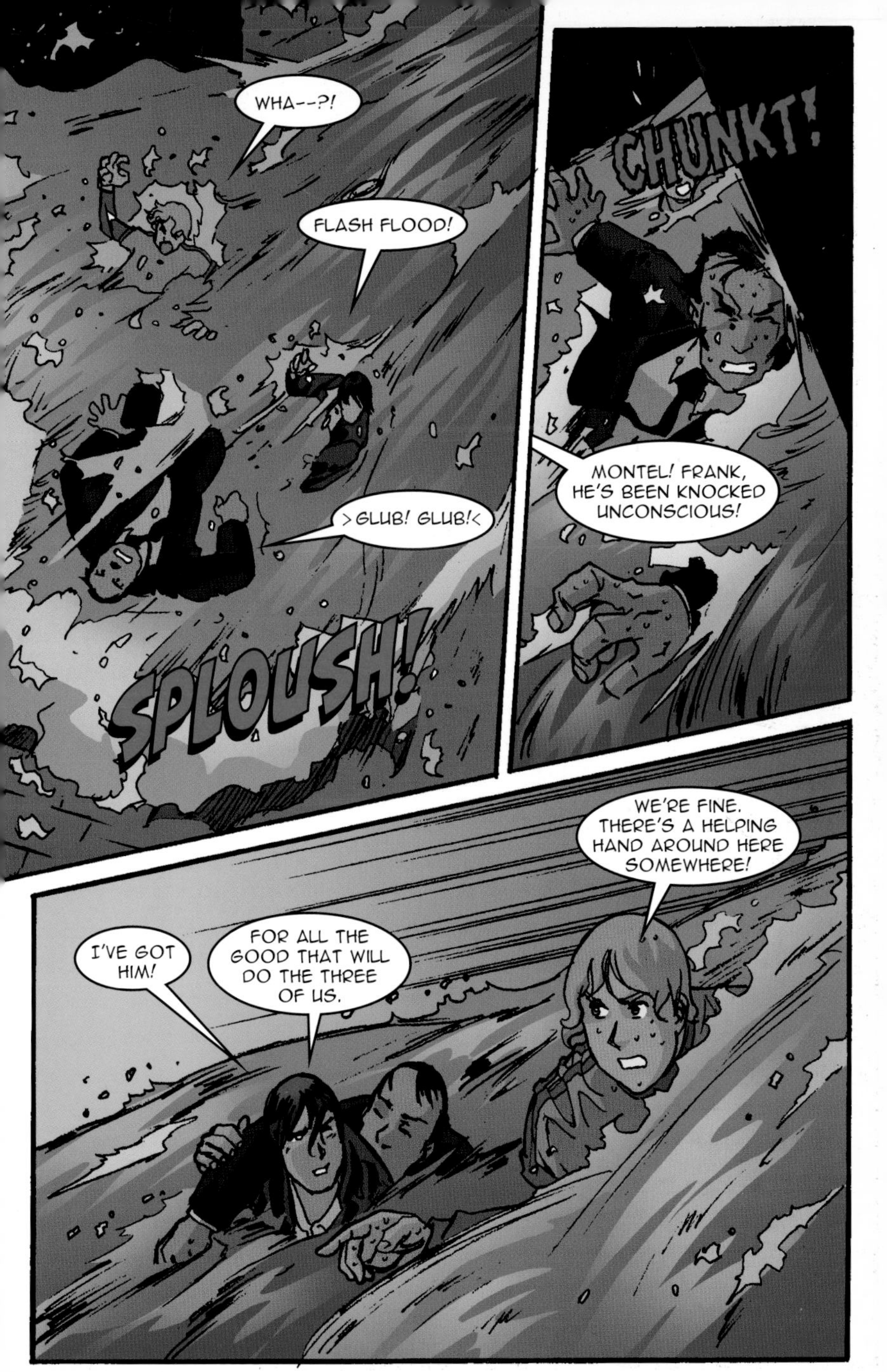
WHA--?!
FLASH FLOOD!
>GLUB! GLUB!<
SPLOUSH!
CHUNKT!
MONTEL! FRANK, HE'S BEEN KNOCKED UNCONSCIOUS!
WE'RE FINE. THERE'S A HELPING HAND AROUND HERE SOMEWHERE!
I'VE GOT HIM!
FOR ALL THE GOOD THAT WILL DO THE THREE OF US.

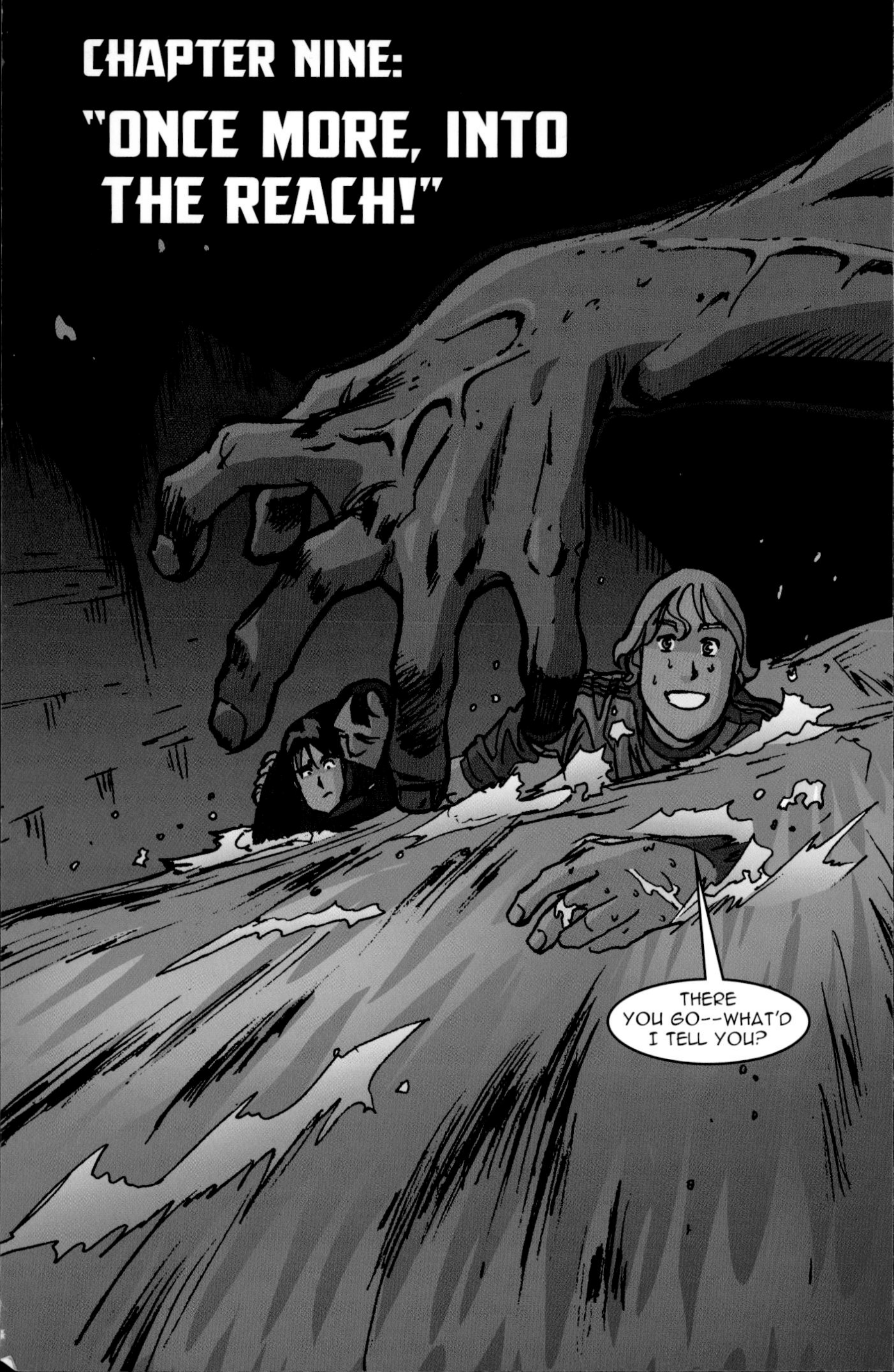
CHAPTER NINE:
"ONCE MORE, INTO THE REACH!"
THERE YOU GO--WHAT'D I TELL YOU?

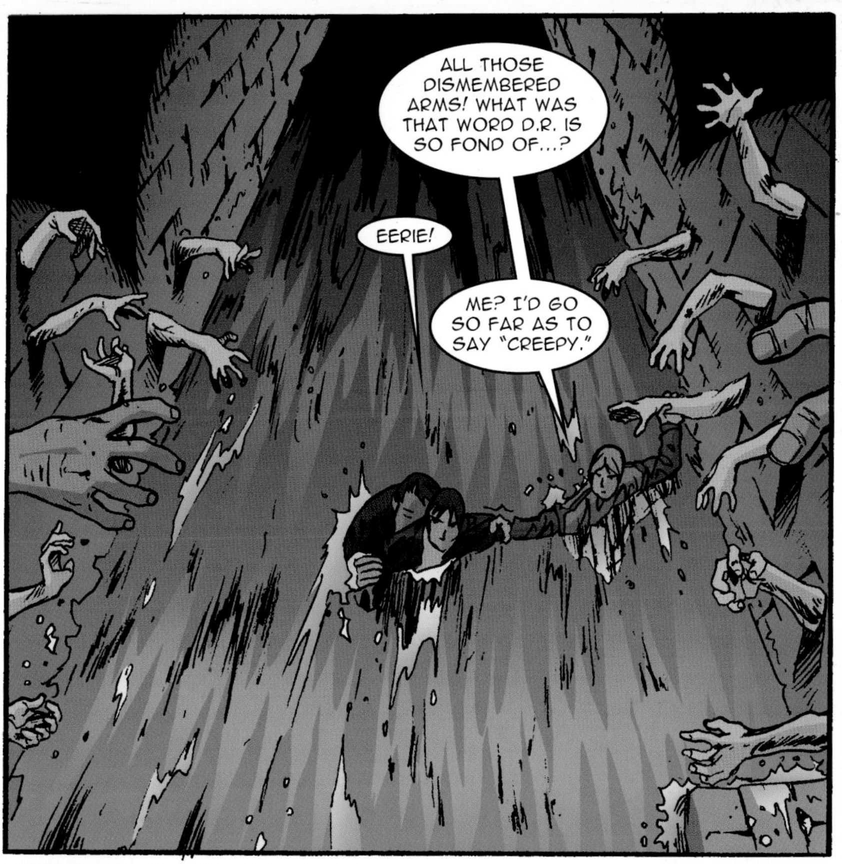
ALL THOSE DISMEMBERED ARMS! WHAT WAS THAT WORD D.R. IS SO FOND OF...?
EERIE!
ME? I'D GO SO FAR AS TO SAY "CREEPY."

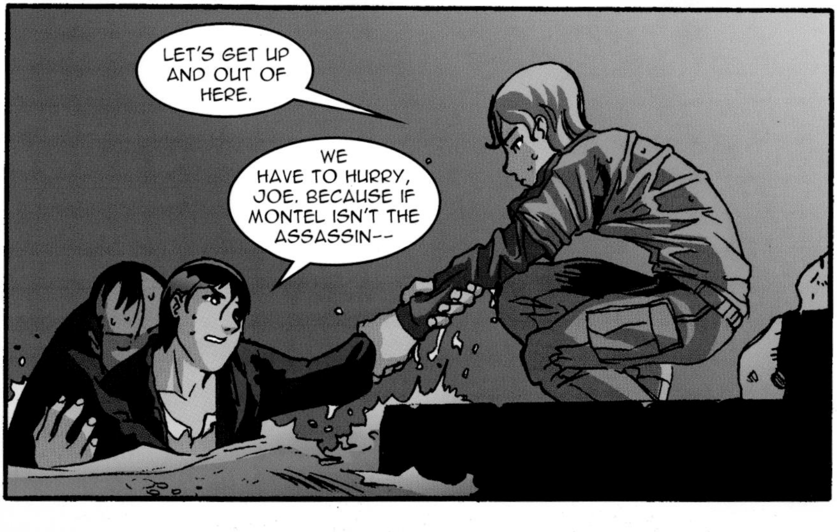
LET'S GET UP AND OUT OF HERE.
WE HAVE TO HURRY, JOE. BECAUSE IF MONTEL ISN'T THE ASSASSIN--

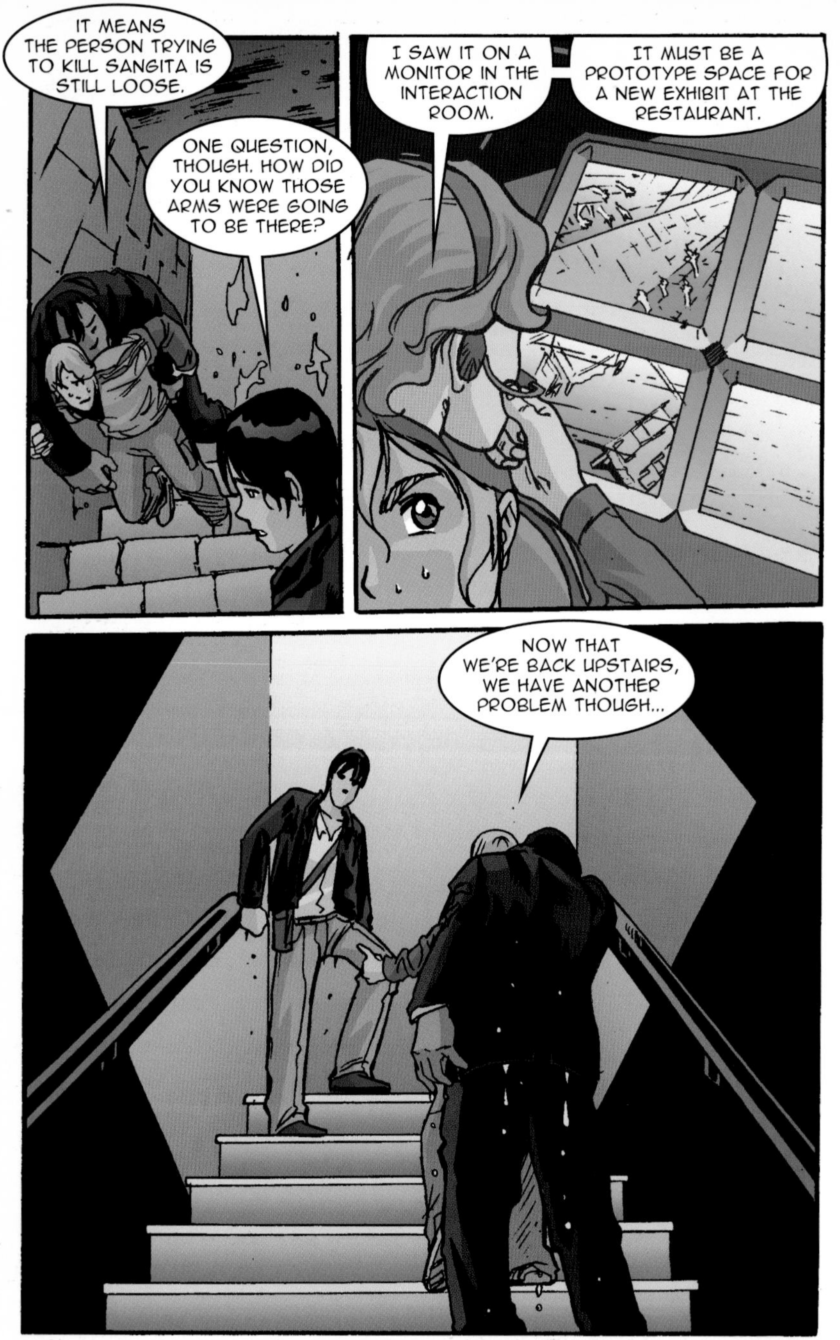
IT MEANS THE PERSON TRYING TO KILL SANGITA IS STILL LOOSE.
ONE QUESTION, THOUGH. HOW DID YOU KNOW THOSE ARMS WERE GOING TO BE THERE?
I SAW IT ON A MONITOR IN THE INTERACTION ROOM.
IT MUST BE A PROTOTYPE SPACE FOR A NEW EXHIBIT AT THE RESTAURANT.
NOW THAT WE'RE BACK UPSTAIRS, WE HAVE ANOTHER PROBLEM THOUGH...

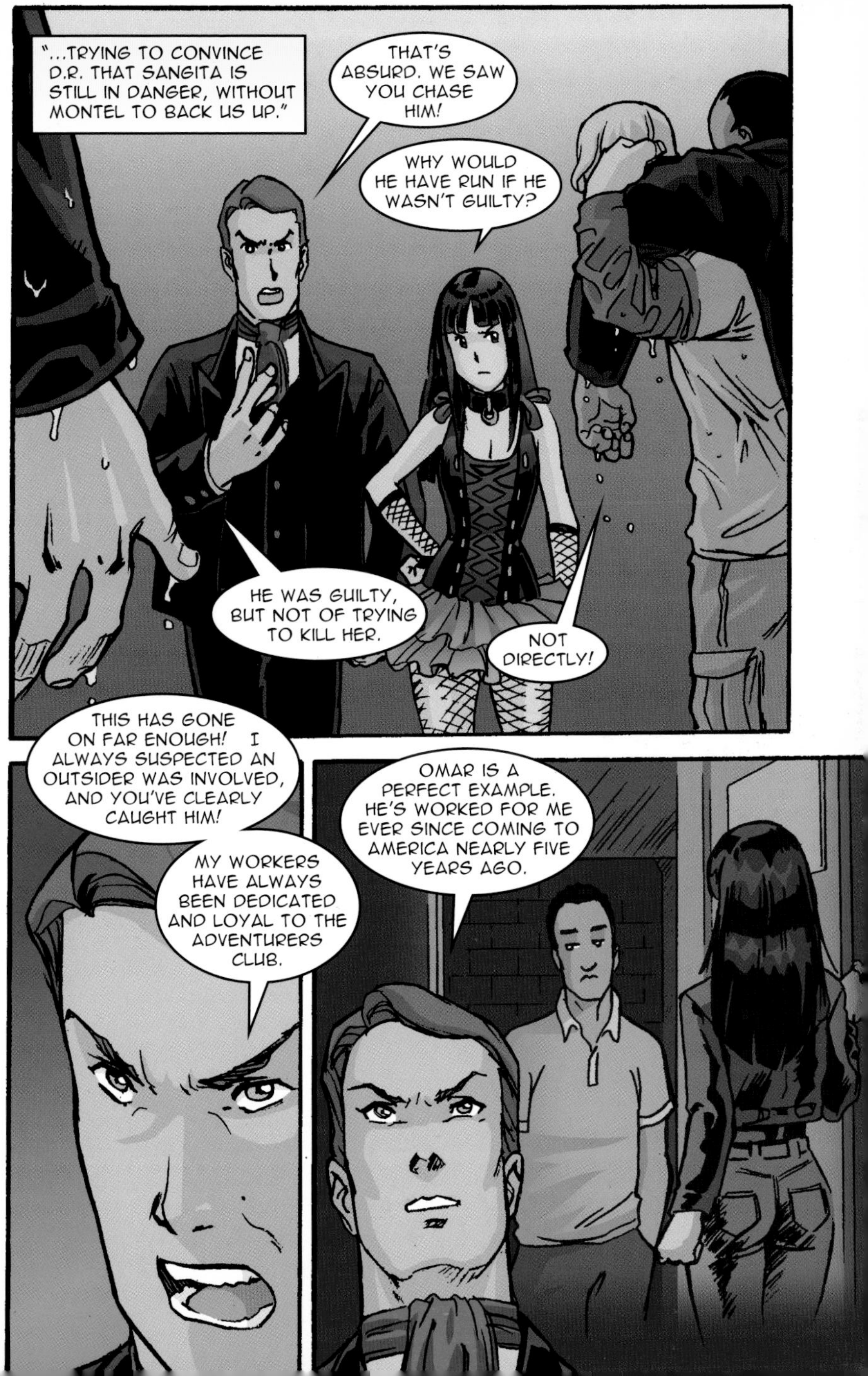
"...TRYING TO CONVINCE D.R. THAT SANGITA IS STILL IN DANGER, WITHOUT MONTEL TO BACK US UP."
THAT'S ABSURD. WE SAW YOU CHASE HIM!
WHY WOULD HE HAVE RUN IF HE WASN'T GUILTY?
HE WAS GUILTY, BUT NOT OF TRYING TO KILL HER.
NOT DIRECTLY!
THIS HAS GONE ON FAR ENOUGH! I ALWAYS SUSPECTED AN OUTSIDER WAS INVOLVED, AND YOU'VE CLEARLY CAUGHT HIM!
MY WORKERS HAVE ALWAYS BEEN DEDICATED AND LOYAL TO THE ADVENTURERS CLUB.
OMAR IS A PERFECT EXAMPLE. HE'S WORKED FOR ME EVER SINCE COMING TO AMERICA NEARLY FIVE YEARS AGO.

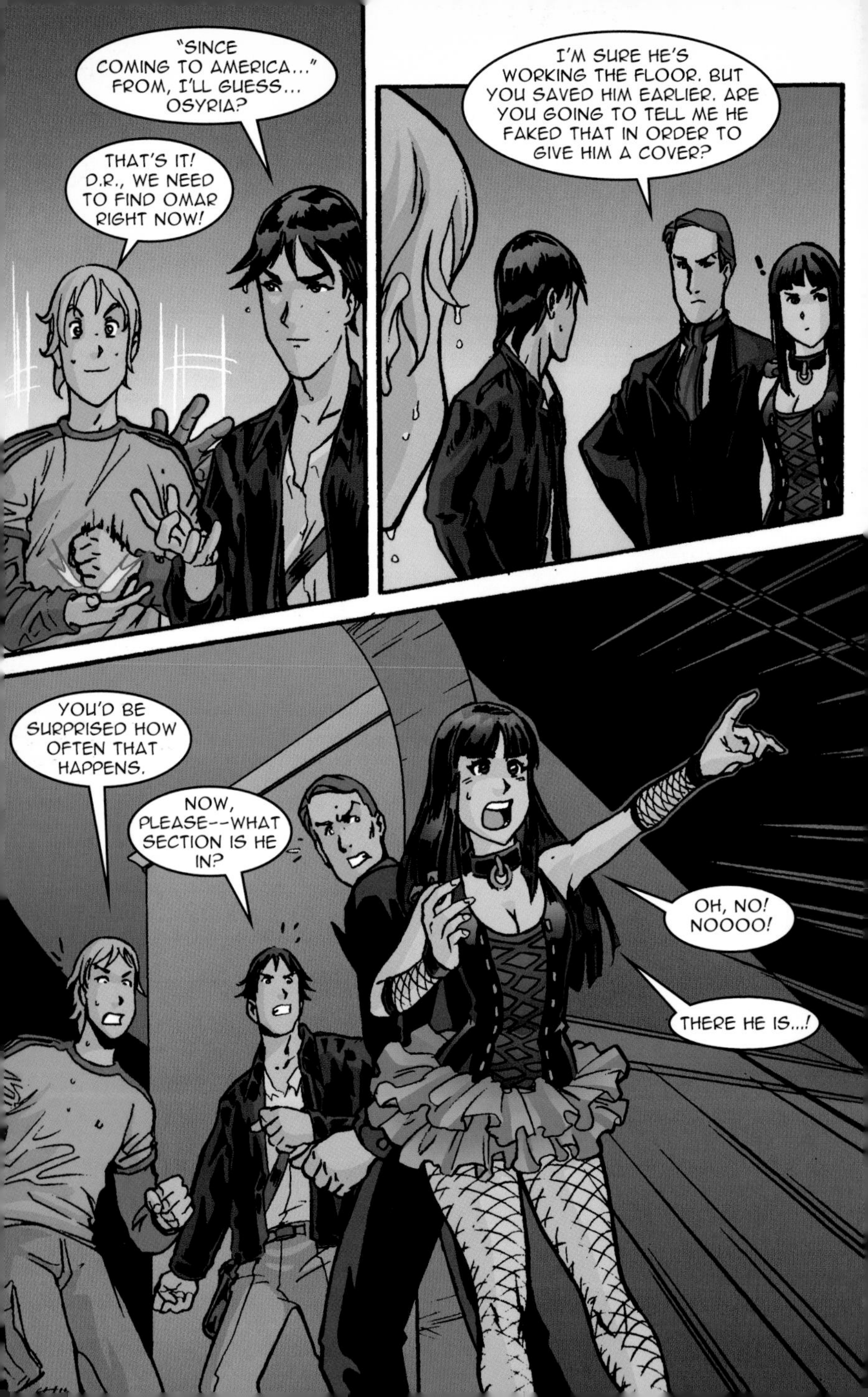
"SINCE COMING TO AMERICA..." FROM, I'LL GUESS... OSYRIA?
THAT'S IT! D.R., WE NEED TO FIND OMAR RIGHT NOW!
I'M SURE HE'S WORKING THE FLOOR. BUT YOU SAVED HIM EARLIER. ARE YOU GOING TO TELL ME HE FAKED THAT IN ORDER TO GIVE HIM A COVER?
!
YOU'D BE SURPRISED HOW OFTEN THAT HAPPENS.
NOW, PLEASE--WHAT SECTION IS HE IN?
OH, NO! NOOOO!
THERE HE IS...!

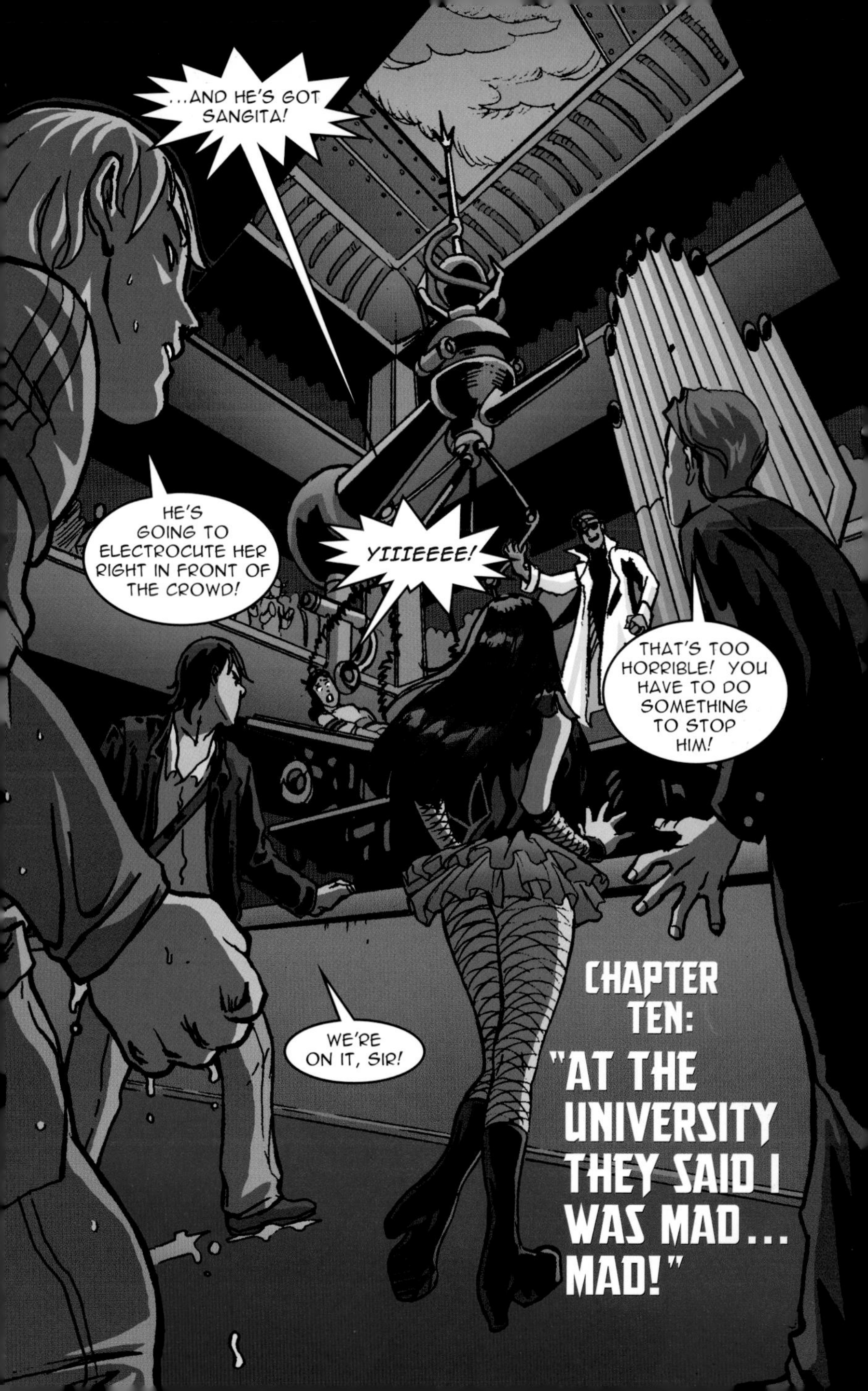
...AND HE'S GOT SANGITA!
HE'S GOING TO ELECTROCUTE HER RIGHT IN FRONT OF THE CROWD!
YIIIEEEE!
THAT'S TOO HORRIBLE! YOU HAVE TO DO SOMETHING TO STOP HIM!
WE'RE ON IT, SIR!
CHAPTER TEN:
"AT THE UNIVERSITY THEY SAID I WAS MAD... MAD!"

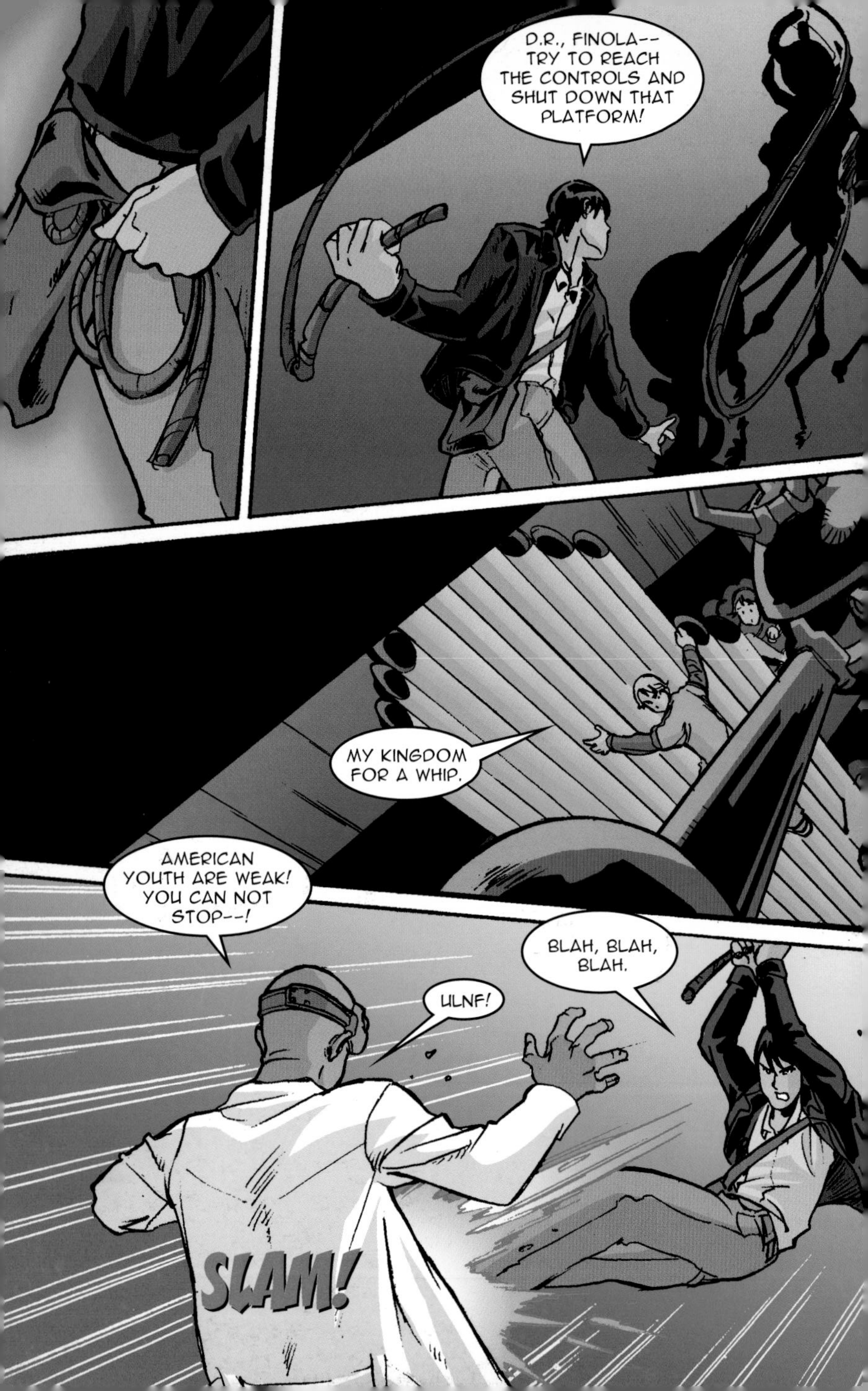
D.R., FINOLA-- TRY TO REACH THE CONTROLS AND SHUT DOWN THAT PLATFORM!
MY KINGDOM FOR A WHIP.
AMERICAN YOUTH ARE WEAK! YOU CAN NOT STOP--!
BLAH, BLAH, BLAH.
ULNF!
SLAM!

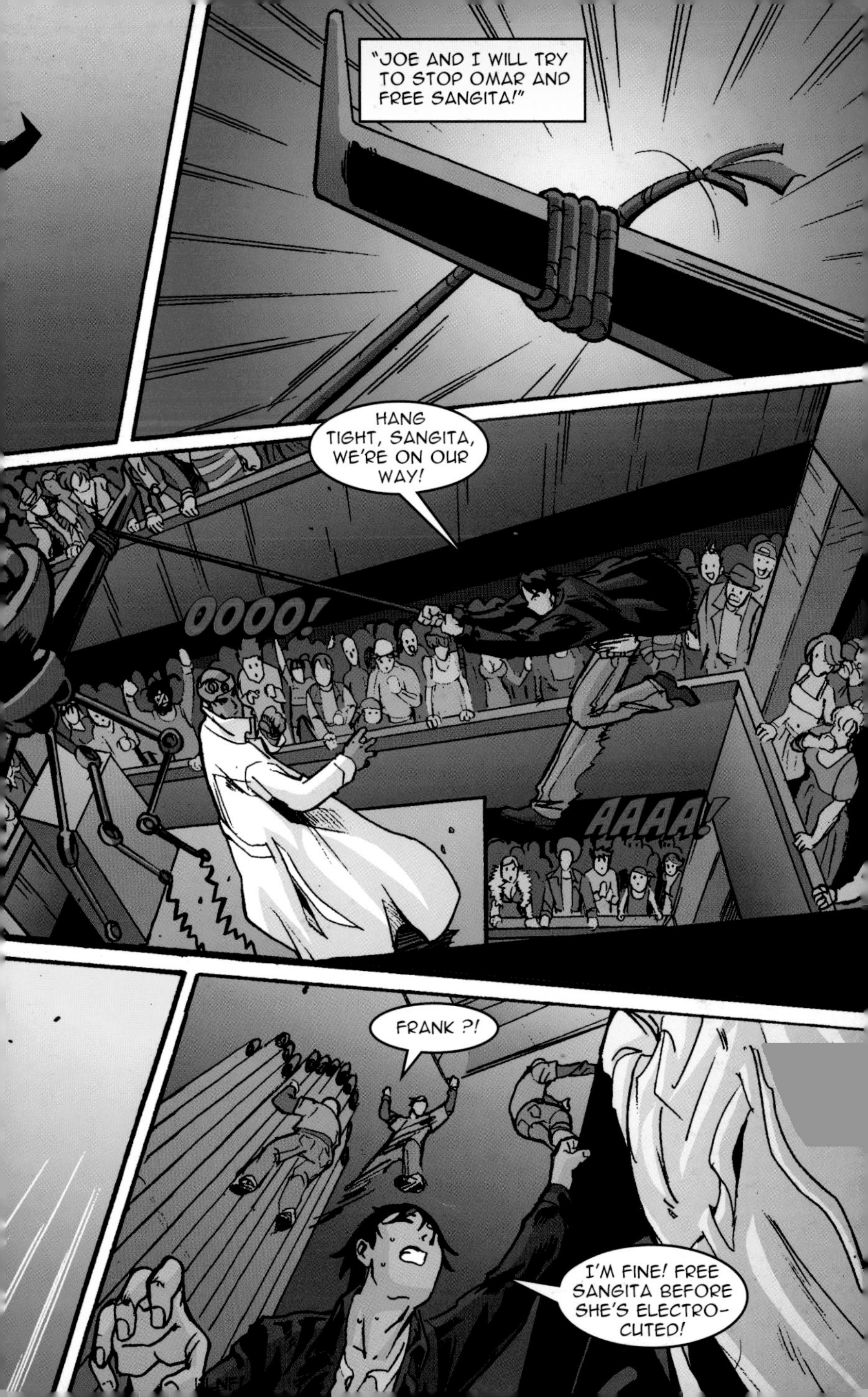
"JOE AND I WILL TRY TO STOP OMAR AND FREE SANGITA!"
HANG TIGHT, SANGITA, WE'RE ON OUR WAY!
OOOO!
AAAA!
FRANK ?!
I'M FINE! FREE SANGITA BEFORE SHE'S ELECTRO-CUTED!

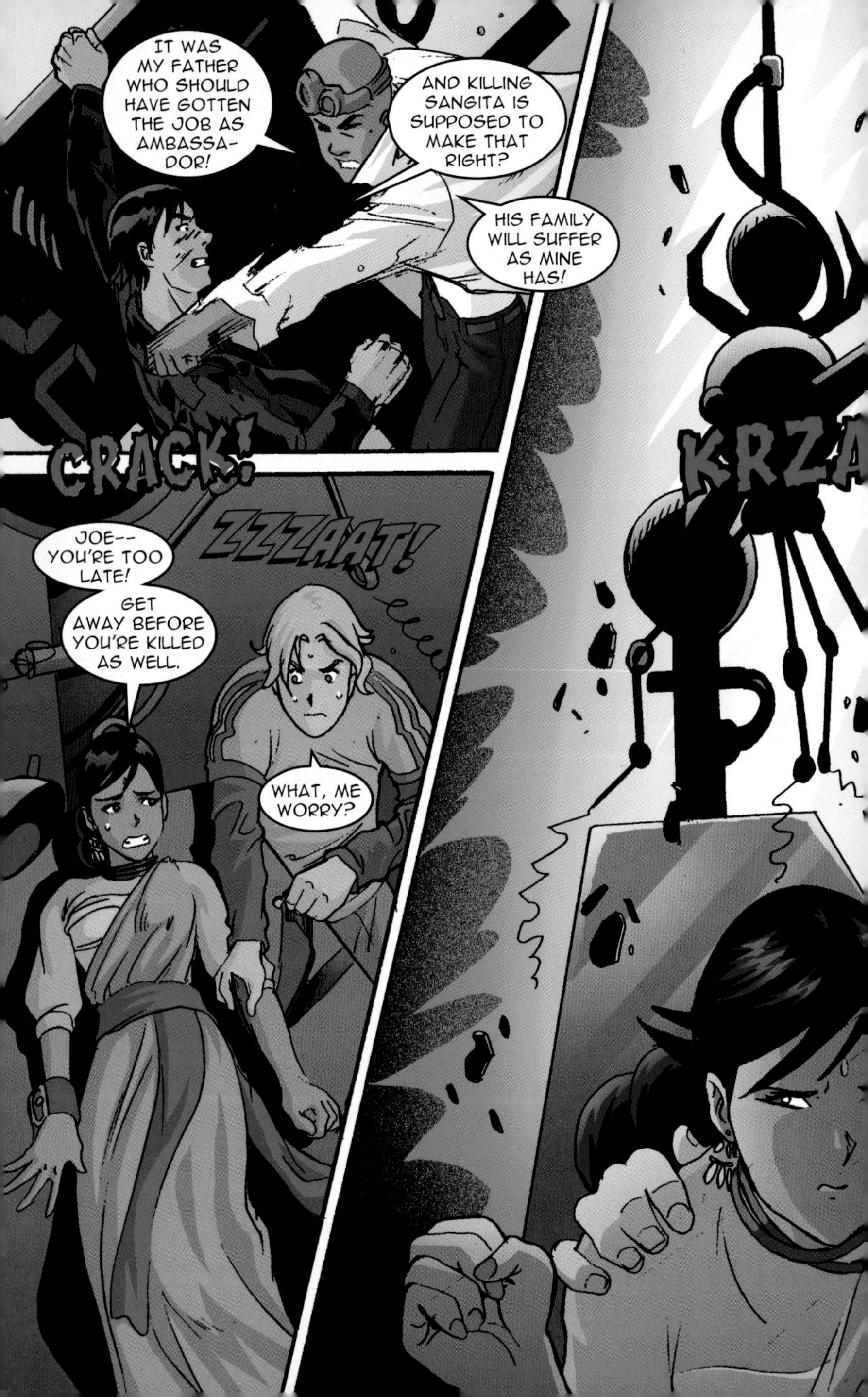
IT WAS MY FATHER WHO SHOULD HAVE GOTTEN THE JOB AS AMBASSA-DOR!
AND KILLING SANGITA IS SUPPOSED TO MAKE THAT RIGHT?
HIS FAMILY WILL SUFFER AS MINE HAS!
CRACK!
ZZZAAT!
JOE-- YOU'RE TOO LATE!
GET AWAY BEFORE YOU'RE KILLED AS WELL.
WHAT, ME WORRY?
KRZA

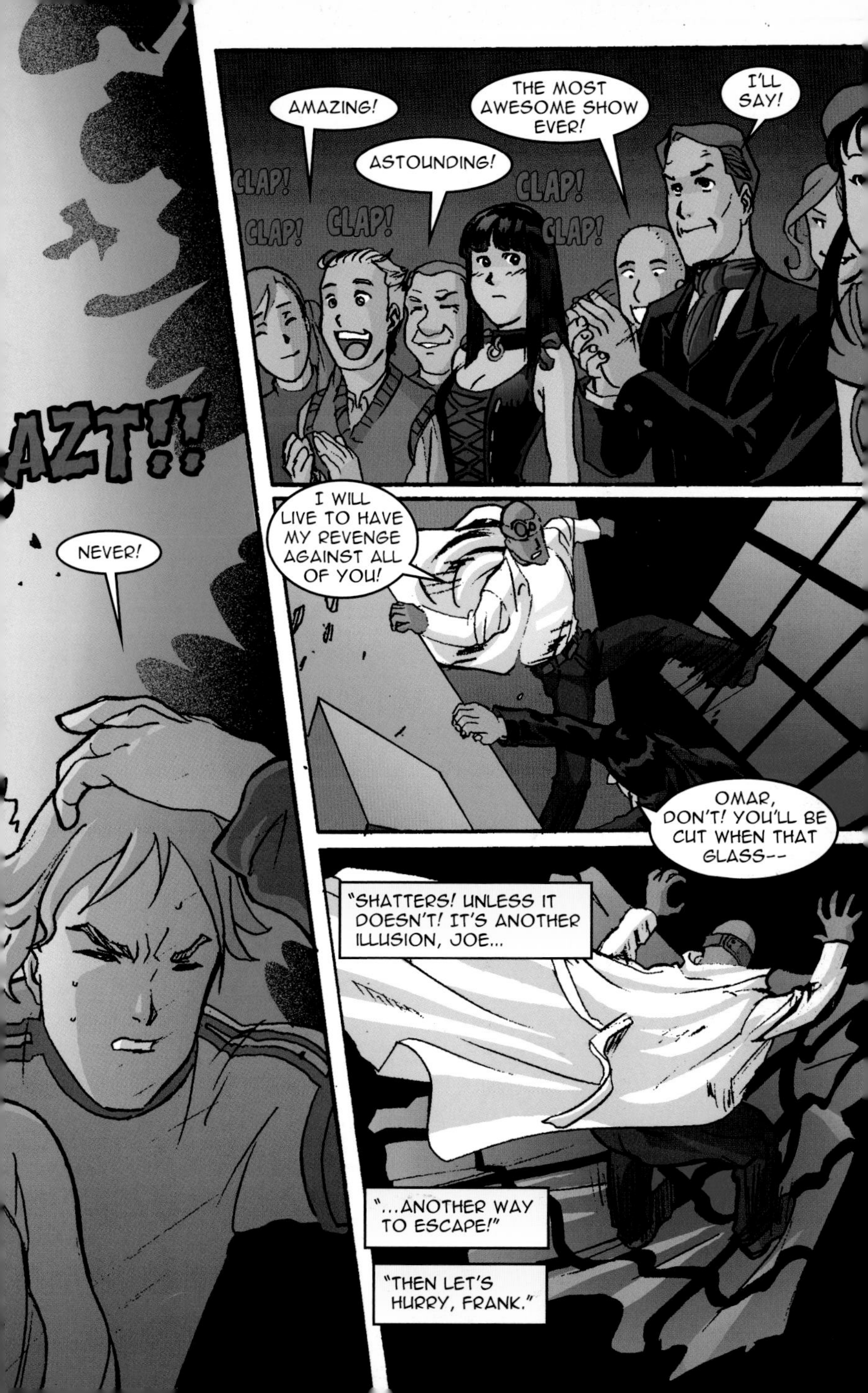
AZT!!
NEVER!
AMAZING!
ASTOUNDING!
THE MOST AWESOME SHOW EVER!
I'LL SAY!
CLAP! CLAP! CLAP! CLAP! CLAP!
I WILL LIVE TO HAVE MY REVENGE AGAINST ALL OF YOU!
OMAR, DON'T! YOU'LL BE CUT WHEN THAT GLASS--
"SHATTERS! UNLESS IT DOESN'T! IT'S ANOTHER ILLUSION, JOE...
"...ANOTHER WAY TO ESCAPE!"
"THEN LET'S HURRY, FRANK."

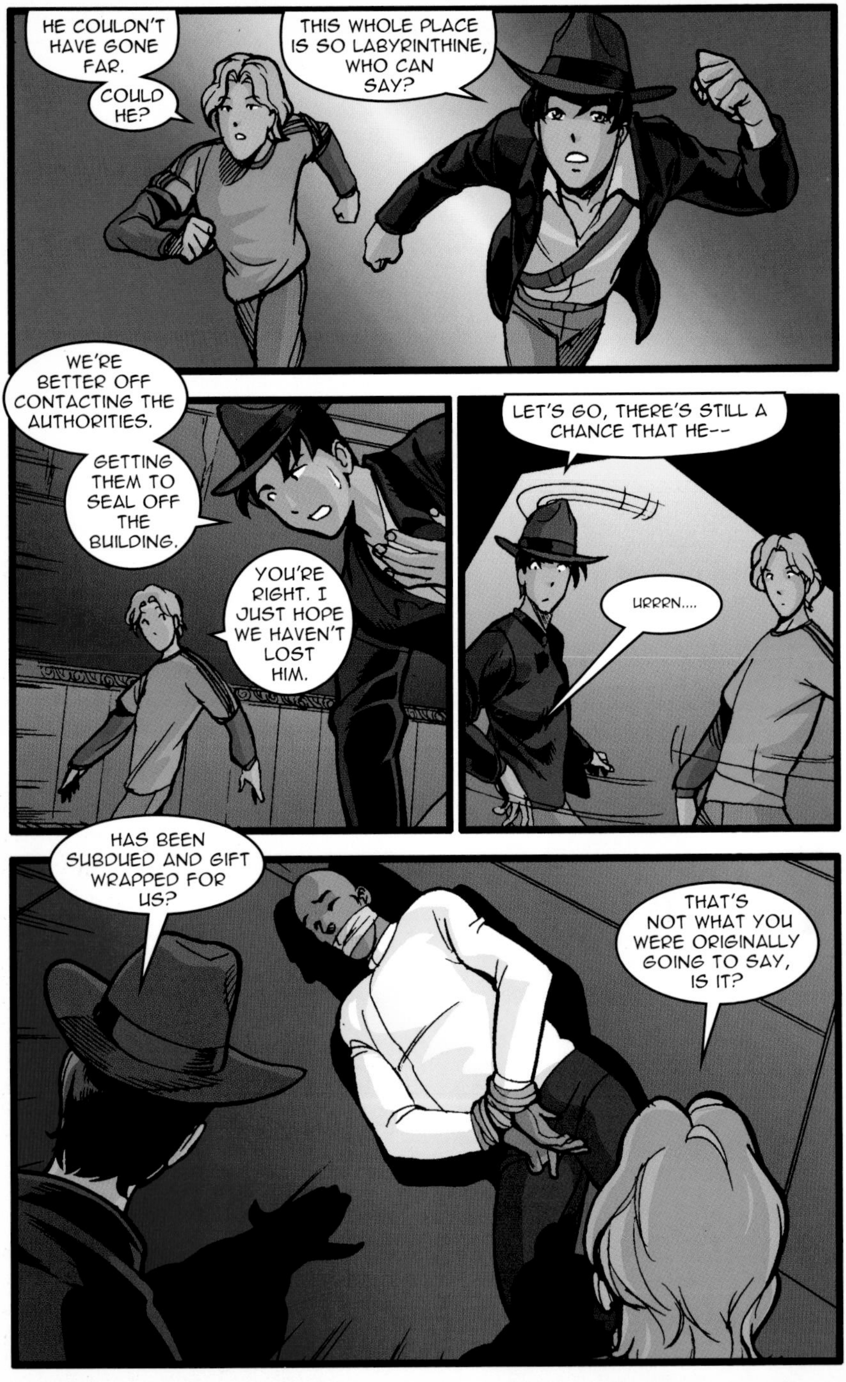
HE COULDN'T HAVE GONE FAR.
COULD HE?
THIS WHOLE PLACE IS SO LABYRINTHINE, WHO CAN SAY?
WE'RE BETTER OFF CONTACTING THE AUTHORITIES.
GETTING THEM TO SEAL OFF THE BUILDING.
YOU'RE RIGHT. I JUST HOPE WE HAVEN'T LOST HIM.
LET'S GO, THERE'S STILL A CHANCE THAT HE--
URRRN....
HAS BEEN SUBDUED AND GIFT WRAPPED FOR US?
THAT'S NOT WHAT YOU WERE ORIGINALLY GOING TO SAY, IS IT?

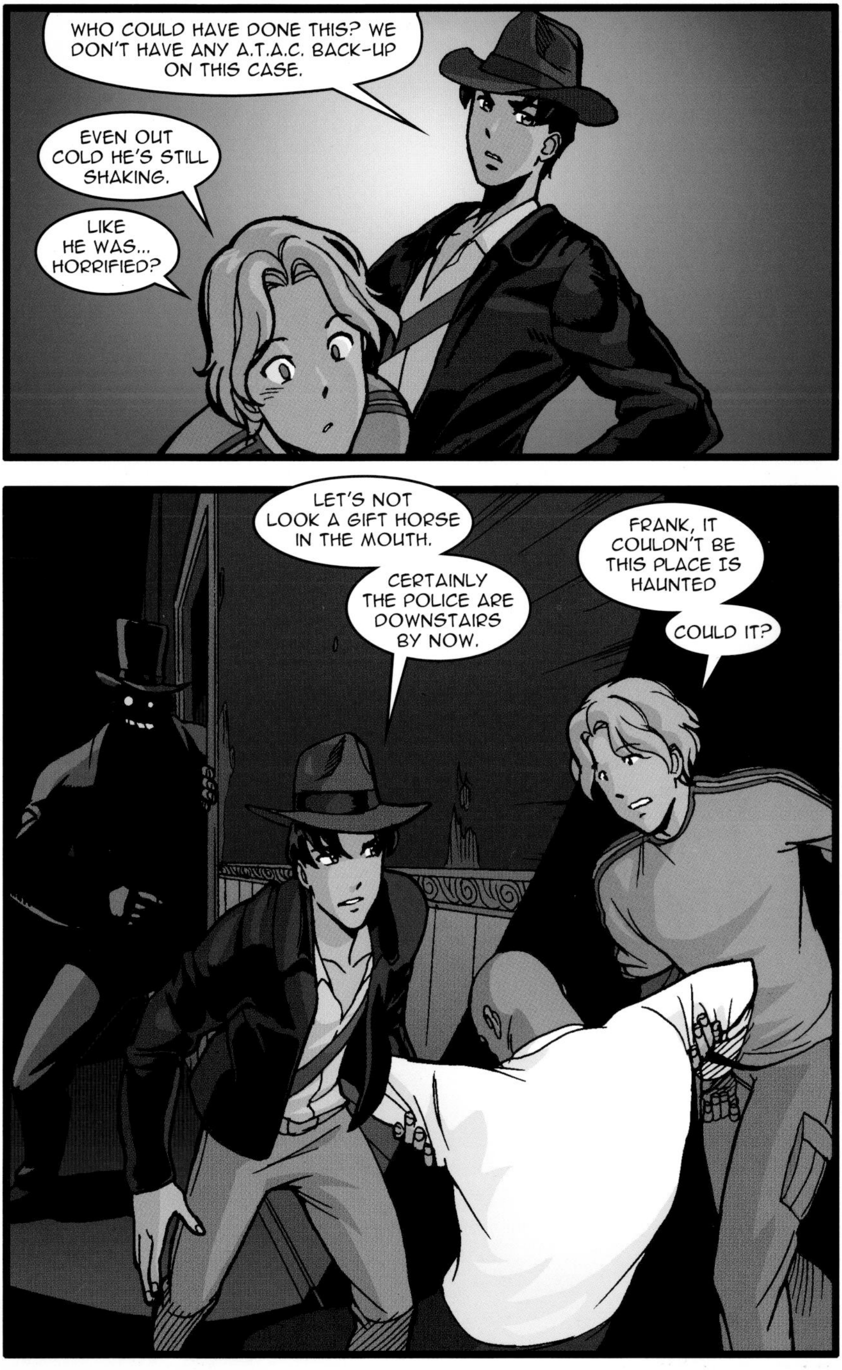
WHO COULD HAVE DONE THIS? WE DON'T HAVE ANY A.T.A.C. BACK-UP ON THIS CASE.
EVEN OUT COLD HE'S STILL SHAKING.
LIKE HE WAS... HORRIFIED?
LET'S NOT LOOK A GIFT HORSE IN THE MOUTH.
CERTAINLY THE POLICE ARE DOWNSTAIRS BY NOW.
FRANK, IT COULDN'T BE THIS PLACE IS HAUNTED
COULD IT?

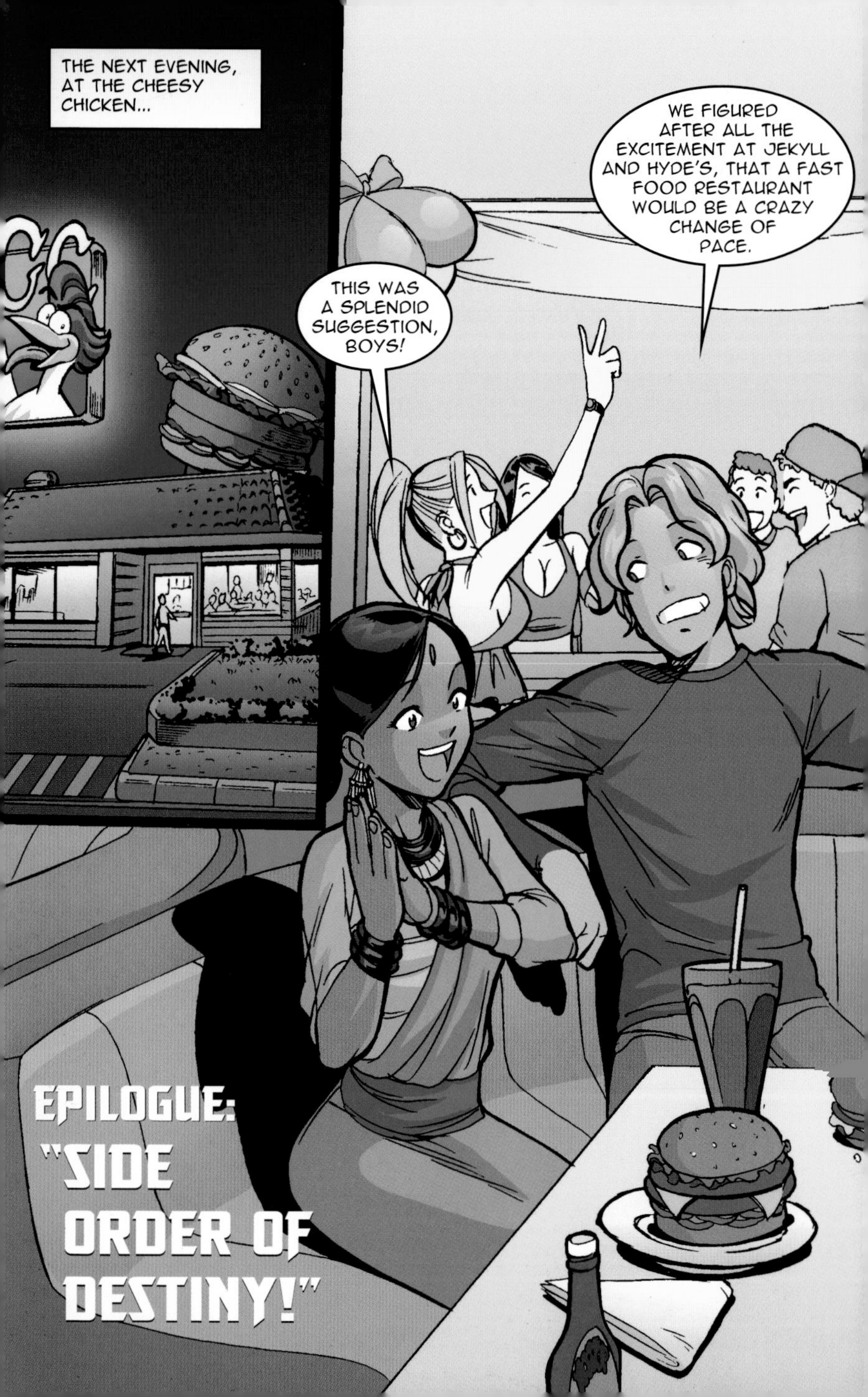
THE NEXT EVENING, AT THE CHEESY CHICKEN...
THIS WAS A SPLENDID SUGGESTION, BOYS!
WE FIGURED AFTER ALL THE EXCITEMENT AT JEKYLL AND HYDE'S, THAT A FAST FOOD RESTAURANT WOULD BE A CRAZY CHANGE OF PACE.
EPILOGUE: "SIDE ORDER OF DESTINY!"

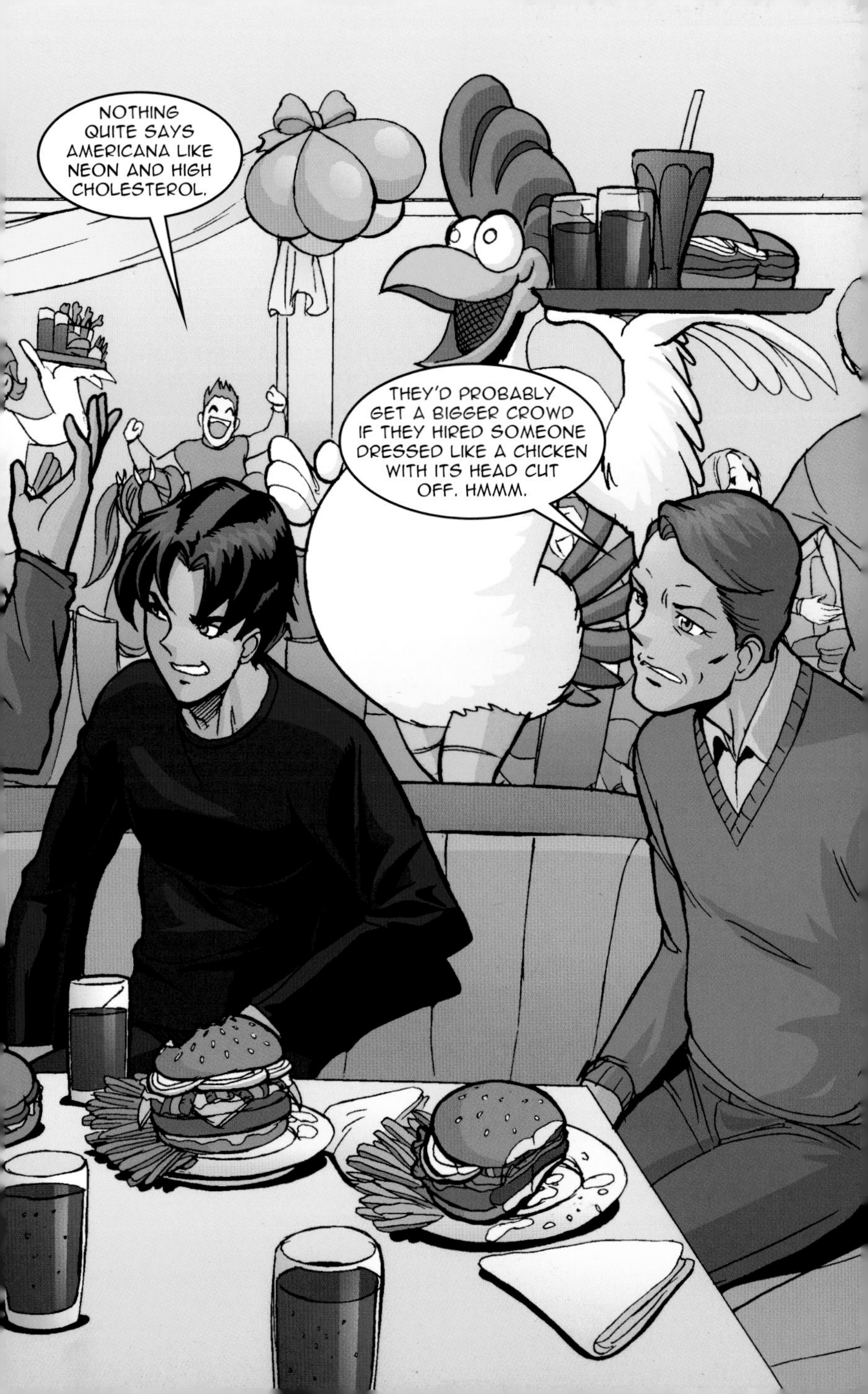
NOTHING QUITE SAYS AMERICANA LIKE NEON AND HIGH CHOLESTEROL.
THEY'D PROBABLY GET A BIGGER CROWD IF THEY HIRED SOMEONE DRESSED LIKE A CHICKEN WITH ITS HEAD CUT OFF. HMMM.

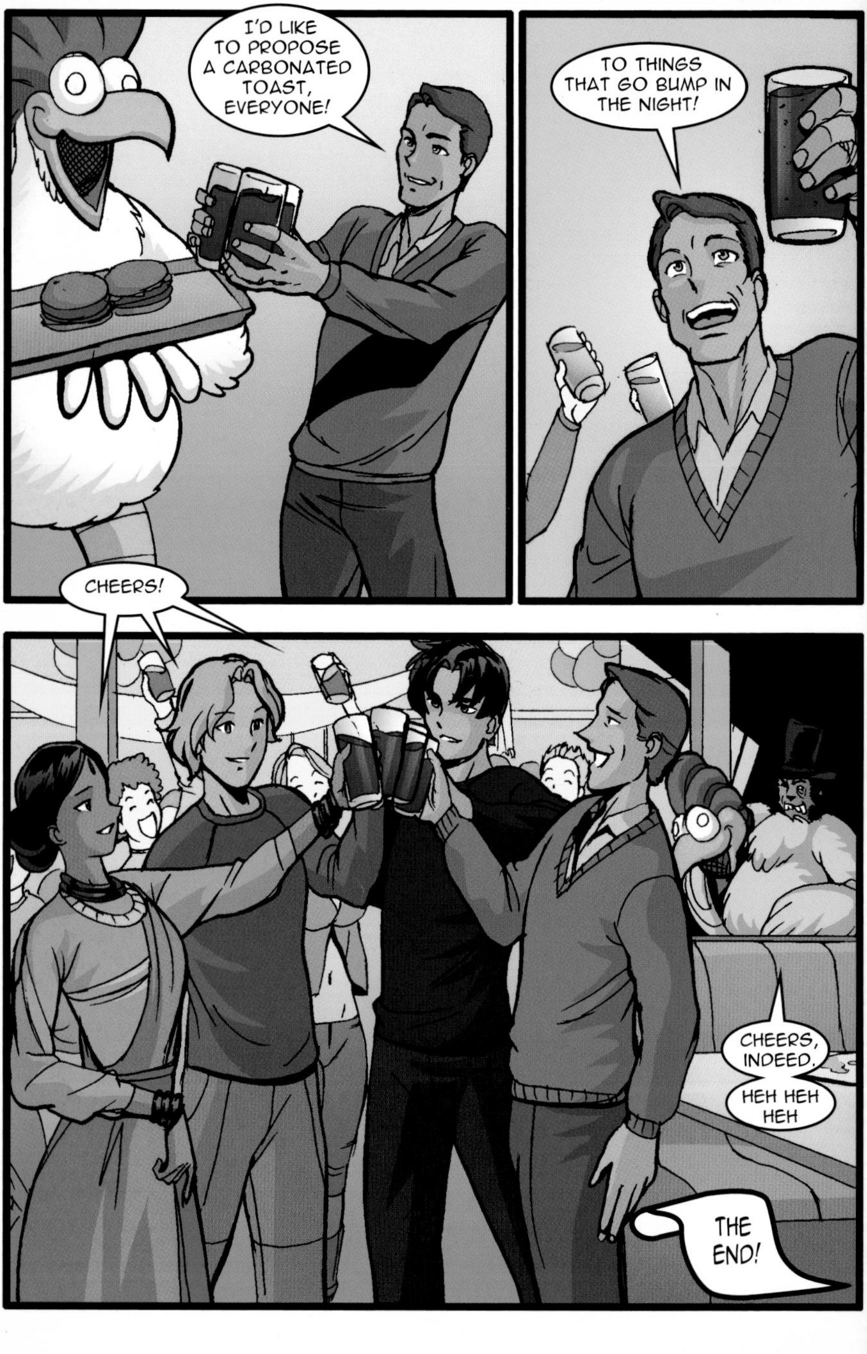
I'D LIKE TO PROPOSE A CARBONATED TOAST, EVERYONE!
TO THINGS THAT GO BUMP IN THE NIGHT!
CHEERS!
CHEERS, INDEED.
HEH HEH HEH
THE END!

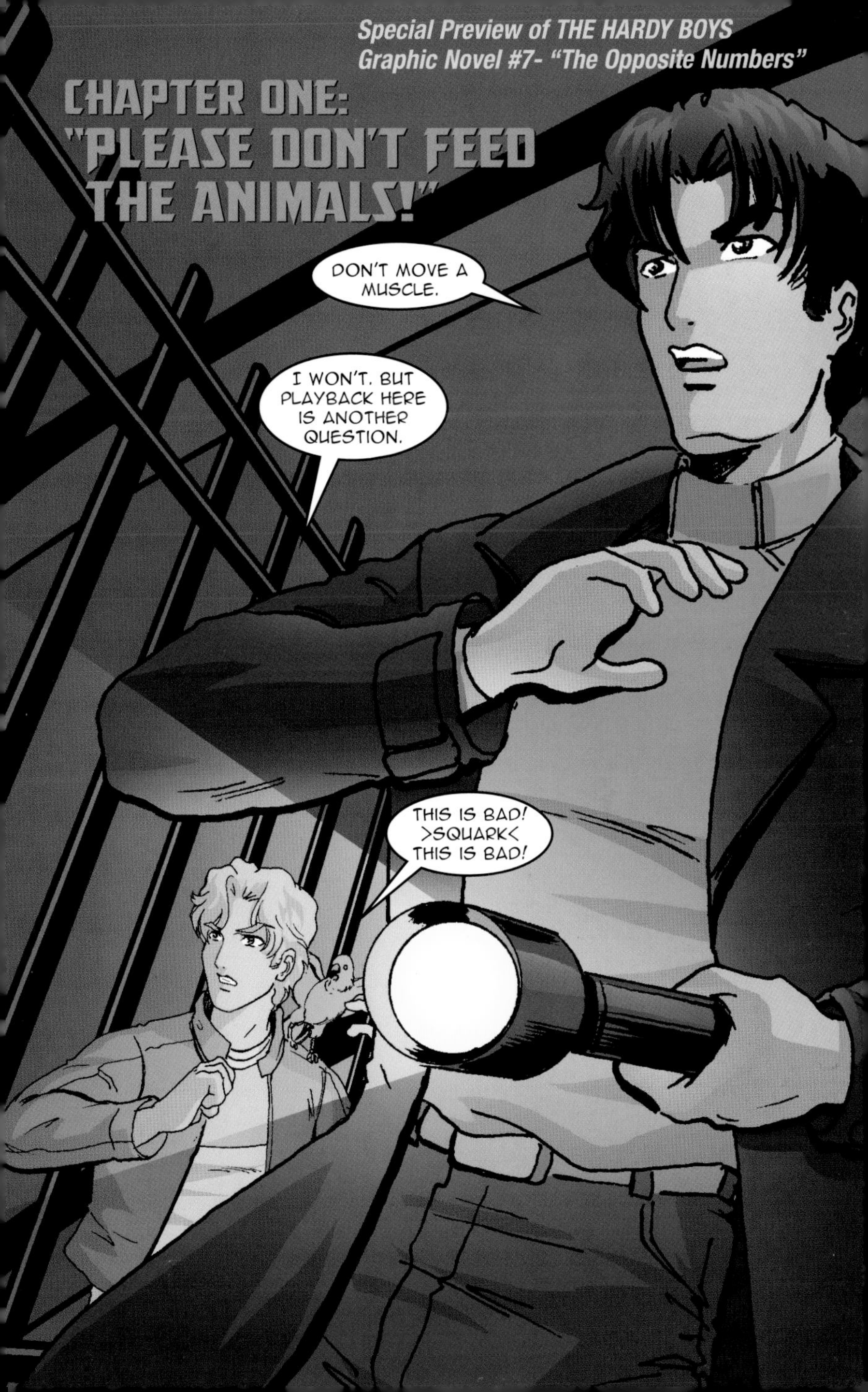
Special Preview of THE HARDY BOYS
Graphic Novel #7- "The Opposite Numbers"
CHAPTER ONE:
"PLEASE DON'T FEED THE ANIMALS!"
DON'T MOVE A MUSCLE.
I WON'T. BUT PLAYBACK HERE IS ANOTHER QUESTION.
THIS IS BAD! >SQUARK< THIS IS BAD!

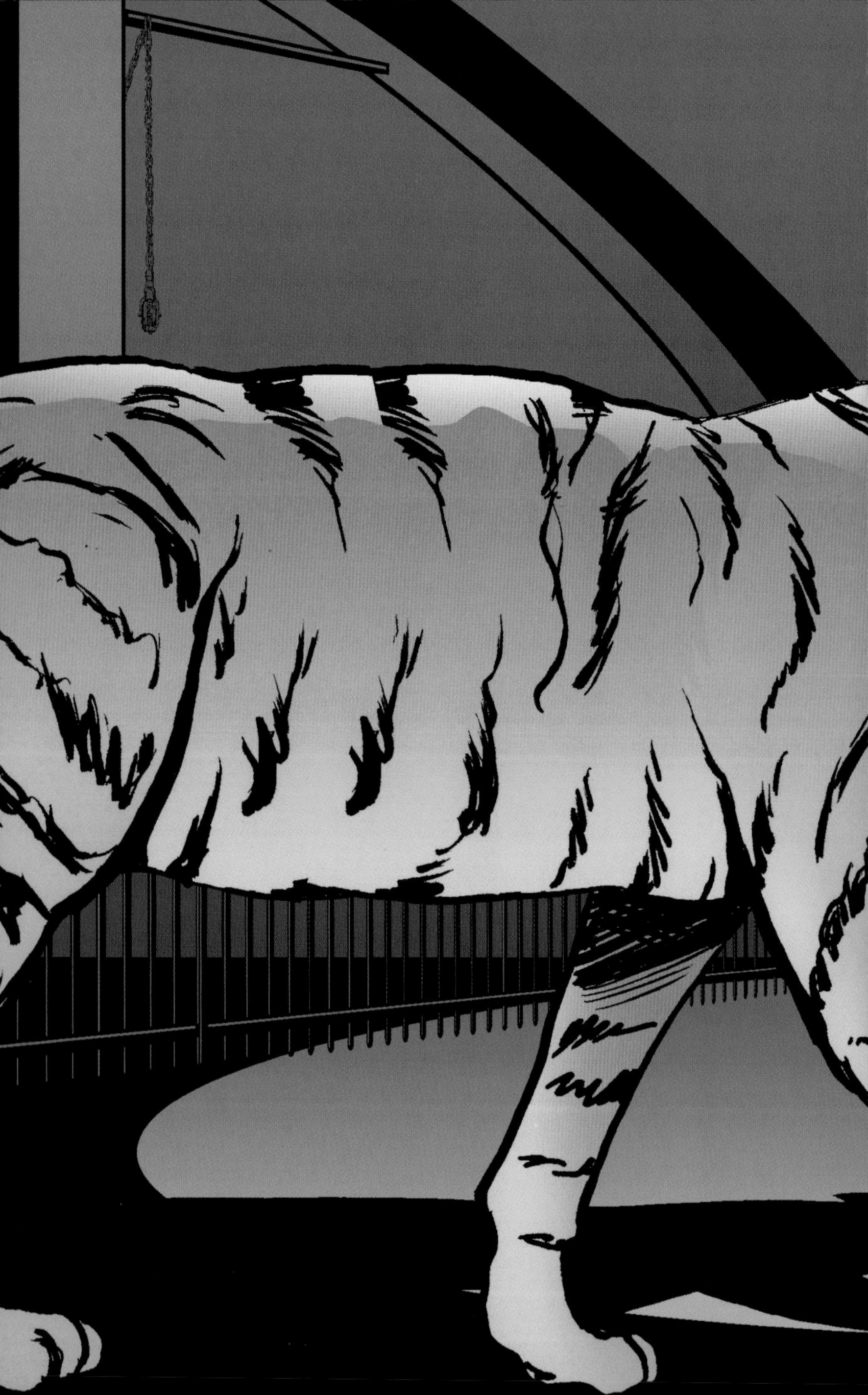

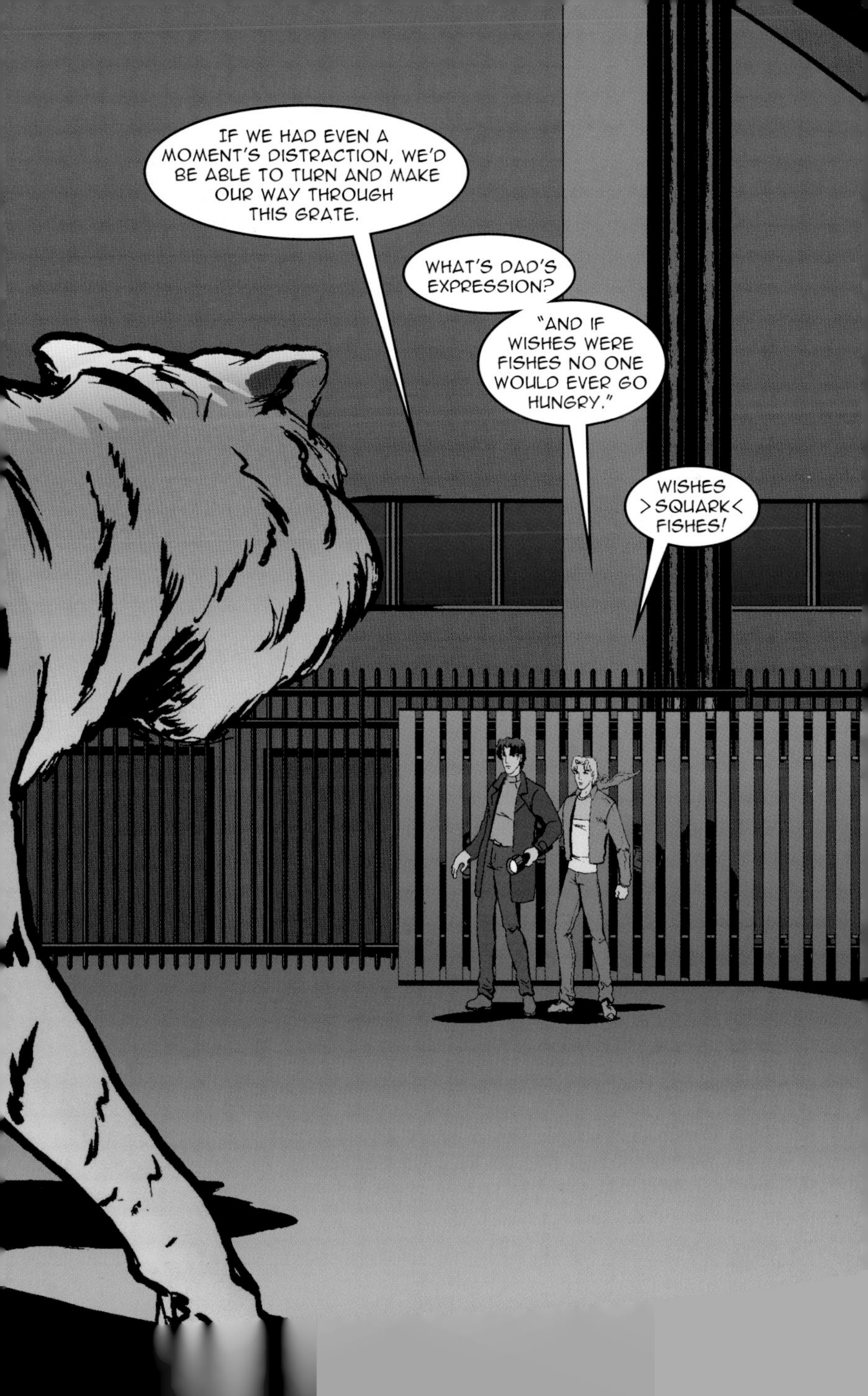
IF WE HAD EVEN A MOMENT'S DISTRACTION, WE'D BE ABLE TO TURN AND MAKE OUR WAY THROUGH THIS GRATE.
WHAT'S DAD'S EXPRESSION?
"AND IF WISHES WERE FISHES NO ONE WOULD EVER GO HUNGRY."
WISHES >SQUARK< FISHES!

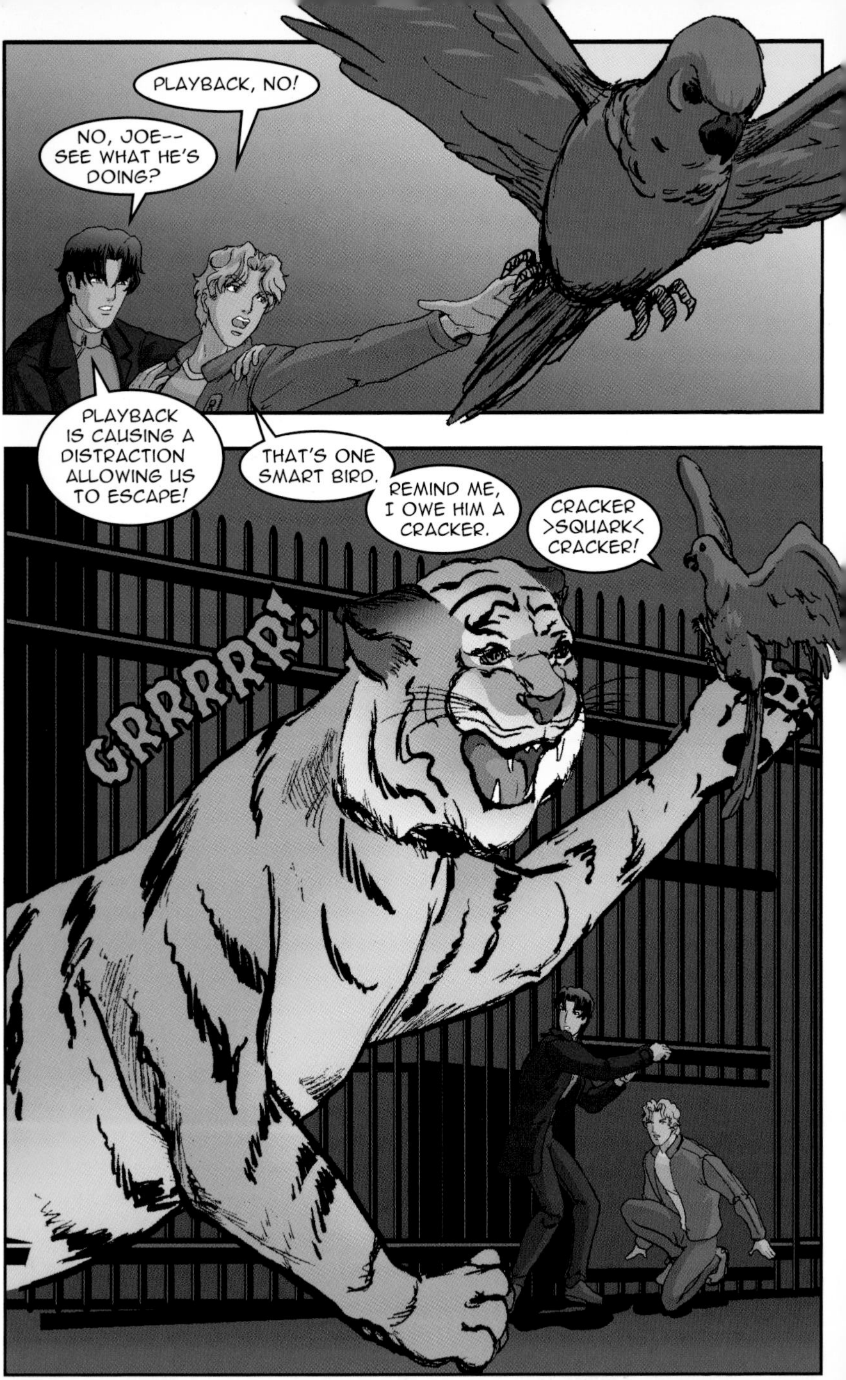
PLAYBACK, NO!
NO, JOE-- SEE WHAT HE'S DOING?
PLAYBACK IS CAUSING A DISTRACTION ALLOWING US TO ESCAPE!
THAT'S ONE SMART BIRD.
REMIND ME, I OWE HIM A CRACKER.
CRACKER >SQUARK< CRACKER!
GRRRRR!

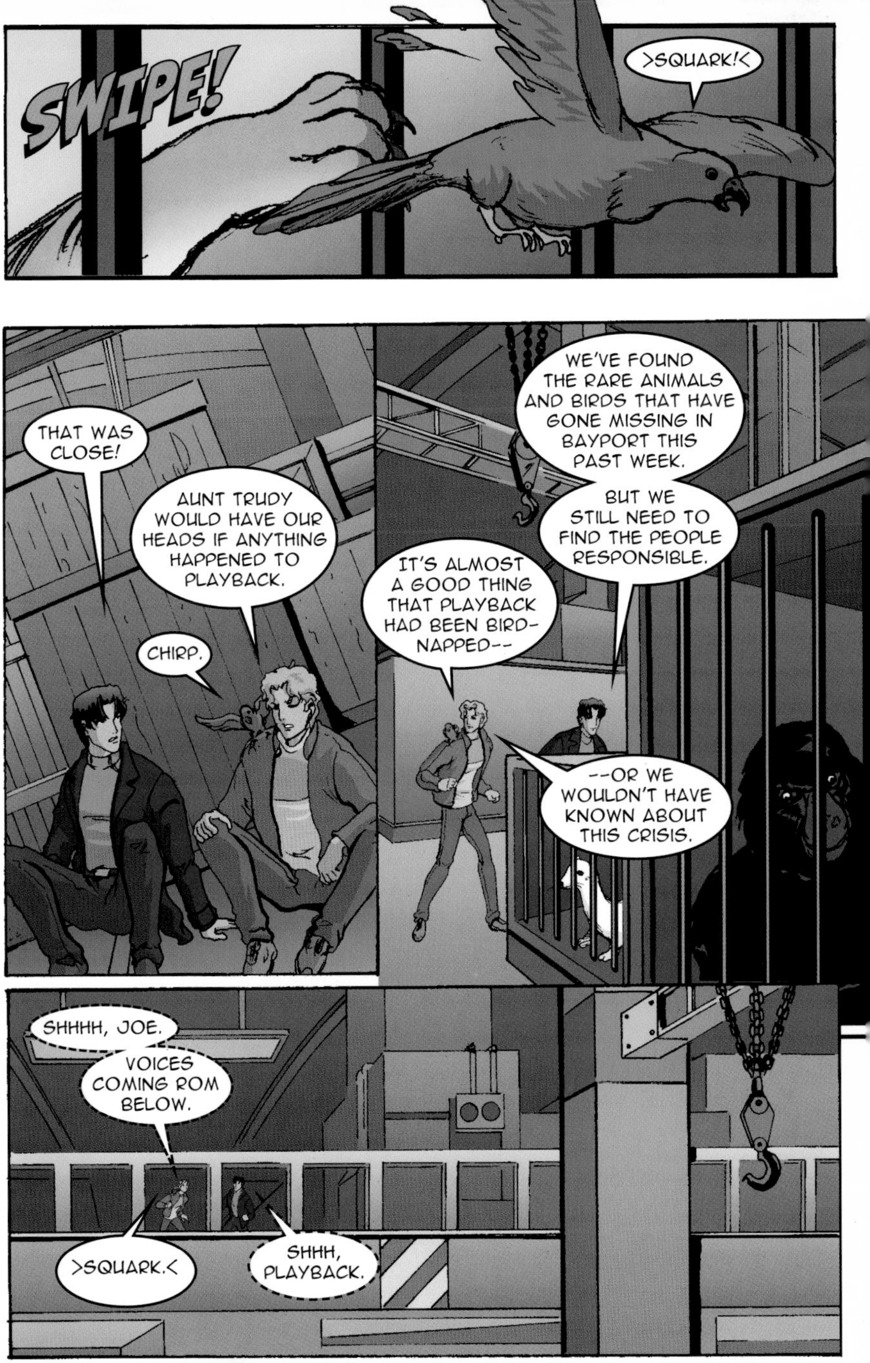
SWIPE!
>SQUARK!<
THAT WAS CLOSE!
AUNT TRUDY WOULD HAVE OUR HEADS IF ANYTHING HAPPENED TO PLAYBACK.
CHIRP.
WE'VE FOUND THE RARE ANIMALS AND BIRDS THAT HAVE GONE MISSING IN BAYPORT THIS PAST WEEK.
BUT WE STILL NEED TO FIND THE PEOPLE RESPONSIBLE.
IT'S ALMOST A GOOD THING THAT PLAYBACK HAD BEEN BIRD-NAPPED--
--OR WE WOULDN'T HAVE KNOWN ABOUT THIS CRISIS.
SHHHH, JOE.
VOICES COMING ROM BELOW.
>SQUARK.<
SHHH, PLAYBACK.

Don't miss THE HARDY BOYS Graphic Novel #7- "The Opposite Numbers"

Uncover a Trail of Secrets
as Nancy Drew® in
The White Wolf of Icicle Creek

Unexplained explosions and a lone white wolf haunt the bewildered guests of the Icicle Creek Lodge in the Canadian Rockies. Former guests say the resort is jinxed, but the staff blames a mysterious wolf. Is there a plot to undermine this resort or are bigger dangers hidden beneath the old foundation?

It's up to you, as Nancy Drew, to go undercover as a lodge employee and track down the culprit in this PC adventure game!

dare to play™

FOR MYSTERY FANS 10 to Adult

Nancy Drew PC Adventure Game #16
**Order online at www.HerInteractive.com
or call 1-800-461-8787. Also in stores!**
Compatible with WINDOWS® XP/Vista

EVERYONE
E
Mild Violence
ESRB CONTENT RATING   www.esrb.org

NANCY DREW

A NEW ONE EVERY 3 MONTHS!

#1 "The Demon of River Heights"
ISBN 1-59707-000-9

#2 "Writ In Stone"
ISBN 1-59707-002-5

#3 "The Haunted Dollhouse"
ISBN 1-59707-008-4

#4 "The Girl Who Wasn't There"
ISBN 1-59707-012-2

#5 "The Fake Heir"
ISBN 1-59707-024-6

#6 "Mr. Cheeters Is Missing"
ISBN 1-59707-030-0

#7 "The Charmed Bracelet"
ISBN 1-59707-036-X

#8 "Global Warning"
ISBN 1-59707-051-3

#9 "Ghost in the Machinery"
ISBN 1-59707-058-0

#10 "The Disoriented Express"
ISBN 1-59707-066-1

#11 "Monkey Wrench Blues"
ISBN 1-59707-076-9

NEW! #12 "Dress Reversal"
ISBN 1-59707-086-9

All: Pocket sized, 96-112pp., full color, $7.95
Also available in hardcover! $12.95 each.

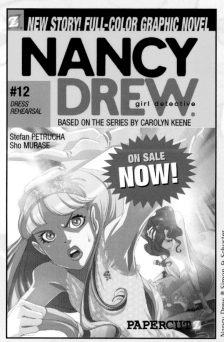

Nancy Drew
Boxed Set, #1-4
384 pages of color comics! $29.95,
ISBN 1-59707-038-6

Nancy Drew
Boxed Set, #5-8
432 pages of color comics! $29.95,
ISBN 1-59707-074-2

TOTALLY SPIES!

#1 "The O.P." ISBN 1-59707-043-2
#2 "I Hate the 80's" ISBN 1-59707-045-9
#3 "Evil Jerry" ISBN 1-59707-047-8
#4 "Spies in Space" ISBN 1-59707-055-6
Each: 5x7½, 112pp., full color paperback: $7.95
Also available in hardcover! $12.95 each

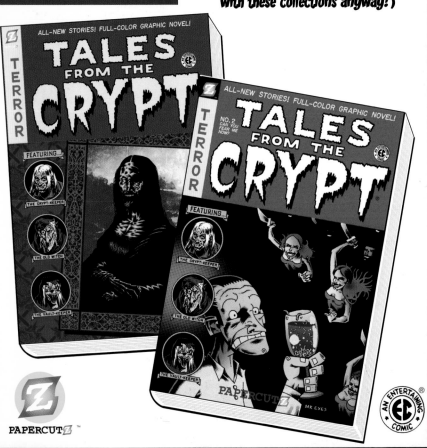

WATCH OUT FOR PAPERCUTZ™

If this is your very first Papercutz graphic novel, then allow me, Jim Salicrup, your humble and lovable Editor-in-Chief, to welcome you to the Papercutz Backpages where we check out what's happening in the ever-expanding Papercutz Universe! If you're a long-time Papercutz fan, then welcome back, friend!

Things really have been popping at Papercutz! In the last few editions of the Backpages we've announced new titles such as TALES FROM THE CRYPT, CLASSICS ILLUSTRATED, and CLASSICS ILLUSTRATED DELUXE. Well, guess what? The tradition continues, and we're announcing yet another addition to our line-up of blockbuster titles. So, what is our latest and greatest title? We'll give you just one hint -- the stars of the next Papercutz graphic novel series just happen to be the biggest, most exciting line of constructible action figures ever created! That's right -- BIONICLE is coming! Check out the power-packed preview pages ahead!

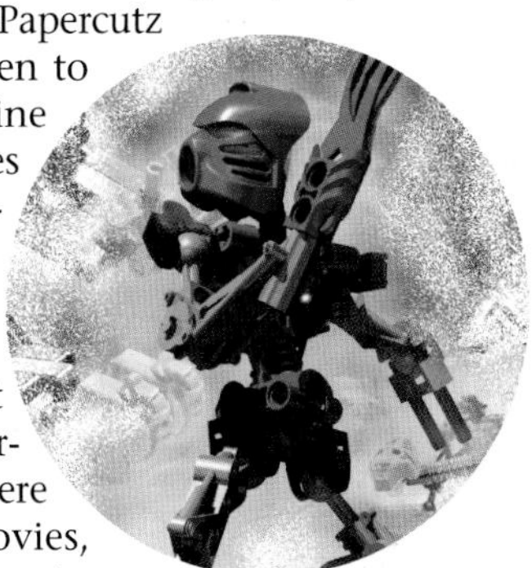

Before I run out of room, let me say that we're always interested in what you think! Are there characters, TV shows, movies, books, videogames, you-name-it, that you'd like to see Papercutz turn into graphic novels? Don't be shy, let's us know! You can contact me at salicrup@papercutz.com or Jim Salicrup, PAPERCUTZ, 40 Exchange Place, Ste. 1308, New York, NY 10005 and let us know how we're doing. After all, we want you to be as excited about Papercutz as we are!

Thanks,

Jim

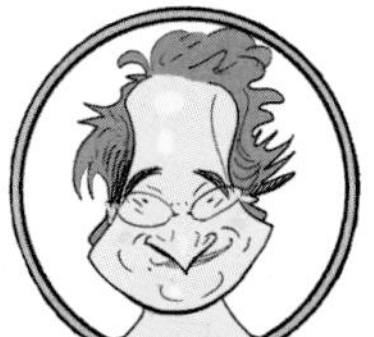
EDITOR-IN-CHIEF

Caricature drawn by Steve Brodner at the MoCCA Art Fest.

TWO DOZEN TEEN DETECTIVE GRAPHIC NOVELS NOW IN PRINT!

NEW STORY! FULL-COLOR GRAPHIC NOVEL
NANCY DREW
girl detective
#12
DRESS REVERSAL
BASED ON THE SERIES BY CAROLYN KEENE
PETRUCHA & KINNEY
MURASE & GUZMAN
PAPERCUTZ

You know, while it's exciting to be adding so many new titles, we don't want anyone to think we've forgotten any of our previous Papercutz publications! For example, can you believe there are now two dozen all-new, full-color graphic novels starring America's favorite teen sleuths?! Let's check out what's happening in the 12th volume of NANCY DREW...

Writers Stefan Petrucha and Sarah Kinney and artists Sho Murase and Carlos Jose Guzman present Nancy's latest case, "Dress Reversal." After showing up at River Height's social event of the year, in the identical dress as the party's hostess, Deirdre Shannon, things get worse for Nancy when she's suddenly kidnapped! That leaves Bess, George, and Ned to solve the mystery of the missing Girl Detective.

That's all in NANCY DREW #12 "Dress Reversal," on sale sale at bookstores everywhere and online booksellers.

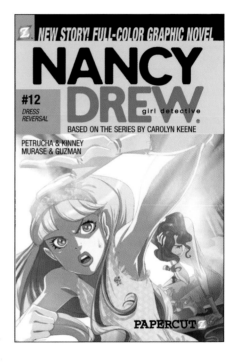

Behold. . .

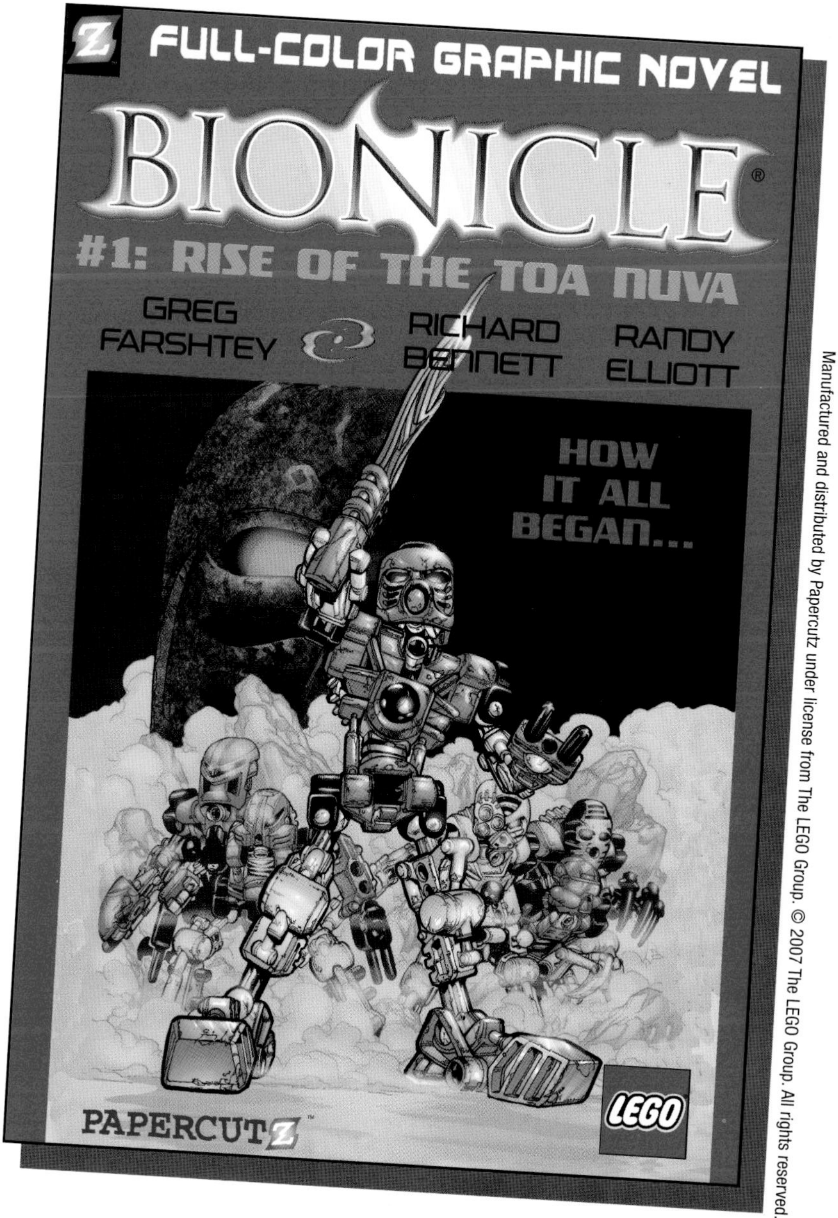

FULL-COLOR GRAPHIC NOVEL
BIONICLE®
#1: RISE OF THE TOA NUVA
GREG FARSHTEY
RICHARD BENNETT
RANDY ELLIOTT
HOW IT ALL BEGAN...
PAPERCUTZ™
LEGO

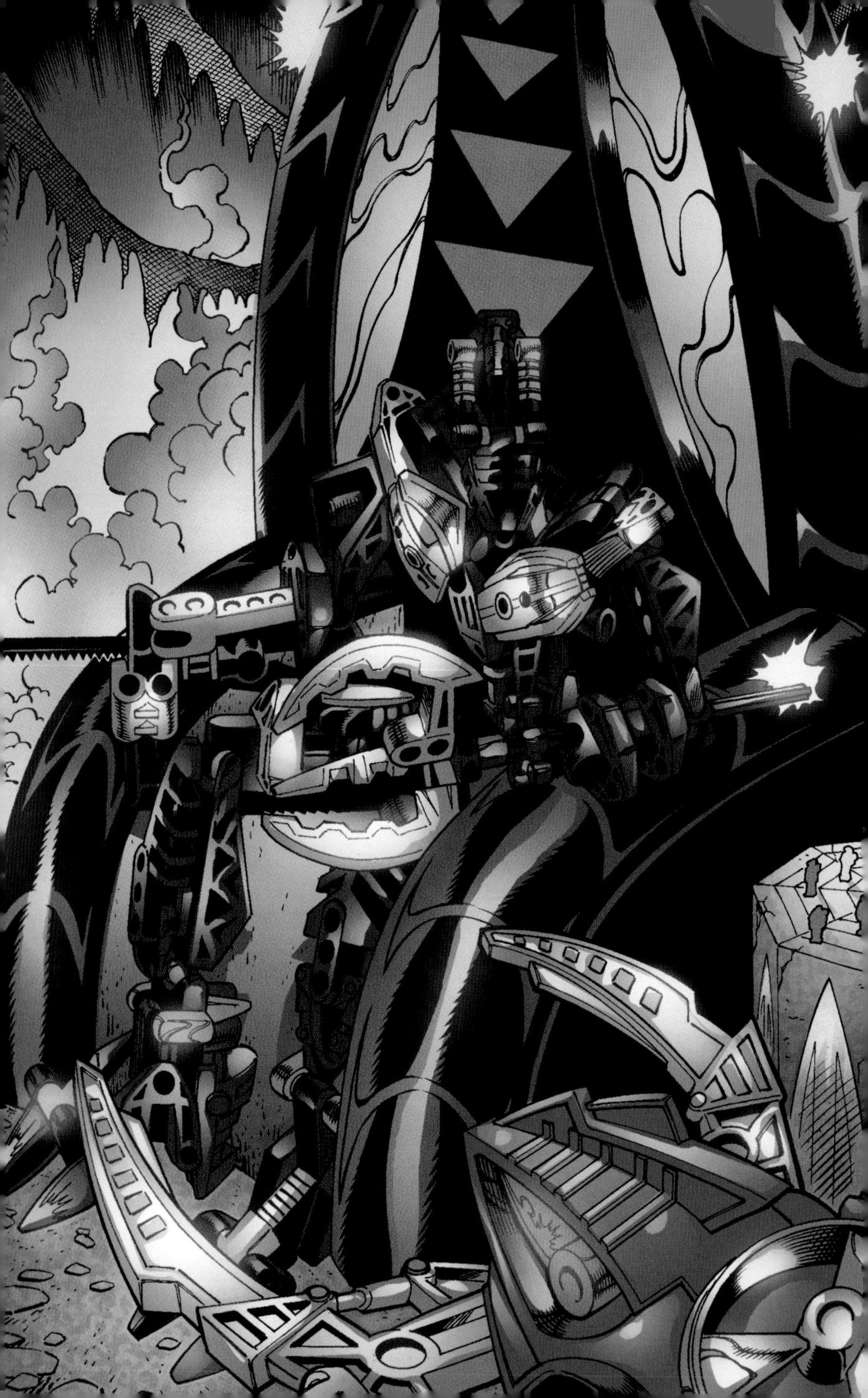

At the start of the new millennium, a new line of toys from LEGO made their dramatic debut. Originally released in six color-coded canisters, each containing a constructible, fully-poseable, articulated character, BIONICLE was an instant hit!

The BIONICLE figures were incredibly intriguing. With their exotic names hinting at a complex history, fans were curious to discover more about these captivating characters. Even now, over six years later, there are still many unanswered questions surrounding every facet of the ever-expanding BIONICLE universe.

A comicbook, written by leading BIONICLE expert and author of most of the BIONICLE novels Greg Farshtey, was created by DC Comics and given away to members of the BIONICLE fan club. The action-packed comics revealed much about these mysterious biomechanical (part biological, part mechanical) beings and the world they inhabited. A world filled with many races, most prominent being the Matoran. A world once protected millennia ago by a Great Spirit known as Mata Nui, who has fallen asleep. A world that has begun to decay as its inhabitants must defend themselves from the evil forces of Makuta.

The first story arc of the comics called "The BIONICLE Chronicles," begins when six heroic beings known as Toa arrive on a tropical-like island which is also named Mata Nui. The Toa may just be the saviors the people of Mata Nui need, if they can avoid fighting with themselves, not to mention the Bohrok and the Rahkshise early comics are incredibly hard-to-find, and many new BIONICLE fans have never seen these all-important early chapters in this epic science fantasy. But soon, those comics will be collected as the first two volumes in the Papercutz series of BIONICLE graphic novels.

These early comics are incredibly hard-to-find, and many new BIONICLE fans have never seen these all-important early chapters in this epic science fantasy. But soon, those comics will be collected as the first two volumes in the Papercutz series of BIONICLE graphic novels.

In the following pages, enjoy a special preview of BIONICLE graphic novel #1...

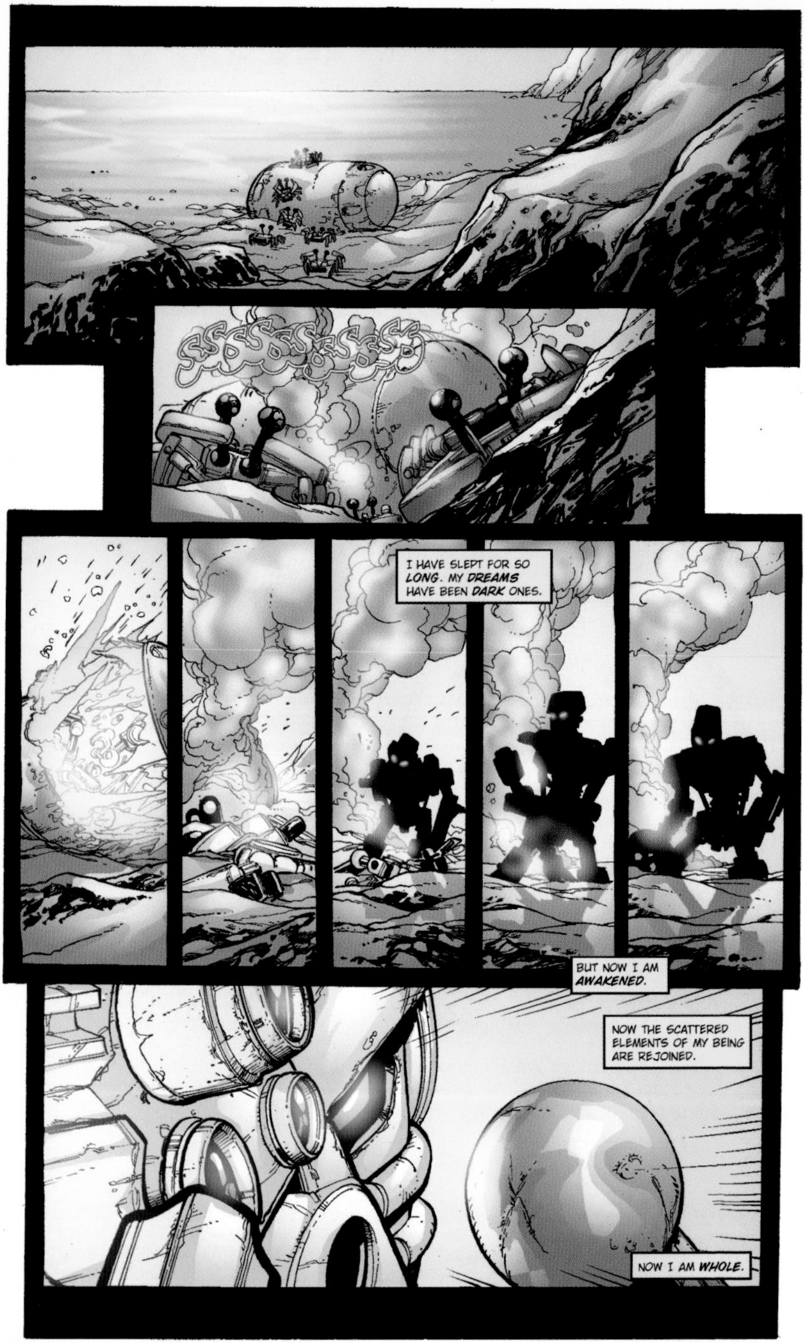
I HAVE SLEPT FOR SO LONG. MY DREAMS HAVE BEEN DARK ONES.
BUT NOW I AM AWAKENED.
NOW THE SCATTERED ELEMENTS OF MY BEING ARE REJOINED.
NOW I AM WHOLE.

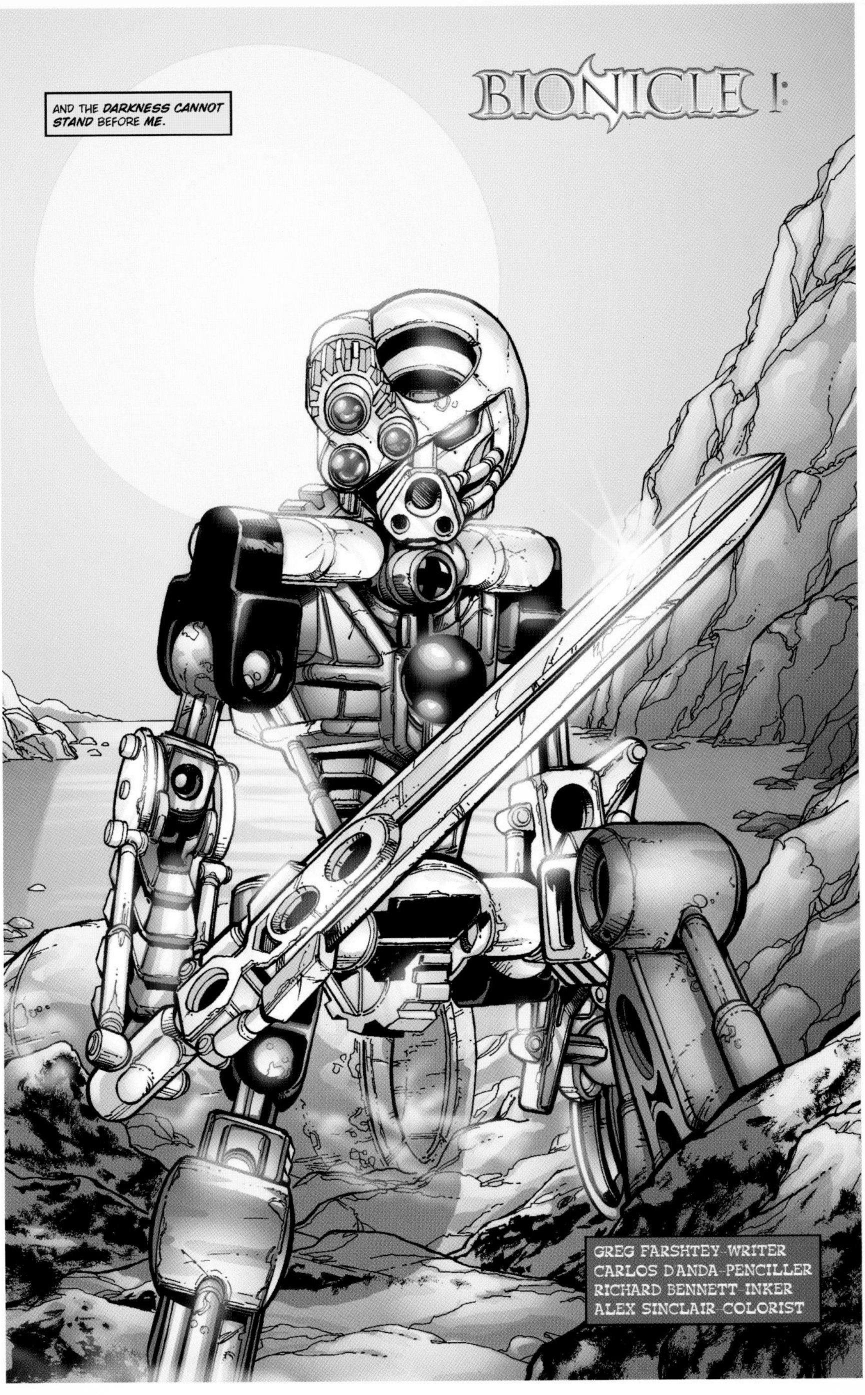
AND THE DARKNESS CANNOT STAND BEFORE ME.
BIONICLE I:
GREG FARSHTEY-WRITER
CARLOS D'ANDA-PENCILLER
RICHARD BENNETT-INKER
ALEX SINCLAIR-COLORIST

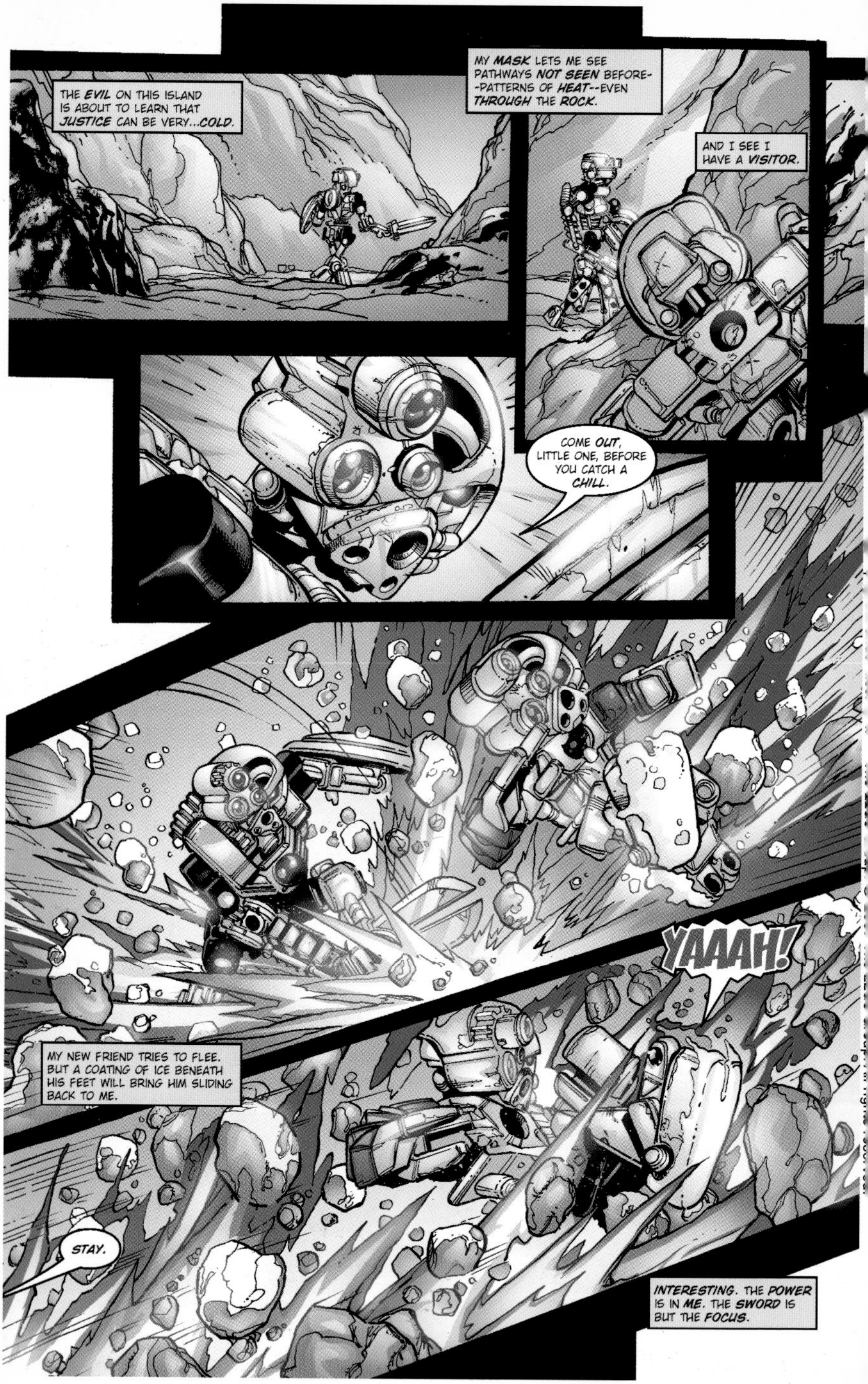

THE *EVIL* ON THIS ISLAND IS ABOUT TO LEARN THAT *JUSTICE* CAN BE VERY...*COLD*.
MY *MASK* LETS ME SEE PATHWAYS *NOT SEEN* BEFORE--PATTERNS OF *HEAT*--EVEN *THROUGH* THE *ROCK*.
AND I SEE I HAVE A *VISITOR*.
COME *OUT*, LITTLE ONE, BEFORE YOU CATCH A *CHILL*.
YAAAH!
MY NEW FRIEND TRIES TO FLEE. BUT A COATING OF ICE BENEATH HIS FEET WILL BRING HIM SLIDING BACK TO ME.
STAY.
INTERESTING. THE *POWER* IS IN *ME*. THE *SWORD* IS BUT THE *FOCUS*.

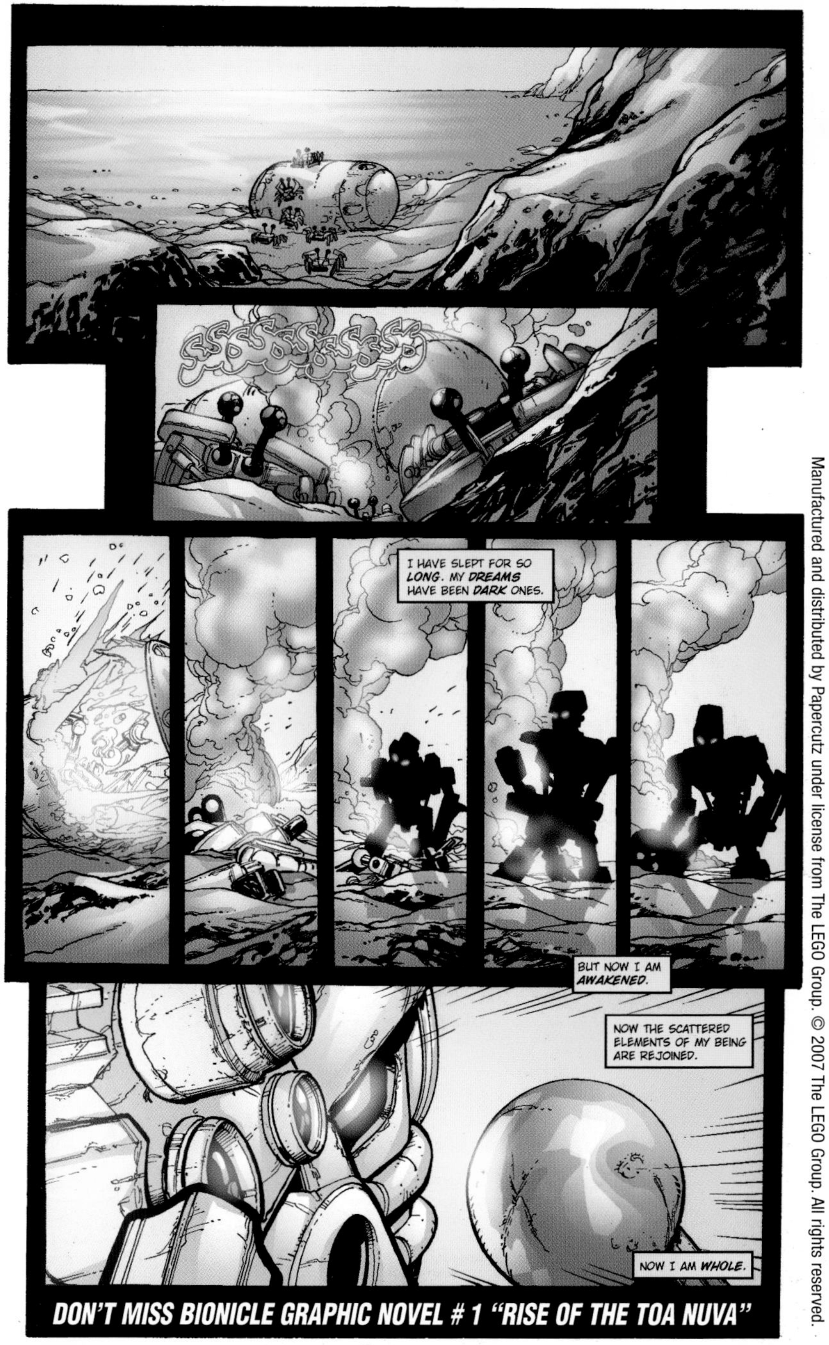
I HAVE SLEPT FOR SO LONG. MY DREAMS HAVE BEEN DARK ONES.
BUT NOW I AM AWAKENED.
NOW THE SCATTERED ELEMENTS OF MY BEING ARE REJOINED.
NOW I AM WHOLE.

DON'T MISS BIONICLE GRAPHIC NOVEL # 1 "RISE OF THE TOA NUVA"

CLASSICS *Illustrated*

Featuring Stories by the World's Greatest Authors

Returns in two new series from Papercutz!

The original, best-selling series of comics adaptations of the world's greatest literature, CLASSICS ILLUSTRATED, returns in two new formats--the original, featuring abridged adaptations of classic novels, and CLASSICS ILLUSTRATED DELUXE, featuring longer, more expansive adaptations-from graphic novel publisher Papercutz. "We're very proud to say that Papercutz has received such an enthusiastic reception from librarians and school teachers for its NANCY DREW and HARDY BOYS graphic novels as well as THE LIFE OF POPE JOHN PAUL II...*IN COMICS!*, that it only seemed logical for us to bring back the original CLASSICS ILLUSTRATED comicbook series beloved by parents, educators, and librarians," explained Papercutz Publisher, Terry Nantier. "We can't thank the enlightened librarians and teachers who have supported Papercutz enough. And we're thrilled that they're so excited about CLASSICS ILLUSTRATED."

CLASSICS Illustrated
THE INVISIBLE MAN
By H.G. Wells
Adapted by Rick Geary

CLASSICS Illustrated Deluxe
TALES FROM THE BROTHERS GRIMM
Adapted by Mazan, Cecile Chicault, and Philip Petit
PAPERCUT

CLASSICS Illustrated Deluxe
ROBINSON CRUSOE
PAPERCUT

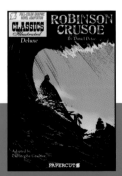

Upcoming titles include The Invisible Man, Tales from the Brothers Grimm, and Robinson Crusoe.

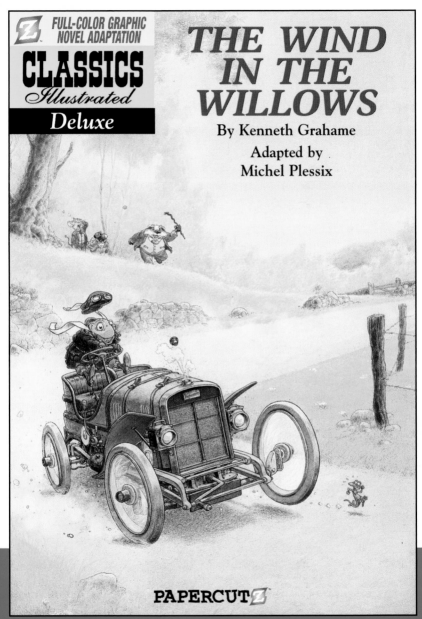

FULL-COLOR GRAPHIC NOVEL ADAPTATION

CLASSICS *Illustrated*
Deluxe

THE WIND IN THE WILLOWS

By Kenneth Grahame

Adapted by Michel Plessix

PAPERCUT**Z**

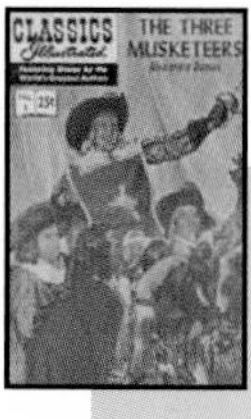
CLASSICS Illustrated
THE THREE MUSKETEERS
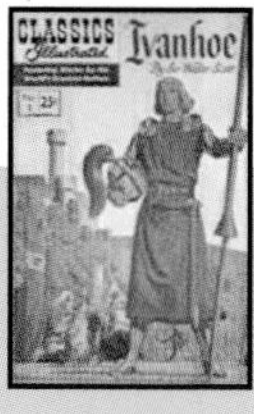
CLASSICS Illustrated
Ivanhoe
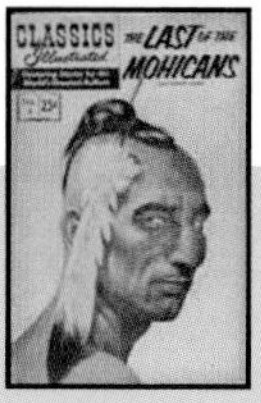
CLASSICS Illustrated
THE LAST OF THE MOHICANS
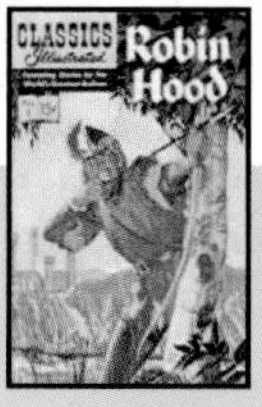
CLASSICS Illustrated
Robin Hood
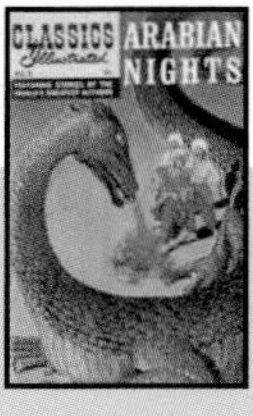
CLASSICS Illustrated
ARABIAN NIGHTS
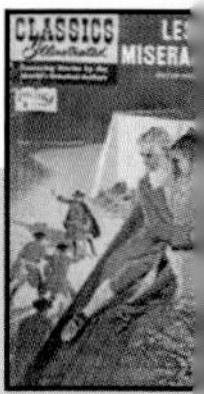
CLASSICS Illustrated
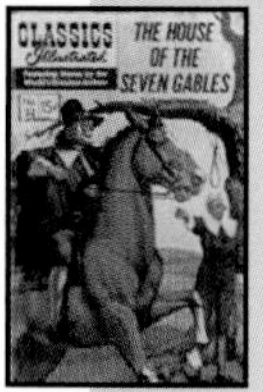
CLASSICS Illustrated
THE HOUSE OF THE SEVEN GABLES

A Short History of CLASSICS ILLUSTRATED...

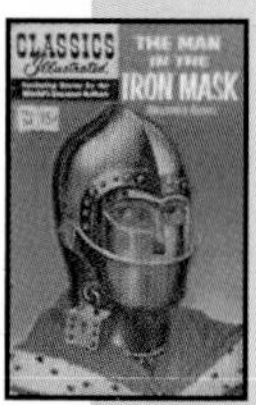
CLASSICS Illustrated
THE MAN IN THE IRON MASK

William B. Jones Jr. is the author of Classics Illustrated: A Cultural History, which offers a comprehensive overview of the original comic-book series and the writers, artists, editors, and publishers behind-the-scenes. With Mr. Jones Jr.'s kind permission, here's a very short overview of the history of CLASSICS ILLUSTRATED adapted from his 2005 essay on Albert Kanter.

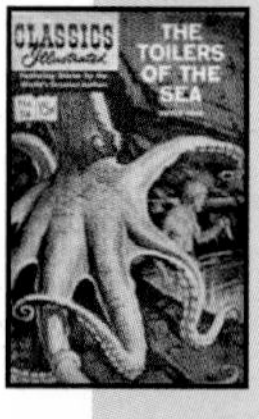
CLASSICS Illustrated
THE TOILERS OF THE SEA

CLASSICS ILLUSTRATED was the creation of Albert Lewis Kanter, a visionary publisher, who from 1941 to 1971, introduced young readers worldwide to the realms of literature, history, folklore, mythology, and science in over 200 titles in such comicbook series as CLASSICS ILLUSTRATED and CLASSICS ILLUSTRATED JUNIOR. Kanter, inspired by the success of the first comicbooks published in the early 30s and late 40s, believed he

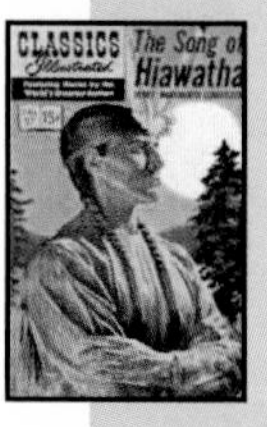
CLASSICS Illustrated
Hiawatha

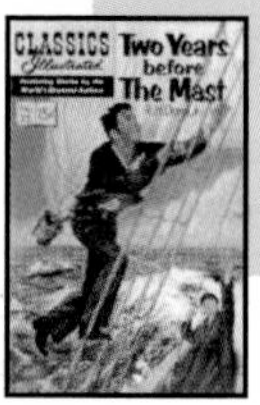
CLASSICS Illustrated
Two Years before The Mast
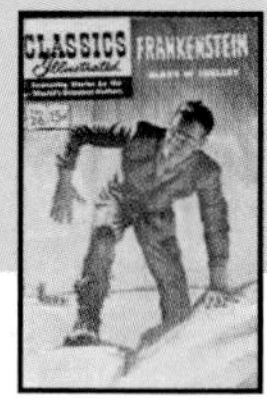
CLASSICS Illustrated
FRANKENSTEIN
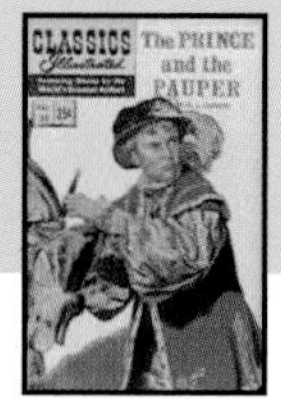
CLASSICS Illustrated
The PRINCE and the PAUPER
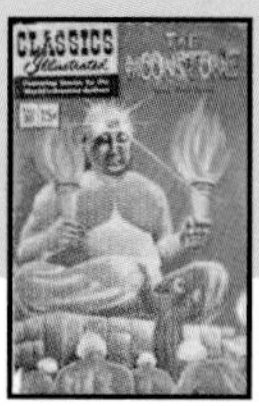
CLASSICS Illustrated
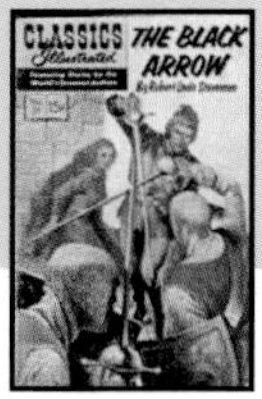
CLASSICS Illustrated
THE BLACK ARROW
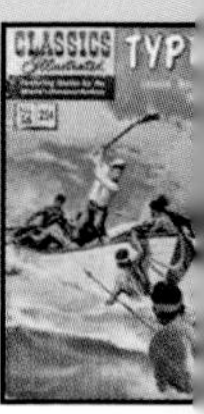
CLASSICS

DON QUIXOTE

CLASSICS Illustrated
Rip Van Winkle

CLASSICS Illustrated
UNCLE TOM'S CABIN

CLASSICS Illustrated
GULLIVER'S TRAVELS

CLASSICS Illustrated
The CORSICAN BROTHERS

CLASSICS Illustrated
OLIVER TWIST

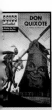

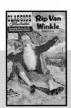

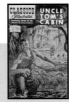

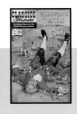

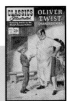

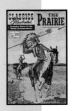

could use the same medium to introduce young readers to the world of great literature. CLASSIC COMICS (later changed to CLASSICS ILLUSTRATED in 1947) was launched in 1941, and soon the comicbook adaptations of Shakespeare, Stevenson, Twain, Verne, and other authors, were being used in schools and endorsed by educators.

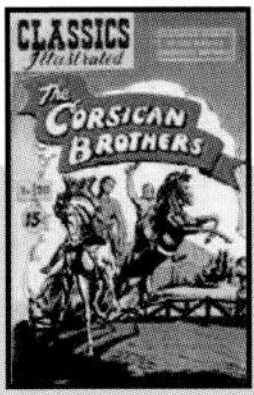

CLASSICS ILLUSTRATED was translated and distributed in countries such as Canada, Great Britain, the Netherlands, Greece, Brazil, Mexico, and Australia. The genial publisher was hailed abroad as "Papa Kassiker." By the beginning of the 1960s, CLASSICS ILLUSTRATED was the largest childrens publication in the world. The original CLASSICS ILLUSTRATED series adapted into comics 169 titles; among these were Frankenstein, 20,000 Leagues Under the Sea, Treasure Island, Julius Caesar, and Faust.

Albert L. Kanter died, March 17, 1973, leaving behind a rich legacy for the millions of readers whose imaginations were awakened by CLASSICS ILLUSTRATED.

CLASSICS Illustrated
THE PRAIRIE

CLASSICS Illustrated
WUTHERING HEIGHTS

CLASSICS Illustrated
BLACK BEAUTY

CLASSICS Illustrated
WESTERN STORIES

TWENTY YEARS AFTER

CLASSICS Illustrated
GREAT EXPECTATIONS

CLASSICS Illustrated
Kidnapped

CLASSICS Illustrated
DAVID COPPERFIELD

CLASSICS Illustrated
The Adventures of TOM SAWYER

CLASSICS Illustrated
THE SPY

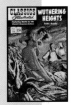

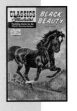

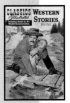

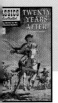

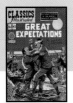

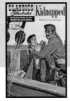

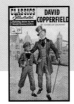

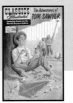

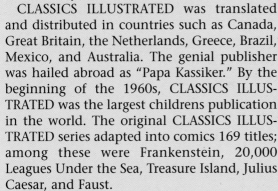

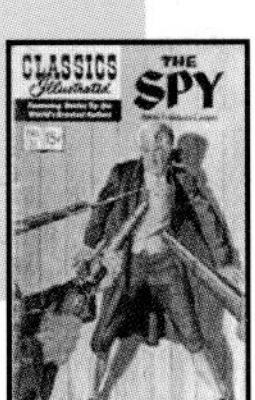

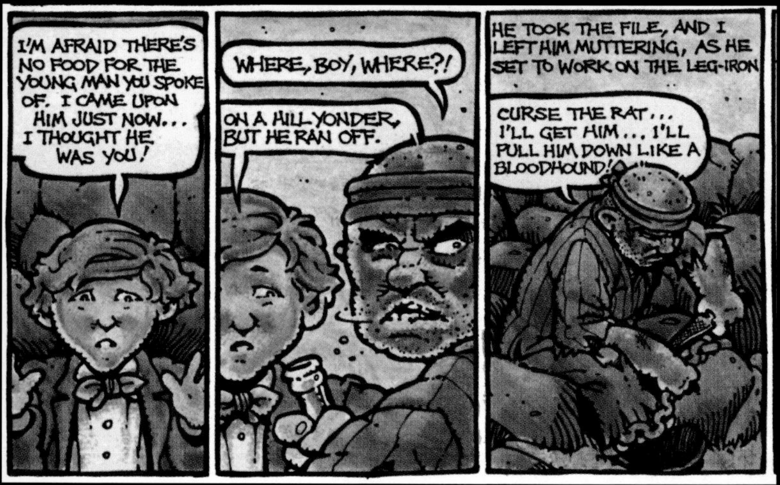
I'M AFRAID THERE'S NO FOOD FOR THE YOUNG MAN YOU SPOKE OF. I CAME UPON HIM JUST NOW... I THOUGHT HE WAS YOU!
WHERE, BOY, WHERE?!
ON A HILL YONDER, BUT HE RAN OFF.
HE TOOK THE FILE, AND I LEFT HIM MUTTERING, AS HE SET TO WORK ON THE LEG-IRON
CURSE THE RAT... I'LL GET HIM... I'LL PULL HIM DOWN LIKE A BLOODHOUND!

CLASSICS ILLUSTRATED was re-launched in 1990 in graphic novel/book form by the Berkley Publishing Group and First Publishing, Inc. featuring all-new adaptations by such top graphic novelists as Rick Geary, Bill Sienkiewicz, Kyle Baker, Gahan Wilson, and others. "First had the right idea, they just came out about 15 years too soon. Now bookstores are ready for graphic novels such as these," Jim explains. Many of these excellent adaptations have been acquired by Papercutz and will make up the new series of CLASSICS ILLUSTRATED titles.

The first volume of the new CLASSICS ILLUSTRATED series presents graphic novelist Rick Geary's adaptation of "Great Expectations" by Charles Dickens, the bittersweet tale of one boy's adolescence, and of the choices he makes to shape his destiny. Into an engrossing mystery, Dickens weaves a heartfelt inquiry into morals and virtues-as the orphan Pip, the convict Magwitch, the beautiful Estella, the bitter Miss Havisham, the goodhearted Biddy, the kind Joe and other memorable characters entwine in a battle of human nature. Rick Geary's delightful illustrations capture the newfound awe and frustrations of young Pip as he comes of age, and begins to understand the opportunities that life presents.

FULL-COLOR GRAPHIC NOVEL ADAPTATION

CLASSICS *Illustrated*®

Featuring Stories by the World's Greatest Authors

GREAT EXPECTATIONS

By Charles Dickens

Adapted by Richard Geary

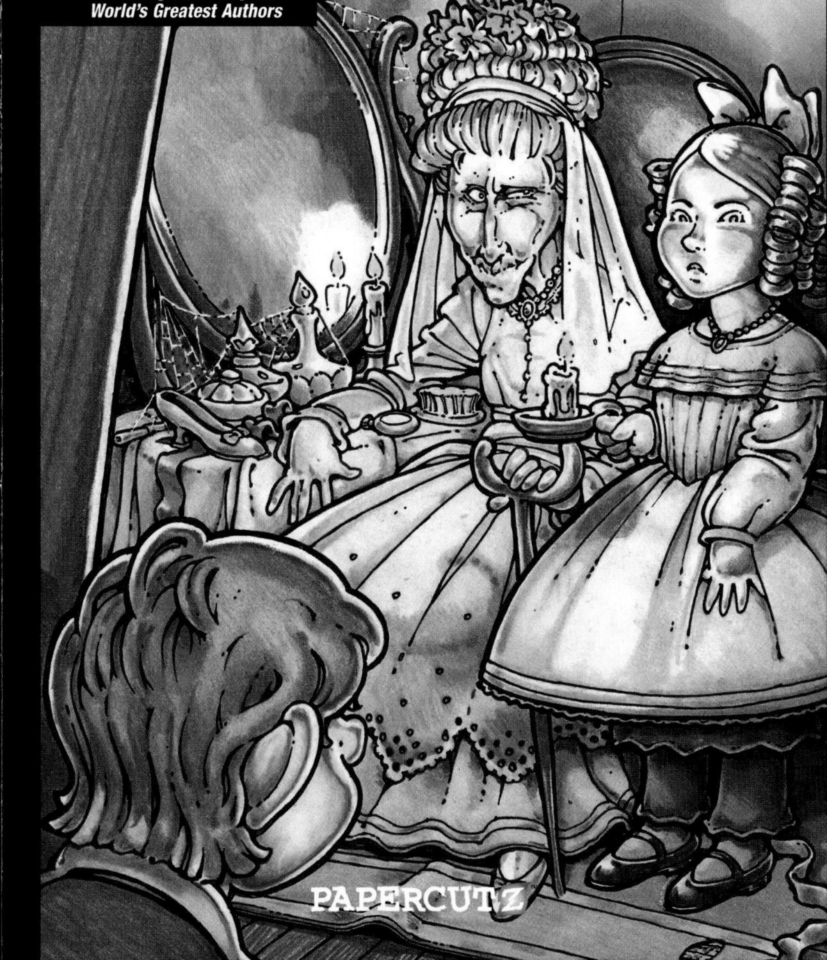

PAPERCUTZ

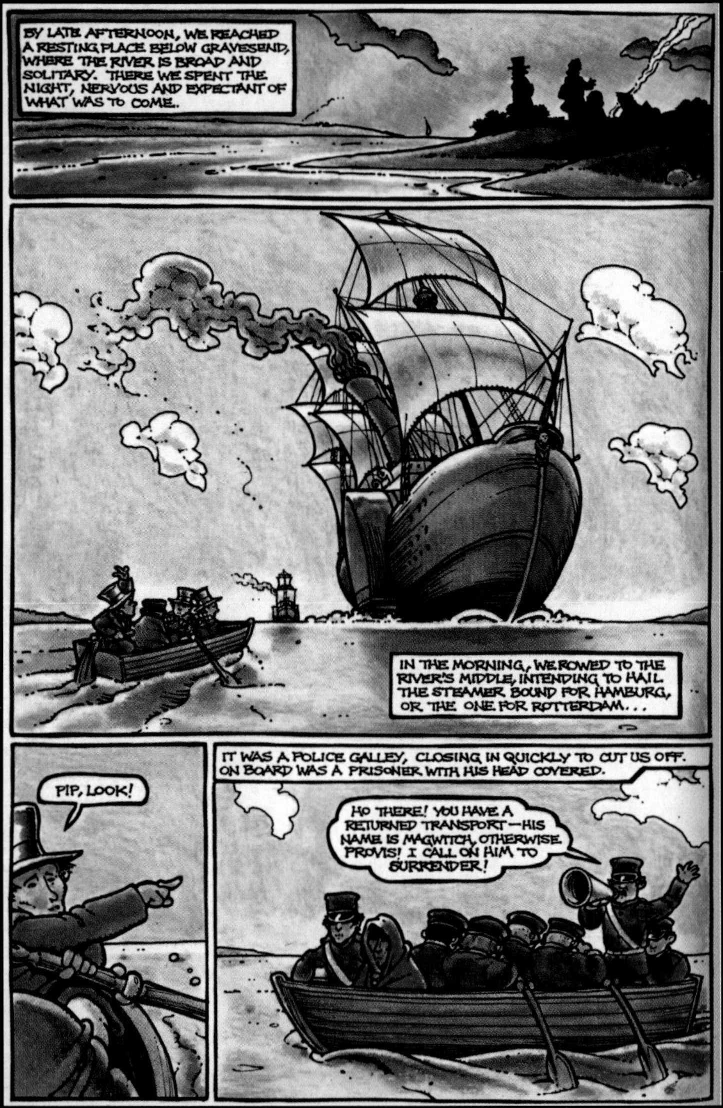
BY LATE AFTERNOON, WE REACHED A RESTING PLACE BELOW GRAVESEND, WHERE THE RIVER IS BROAD AND SOLITARY. THERE WE SPENT THE NIGHT, NERVOUS AND EXPECTANT OF WHAT WAS TO COME.
IN THE MORNING, WE ROWED TO THE RIVER'S MIDDLE, INTENDING TO HAIL THE STEAMER BOUND FOR HAMBURG, OR THE ONE FOR ROTTERDAM...
PIP, LOOK!
IT WAS A POLICE GALLEY, CLOSING IN QUICKLY TO CUT US OFF. ON BOARD WAS A PRISONER WITH HIS HEAD COVERED.
HO THERE! YOU HAVE A RETURNED TRANSPORT—HIS NAME IS MAGWITCH, OTHERWISE PROVIS! I CALL ON HIM TO SURRENDER!

Here is one preview page of CLASSICS ILLUSTRATED #1 "Great Expectations" by Charles Dickens, as adapted by Rick Geary. (CLASSICS ILLUSTRATED will be printed in a larger 6 1/2" x 9" format, so the art will be bigger than what you see here.)